When **Virginia Heath** was a little girl it took her ages to fall asleep, so she made up stories in her head to help pass the time while she was staring at the ceiling. As she got older the stories became more complicated—sometimes taking weeks to get to their happy ending. One day she decided to embrace her insomnia and start writing them down. Virginia lives in Essex, with her wonderful husband and two teenagers. It still takes her for ever to fall asleep.

Also by Virginia Heath

Her Enemy at the Altar
The Discerning Gentleman's Guide
Miss Bradshaw's Bought Betrothal
His Mistletoe Wager

The Wild Warriners miniseries

A Warriner to Protect Her
A Warriner to Rescue Her
A Warriner to Tempt Her
A Warriner to Seduce Her

The King's Elite miniseries

The Mysterious Lord Millcroft

And look out for the next book
coming soon.

Discover more at millsandboon.co.uk.

THE MYSTERIOUS LORD MILLCROFT

Virginia Heath

MILLS & BOON

First Published in Great Britain 2018
by Mills & Boon, an imprint of HarperCollins*Publishers*
1 London Bridge Street, London, SE1 9GF

© 2018 Susan Merritt

ISBN: 978-0-263-93307-9

MIX
Paper from
responsible sources
FSC C007454

This book is produced from independently certified FSC™ paper
to ensure responsible forest management.
For more information visit www.harpercollins.co.uk/green.

Printed and bound in Spain
by CPI, Barcelona

For Ruby Graham-Lovett.

Because special little girls deserve to
have the whole world know they are lovely.

Chapter One

Deepest, darkest, dankest Nottinghamshire
—March 1820

The bullet hole still hurt like the devil, but to add to Seb's current misery, this morning it had started itching, as well. So badly that he was sorely tempted to poke a buttonhook down the tightly bound, pristine bandages encasing his abdomen and vigorously flay the blasted irritation away. Instead he subtly scratched at the area with his fingers, only to have them slapped away by his diligent hostess who was listening to his chest with something which resembled a miniature wooden trumpet.

'You have to leave the wound alone, Seb. The stitches have only just come out and the area is still delicate.'

As was he. With a huff he flung his head back on the pillow and, to his shame, pouted like a pet-

ulant child. 'I'm going mad, Bella. Slowly around
the twist at the sight of these four walls.' He'd been
in bed almost three weeks. Granted he hadn't remembered the first ten days of that, he'd been too
busy fighting for his life, but he had been improv-
ing steadily for the last ten and was desperate to
get back to work. He had smugglers to catch and
one in particular. The Boss. The elusive name-
less, faceless mastermind behind a highly organised, extremely dangerous smuggling ring linked
to Napoleon himself, which not only threatened
the English economy, but had also been indirectly
responsible for killing two of Seb's best men as
well as aerating his chest.

'How much longer is your husband going to
keep me chained to this bed?' Not that he wasn't
grateful. Doctor Joe Warriner had saved his life.
The musket ball had gone deep and the blood loss
had been so significant that most physicians would
have sent for a parson to administer the last rites.
But Joe wasn't most physicians and had battled
to dig the thing out, and had worked tirelessly to
snatch Seb from the snapping jaws of death in the
week afterwards. Who wouldn't be grateful? But
one could still be indebted for ever and frustrated
at being gaoled by the same man simultaneously.
Doctor Joe was both a genius and a tyrant…and
now Seb was thinking petulantly, as well. Being

indoors for long periods of time clearly brought out the worst in him.

'Actually, after your astounding show of ill-tempered belligerence yesterday, he has agreed you can come downstairs today. But *only* to sit in a chair. And *only* for a few hours. Once you've taken your medicine, I shall send someone in to help you get cleaned up while I sort out something appropriate for you to wear. I'm sure Joe must have something that will fit you.'

Whilst sitting in a chair didn't sound the least bit exciting, it was better than lying in a bed like an invalid and, once he was downstairs, they really would have to chain him up to stop him moving around. For a man used to being out in the elements, being cooped up was anathema. Mind you, Seb couldn't complain about the luxury. A soft mattress, warm blankets, clean sheets and three excellent meals a day were a rarity in his line of work. Ten days' worth was unheard of. He might be in purgatory, but it was a sweet-smelling, comfortable cocoon-like ordeal and it could be much worse. He could be worm food.

A male servant came in as soon as Bella left, clutching a steaming bowl of water, soap, towels and razor, clearly intent on bathing him like a baby. Seb sent him packing and groomed himself as best as he could, something which proved to be more challenging than he had first thought.

Being left-handed, and because the bullet which lodged itself in his ribcage had sailed inches shy of his heart, every movement of his arm sent pain shooting through his body. The repetitive action required to scrape the cutthroat over his unruly new beard was impossible. He briefly attempted it with his right hand and almost sliced his nose off, so Seb settled for clipping it as best as he could with scissors while trying to ignore the worrying image of his pale, gaunt face in the mirror and the dark-ringed sunken eyes that stared back.

He looked ill.

Seeing it for himself certainly gave him pause for thought for a moment, until his legendary stubbornness kicked in and he tossed the mirror on the bed. What difference did it make if he was pale and unkempt? In his job, he had to blend in to the shadows and mix with the flotsam and jetsam. His new complexion only served to camouflage him better, made him appear more fearsome, and the thick beard very nearly covered up the ugly jagged scar than ran down his right cheek. The one Seb hated far more than he loathed these four walls. His permanent reminder of his allotted place in the world. Perhaps he'd keep the beard? Even though that, too, itched.

Gingerly he tugged the clean linen shirt over his head and was relieved to see it just about fitted. He might well have lost weight, but the burly muscles he had inherited from his mother's family were still there. Farming stock and not the gentlemanly type. The sweat of his people had fertilised the land they had worked. Like his grandfather and *his* grandfather before him, Seb was still fundamentally as strong as an ox underneath the temporary sickly pallor. He had always been more farm labourer than gentleman and he'd be fighting fit again in no time. Not much ever laid down a Leatham, aside from extreme old age, and neither would one stray bullet. That thought cheered him as he flung his equally sturdy legs over the mattress and planted his big farmer's feet firmly on the floor.

When he tried to stand to dress himself, however, his legs almost gave way and he had to grab the bedpost quickly as his head spun. Then, for the first time in his adult life, Seb had to suffer the indignity of someone else supporting him as he dressed, and then made his way laboriously down the stairs, collapsing in the nearest chair like a wobbly newborn foal. Exhausted. Humbled. And frankly, a little bit scared at the extent of his deterioration.

There was no two ways about it, his recovery was going to take much longer than a week. Suddenly the safe cocoon of his bed didn't seem half as bad as it had half an hour ago, especially as the chair was now his new nemesis and one he could barely hold himself upright in. Perhaps he wouldn't attempt to venture outside today. Being scraped up from the ground would be the ultimate humiliation and one his stubborn pride would never allow. Unconsciously he rubbed the scar beneath his new beard. Seb loathed being beholden to others. He looked after himself and those dear to him. Always had. Always would. Another trait from his proud farming heritage and the harsh realities of life.

A maid came in with a tea tray. 'Good morning, Mr Leatham. How do you take your tea?'

'Milk. No sugar.' He looked down at his hands and cringed at how rude he sounded. 'Thank you.' He also loathed his crass ineptitude around women, especially the young and pretty ones. The ability to smile in their presence and be charming was not one he possessed. Seb wished he did, and it was not for want of trying, but each time he steeled himself to be more erudite than the average granite boulder, the awkward shyness tied his tongue in knots and the ability to string more than two words together evaporated. At best he barked at them so fiercely he scared them, and at worst he was simply mute.

Even the safe, married women had a similar effect. It had taken the best part of the last ten days to be able to converse with Bella properly and only because she had made a concerted ef-

fort to put him at his ease. He probably had all
those gruff farmers in his lineage to thank for that
unfortunate trait as well, because his father had
certainly never suffered from the affliction. He
could charm the birds from the trees to such an
extent he sincerely doubted the man's sheets had
ever been cold. Unlike Seb's, which rarely met
any skin which wasn't his. Yet another depressing thought in a day seemingly filled with them.

He heard the brittle rattle of china and risked
looking at the maid out of the corner of his eye.
He saw her sunny open smile had vanished because he'd been curt and monosyllabic yet again
and all the poor girl had done to deserve it was
bring him some tea. The gruff tone was a defence
mechanism which hid his shyness from the world,
although the maid wouldn't know that. Only his
closest friends knew of his affliction. Seb attempted a smile as she placed it on the side table
next to him and muttered another thank you into
his lap, then groaned as soon as she left the room.
If being fearsome was wholly inappropriate, usually he would be the first person to leave a potentially awkward situation, which was probably
why hiding in the shadows came so naturally to
him. Normally, when not sporting a debilitating
bullet hole, he would have darted out of the room
as soon as he heard the click of female heels on
the floorboards and returned when the coast was

clear—but of course, he could barely stand, let alone dart.

Bella came in next, smiling in that concerned way she and her husband did as a matter of course. 'I've brought you some books. They're a bit of a mixture, as I didn't know what you'd like to read, but I thought they might help pass the time.' She placed them on the side table next to the tea and then poured herself a cup. 'If it's any consolation, I know what it feels like to be bored. Joe is insisting that I stay at home and rest for three hours every day despite the fact I feel as right as rain.' She daintily sat on the sofa opposite him, her hand automatically resting on the increasing baby bump beneath her skirts. 'At least I now have you to keep me company.'

'Lucky you. I'm famous for my scintillating conversation.'

She grinned and took a sip of her tea. 'I've arranged for luncheon to be brought in here. I thought we'd both be more comfortable than sat rigid at the dining table. Would you mind if we ate it a little early? Only I find myself constantly starving nowadays.'

'I could eat.' Now that she mentioned it, Seb was hungry. Another good sign, he supposed. Evidence of the tiny steps of improvement he was making.

'Oh, I'm so relieved to hear that.' Bella grabbed

the bell and rang it. 'I will tell them to bring it immediately and use you as the excuse.'

Five minutes later and the same maid who had brought him tea came in with another tray. This one contained some delicate sandwiches and cakes and, to his abject horror, the dreaded invalid cup he had come to despise. He eyed it with distaste. 'Please tell me that's not more of your insipid broth!'

'It most certainly is and if you refuse to drink it again I shall tell Joe that I don't think you are quite ready to be out of bed. That broth is a carefully balanced recipe designed to restore your strength and vitality. You do *want* to get better, don't you?'

'Can you at least stop serving it to me through a spout like an infant? I am sat upright in a chair. I could take it just as easily in a teacup as in that monstrosity.'

'A fair point and one I shall certainly take on board at dinnertime—if you drink that one without…' The rattling of carriage wheels on the gravel outside made her pause and frown. 'I'm not expecting anyone… I wonder who that can be?' She placed her forgotten tea on the table and disappeared to investigate, leaving Seb alone with his dented masculinity, the foul restorative broth and the invalid's sipping cup. When she failed to materialise after five minutes, he snatched it up and searched for something close by to pour it into. He soon realised that was a forlorn hope and began to pour the tasteless, lukewarm contents quickly down his throat to get it over with.

'I shall order more tea.' At the sudden sound of Bella's voice so close he nearly choked and spilled the last drops over his chin, just in time for the most beautiful woman he had ever seen to appear at her elbow. Bella grimaced apologetically as he swiped the mess away with the back of one hand while trying to hide the awful cup with the other. 'We have a surprise visitor, Seb. My sister has abandoned the excitement of society to come to stay for a few days... Mr Sebastian Leatham—Lady Clarissa Beaumont.'

The vision, because there was no other word to describe the angelic perfection which had just walked in the room, momentarily appeared as surprised to see him as he was her. Her step faltered and he swore he saw a note of panic in her widened blue eyes before she caught herself. In fascination he watched her transform from startled and almost afraid to supremely confident. She tilted her golden head in acknowledgement, those beautiful eyes now amused at either his clumsiness or the freshly glowing red tips of his ears.

'Mr Leatham.'

The voice matched the face. Lovely. Lingering over the vowels just enough to sound subtly seductive, although Seb hadn't needed to hear it to be totally seduced—and mortified to be so. He was a clumsy oaf around most women, but in front of this goddess of perfection he stood no chance of behaving nonchalantly.

'M'lady.'

To compound his embarrassment, his errant tongue managed to completely slur the words, making him sound every inch the subservient farm labourer from rural Norfolk he truly was. Good manners dictated he stand, because that is what a real gentleman did in the presence of a *real* lady, and so Seb tried, winced and promptly collapsed back into the chair, winded.

'No, please. Don't get up on my account, you poor thing.'

Thing.

That stung.

'I didn't realise you had company, Bella.' She turned to her sister and he saw it again. That crack in her composure. 'Perhaps I picked a bad time to turn up unannounced?'

Bella threaded her arm through her sister's and grinned. 'Not at all. There's room enough for both of you. Don't you remember? I wrote to you about Seb.'

'Yes… Yes, you did. How silly of me to have forgotten.' The vision turned her perfect head and scrutinised him as if properly noticing him for the first time. No doubt she saw the same things he had in the mirror. The gaunt face. The ratty beard. The lack of both a coat and waistcoat because he didn't have the strength to shrug them on. The distinct lack of good breeding which he always tried to deny to the world. The ugly, jagged scar he wore like a badge. '*You* must be the brave hero who threw himself in front of a scoundrel's bullet to save the schoolmistress?'

To nod seemed arrogant, but he allowed his unsightly head to bob once rather than attempt to speak again, not that he had considered his actions particularly brave at the time. He was simply doing his job. Breaking cover and charging towards the gun had given his friend a chance at killing the aforementioned scoundrel and saving the girl. The selfless act had been instinctual. Necessary. To complete their mission and because his friend and an innocent woman had needed him. Only now, with the benefit of hindsight and in view of the fact he had very nearly died as a result, was he privately prepared to acknowledge it had been a ridiculously courageous thing to do. Stupid, too. After weeks to ponder his rash response Seb realised he could have simply shifted his camouflaged position in the bushes and shot the scoundrel himself instead. But then sometimes he did tend to over-complicate things when the simplest solution was staring him right in the face.

'Bella said you are lucky to be alive, Mr Leatham.'

'So they tell me.' Now he sounded typically clipped and unfriendly, his eyebrows already aching with the force of his scowl while the weight of her expectant stare was making his toes curl inside his boots. At a loss as to how to salvage the situation, he stared down at his hands and willed the floor to open up and swallow him.

'I see you are reticent to talk about it.'

'Seb is a man of few words.' He could hear the affectionate smile in Bella's voice and risked glancing up, only to find his eyes immediately lock once again with Lady Clarissa's. She must have seen the heat and longing hidden in their depths because the corners of her plump, pink mouth curved knowingly. He supposed a woman like her was used to being admired, but it still annoyed him to be so transparent, so he resolutely stared back at his coarse, callused hands with the most unfriendly expression he could muster. Why had he gazed winsomely at her? Society ladies weren't for him any more than society was. What a fawning idiot.

'Or Mr Leatham is merely being mysterious to pique my interest?'

Pique her interest! Now she was making fun of him. Seb lifted his eyes defiantly as he glared, his stubborn pride refusing to let him appear less than he wanted the world to see, or revealing his pitiful shyness. 'There's nothing much to tell, my lady. It all happened in a moment.'

'A significant moment, though.'

'Which rendered me blessedly unconscious.' An outright lie as he had lain on the ground in agony in a pool of his own blood far too aware of his life ebbing away. 'I have *no* memories of the event. Nothing to entertain *you* with.' Splendid. He was barking again. Conscious of the vision's eyes still on him, Seb sat silently and hoped she'd quickly lose interest, as ladies were often prone to do when confronted with his legendary charm and lack of real gentlemanly credentials.

A waft of something truly wonderful and feminine tickled his nose as she moved to sit on the sofa with her sister. Whatever it was, it altered the air in the room until everything was enlivened by her fragrance, heightening his remaining senses while he avoided directly looking at either of them in case he appeared smitten as well as struck dumb. He heard rather than saw the rattle of teacups. Mumbled thanks as his forgotten one was removed and replaced with a fresh one, then only risked picking it up when the two ladies were happily chatting about the state of the roads between Nottinghamshire and London. When the topic changed to society gossip, Seb allowed himself to relax while simultaneously trying to blend into the wallpaper. As there was nothing he could add to the conversation and nobody was likely to ask him anything, he took his first sip and covertly studied the vision as she talked.

Lady Clarissa was every inch a beautiful and sophisticated titled lady. Impeccably attired in what he assumed were the latest fashions, there wasn't a single hair out of place on her pretty head despite the fact she had travelled two hundred miles in a carriage. The symmetrical and casually loose ringlets which framed her cheeks were too bouncy, the intoxicating perfume too vibrant. If he were a betting man, Seb would lay good money on the fact she had stopped at an inn close by so that she could repair any damage and arrive looking as fresh as a daisy, rather than as wilted as a wet lettuce leaf like all the mere mortals would after days on the road. Surely nobody was that perfect? Judging by the creaseless silk of her becoming travelling dress, she had changed, too. No fabric looked that good after a jaunt up the Great North Road, especially when it moulded to her upper body like a second skin.

And it wasn't just the external façade which both bothered and intrigued him. Her voice was like warm honey, slow yet animated at the same time. Perfect for story-telling and he found his own ears hanging on her every word while his eyes kept being pulled by some invisible force to watch her. Whilst that was no hardship, the more he observed, the more he saw.

She had that practised way of moving he had noticed in others of her ilk, only magnified, which showed off her face and figure to perfection, yet the effortless grace didn't quite ring true either. A tad too choreographed to be natural. Even the position of her fingers as she held her tea-cup smacked of previous rehearsal, as if she had spent hours sat in front of a mirror, trying to discern the very best position to show off the delicate bones and the slimness of her wrist beneath the gossamer lace at her cuffs. Too perfect once again. Everything about her was too perfect, from her ridiculously long and seductive lashes to the oh-so-casual flick of that precisely positioned wrist.

Seb spent most of his life pretending to be someone else, usually a better man than he was, so he recognised an act when he saw one. Lady Clarissa Beaumont was a good actress. So good that her own sister didn't appear to notice the brittleness of some of her smiles or the flashes of sadness in her lovely cornflower eyes between blinks. The unconscious jerkiness of some of those movements that suggested she was nervous or uncomfortable.

While there was no doubting the instant and wholly male reaction he had experienced upon first meeting her, because she truly was the most exquisite woman he had ever seen, it was that hidden mystery which now piqued *his* interest. Those little clues to the real woman she might be beneath the carefully constructed mask she wore so well.

She must have sensed him watching her, because her eyes suddenly locked again with his. 'Don't think for a minute I have forgotten *you*, Mr Leatham.' Hot tea sloshed out of his cup and on to his leg at his being so hideously caught out. Only sheer pride held back the yelp of pain as he forced himself to return her gaze. For several long moments she searched his almost snarling face, then she picked up her teacup again and slanted him a coquettish glance over the rim.

'There is nothing I adore as much as a mysterious man. Is there a *Mrs* Leatham I should know about?'

The sudden and unexpected flirting tied his damn tongue into gauche knots again, although while he faltered he also knew with certainty she had done it on purpose. Another layer of artful trickery to hide the real her.

Chapter Two

Clarissa maintained the forced smile until the bedchamber door closed with a soft click, then her expression crumpled as the ever-threatening tears finally leaked their way out. Pretending everything was normal was proving exhausting, especially in front of a handsome stranger whose intelligent, hostile eyes seemed to bore into her very soul to the panicked and terrified girl inside.

Even if Mr Leatham hadn't been here, Clarissa acknowledged she wouldn't have shared her shame with her sister, because there was so much about herself she was ashamed of that hiding it was second nature. But at least if it were just them she would take solace in her younger sibling's calm and straightforward manner. Bella had always been the sensible one. Clarissa had fled here needing that honesty and forthrightness, needing to know that there were no subtle nuances or hidden meanings in conversations, hoping that a few days of not having to pretend to be perfect would fortify her enough to endure the rest of the awful Season—no matter what was thrown at her.

However, in just a few short minutes, her hasty flight from Mayfair to the north was not looking like the most prudent course of action. She had quite forgotten Bella was nursing a hero back to health. Clarissa still missed her sister dreadfully, and usually took great interest in the chatty, weekly letters Bella sent her. The letters she pretended she was far too busy to read. The same letters Clarissa laboriously read alone in her bedchamber, smiled over yet never replied to. Their mother's letters kept Bella up to speed with all Clarissa's news, assuming her eldest daughter was too busy or flighty to bother with such things, and out of pride she never corrected that false assumption because she had worked very hard to achieve it.

Whilst it wasn't the same as having Bella in London, those triangulated missives still felt like a conversation of sorts and reinforced their sisterly bond. But events in Clarissa's own life had rocked her to her core and quite overshadowed everything else, leaving her floundering and feeling so dreadfully alone and bereft. It had been instinctual to need Bella even though she knew she would never pluck up the courage to confide in her or anyone. There were too many lies now. A decade-and-a-half's worth. But with Bella she could at least lick her wounds in private and decide on the best move to make upon her return to fix the horrendous mess Clarissa had not seen coming.

None of those things would be easy to do with a stranger in their midst. Not only would Mr Leatham be here for the duration of her brief visit and beyond, Clarissa had not considered how painful it would be to see her brilliant baby sister blissfully happy, head over heels in love with a worthy man who obviously adored her. It rubbed even more salt into an already open wound and made her feel unbelievably stupid once again. Not that she really needed the extra reminders. She'd lived with them all her life.

She felt ashamed at envying Bella's happiness. Bella was not only brilliant and clever, she was kind, ridiculously brave and the most selfless individual Clarissa had ever known. Bella had worked hard to overcome her insecurities, while Clarissa worked hard to hide all hers. Her only ambition had always been to secure a good marriage to a decent man, one who loved her despite her flaws, become a mother and do wifely things. Frankly, with her limited abilities at anything else, that had seemed ambition enough. Her husband would shield her failings from the world and her life would have some purpose.

But then her face and figure had been lauded

as special and her head had been turned by the compliments. If she couldn't be brilliant, slightly clever or even of average intelligence, being beautiful and sought after had become far more important than it should. Why marry a decent man when she could marry a real catch? A duke, even? It would be the single most triumphant achievement of her life and something few young ladies could ever aspire to. And as the wife of a duke she could employ people to make up for all her failings. Duchesses were too busy to school their own children or reply to their own correspondence. As a duchess, no one—not even her illustrious husband—would ever need to know how truly stupid she was. The allure of perpetuating that lie had sucked her in and Clarissa had quite lost sight of her goals.

What a foolish dream! And yet another example of her lack of wits. She should have settled that first Season when the beaus had been plentiful. Now she was trapped in a nightmare she didn't dare leave, while sensible Bella was living Clarissa's only dream. She was loved for who she was—flaws and all.

As much as she loved her sister, she hated walking in her shadow. Bella had always been better than Clarissa in everything. More intelligent. More practical. More academic. More altruistic. She could play the piano, speak passable French in conversation and set a broken bone without any real effort at all. In the two years she had been married to her handsome physician, Bella was practically a fully trained physician herself, albeit one who would never hold the lofty title of doctor on account of her sex, and now she was to become a mother, as well. Unwittingly, she had achieved everything Clarissa had always hoped for and all without trying. While Clarissa had tried everything to win her a man and was still left sitting on the shelf. Unless she thought of a way out of her current, perilous situation quickly, that shelf was beginning to look as if it would become her permanent residence.

Of course, it hadn't helped that her sister had ribbed her over luncheon in front of Mr Leatham.

'Back in town Clarissa is highly sought after. She's considered an *Incomparable*. A *diamond* of the *first water*.' Bella had grinned mischievously and Clarissa had forced herself to shake her head and laugh.

'A preposterous title.' One she had simultaneously grown to loathe while also fearing the day when she was *not* being referred to as such. All the signs pointed to that day coming very soon. 'A silly nonsense thought up by the scandal sheets.' Who now had labelled other girls as beyond compare. Younger girls. Far more intelligent girls.

Girls who hadn't seen too many Seasons go by and were the new fresh faces competing for the very best gentlemen and one in particular. The Duke of Westbridge. The wealthiest and most eligible bachelor in London, who up until recently solely had eyes for Clarissa. Until his eyes had wandered to pastures new.

'A gem?'

Mr Leatham said this with a smile, the only one he had bestowed upon her, and for once it was a genuine smile, she could tell. His dark eyes had crinkled in the corners before he had scowled and quickly looked away. Perhaps he wasn't quite as brash and ferocious as he seemed?

He was not immune to her charms. Clarissa could see through his short, sharp answers and borderline rudeness because he couldn't seem to take his eyes off her. She was still pretty. Her only saving grace was intact. A reassuring piece of knowledge when her pride and her confidence were so severely damaged, although his charming reaction to her customary flirting came nowhere near close enough to repairing that damage. But then Mr Leatham was no duke and as such lacked the cold self-assurance such men wielded with cruel precision.

He was handsome though, in a rough and ready sort of way. The way he filled out the soft linen shirt he wore open at the neck was quite magnificent.

Broad shoulders, muscular arms, big hands which positively engulfed the delicate china teacup he was trying to hide behind. Nothing at all like the usual men of her acquaintance who padded their coats extensively to achieve half the effect. Nor did he try to impress her with bravado, as men usually did. He was a genuine hero. A man who had selflessly been prepared to sacrifice his own life to save another and was lucky to be alive. Every gentleman she knew would have crowed about his bravery from the highest rooftops, revelling in the deserved admiration he received from his peers. Not so Mr Leatham. As her sister had promised, he was a man of few words and those he did utter were curt. That curtness didn't put her off him in the slightest because behind his brief, gruff answers and standoffishness, he had nice eyes. Kind eyes. Eyes that told her he listened carefully to everything she said rather than treat her as a purely decorative companion whose only purpose was to listen to what *he* said. Eyes that frequently, shyly struggled to hold her gaze as he spoke.

How adorable was that?

Once or twice, between glares, Clarissa was convinced he even blushed—which was an unusually endearing trait in a man in his prime and one which made her predisposed to like Mr Leatham a great deal. Even though she knew next to nothing about him and had promised herself not to be so trusting ever again with so little background knowledge of a man's true character.

'I can't say I know any Leathams. Who are your people?' A ploy to change the subject, although she was curious about the enigmatic man who said so little but she suspected saw so much.

'They were farmers. In Norfolk.'

'Were?'

'I'm the last of the line.'

He said it in such a matter-of-fact way, as if being all alone in the world didn't matter, but immediately her heart went out to him. Clarissa hated being alone at the best of times because it allowed the doubts to creep in. She preferred to be in company because when socialising her mind was occupied and socialising was one of the few things she was good at. To have no one who cared about you—loved you—to be all alone with your thoughts didn't bear thinking about. How awful must it be to have nobody to go to in times of need? Nowhere safe and comforting to escape to when you felt inadequate, which she did daily. Or when the bottom had fallen out of your world and your poor heart was bleeding.

'Is the Season very dull this year?' Bella stepped in to save him and inadvertently hit another sore spot with her question. They both knew that the most exciting entertainments happened in the spring when everyone was in town because the weather was at its best.

'It is the same as it always is.' Except it wasn't. 'I thought I would squeeze in a quick visit to my favourite sister before the garden parties begin in earnest.' She flicked her eyes towards the reticent man in the chair opposite and hoped she appeared and sounded nonchalant. 'It all becomes very tiring Mr Leatham.'

'I wouldn't know, my lady.' Although something in his dark, intelligent eyes told her he knew much more than he let on. Saw far more than he said, which was unnerving and this time it was Clarissa who looked away first because she was frightened he would see the truth. Beneath the pretty face there was nothing else. An empty void of disappointing, below-average woman.

'Clarissa is being courted by a *duke*.'

'Is she now.'

'Yes indeed.' Bella had turned to her conspiratorially. 'Do we anticipate the announcement of your engagement imminently?'

The canny Mr Leatham had seen her lip tremble, his dark eyes had flicked to it, then back to look into hers, but regardless the practised lie still tripped off her tongue.

'I haven't said yes yet.'

Because the Duke still hadn't asked. Not once in the eighteen months of their much-gossiped-about acquaintance had the word *marriage* come up in conversation, let alone talk of affection, and Clarissa had become quite overt in her hints. He waltzed with her at every party. Sent her a bouquet of scarlet hot-house roses every Wednesday, drove her up and down Rotten Row each Saturday when the rest of Mayfair was there, all of which had served to scare off every other suitor she'd had, but the wretch hadn't so much as hinted at making their liaison official or once tried to steal a kiss. The conflicting behaviours had kept her on tense tenterhooks from the outset, something the Duke doubtless knew, but didn't seem to care about.

At first, Clarissa had assumed those things would come with time, that he was just being careful as a man befitting his high station *should* be careful when choosing a wife, but now she knew better. The Duke of Westbridge, although enamoured, wasn't nearly enamoured enough. She had accidentally overheard his own mother say as much in the retiring room at the Renshaws' ball only last week. A cruel coincidence seeing as that was the second ball at which he had failed to waltz with her once despite the fact she had saved both for him, and the third in which he had waltzed with Lady Olivia Spencer. The latest and brightest *Incomparable*—now Clarissa's significantly younger rival. If the gossip columns were to be believed—and she had no reason to doubt them—Lady Olivia had also received a bouquet of scarlet roses last Wednesday.

Thankfully, they hadn't learned that Clarissa's roses had suddenly been relegated to pink else she'd be a laughing stock as well as yesterday's news. She'd stamped on the damning stems before packing her bags and dragging her surprised maid halfway up the country, praying that absence really did make the heart grow fonder. At the ripe old age of twenty-three, it was now her only remaining hope of securing a suitable husband and making something of the poor arsenal of attributes the good Lord had graced her with.

'I'm sure it's only a matter of time before we all have to refer to you as *your Grace.*'

Bella's teasing tone was almost her undoing, but she managed to force a smile in response before hiding behind her own teacup, thoroughly disgusted at her own youthful foolishness at allowing herself to be seduced by the idea of being better than she was. Then she caught Mr Leatham staring at her quizzically. Almost as if he knew that the whole *Incomparable* Lady Clarissa was indeed one big, fat sham and the real Clarissa wasn't much of a catch for anyone. A sad truth which couldn't be denied.

After that, the rest of the lunch was pure torture. Mr Leatham listened to Bella regale tale after tale about Clarissa's legions of suitors, expecting her to embellish certain stories in her customary witty manner. It was exhausting and humbling to remember exactly how far she had fallen since her empty head had been turned. When Bella had insisted her patient return to bed because he looked worn out, Clarissa, too, pleaded tiredness from her travels. She needed time to lick her wounds in private and to repair her mask before dinner, which had been more of the same—only worse. Much worse.

Throughout the evening she had not only had to contend with Mr Leatham's intelligent, silent assessment as she pretended to be engrossed in a book to avoid conversation, but the sight of her baby sister and her husband together. Deliriously happy, perfectly content. Hopelessly in love. A stark reminder that Clarissa had failed to manage that in much the same way as she failed at everything else Bella excelled at. Yet hardly a surprise really. Bella had substance and Clarissa had none. Dreaming of finding a man who loved her was as futile as believing she could pull the wool over the eyes of the *ton* indefinitely.

Fleeing here had been a huge mistake. Her unexpected visit would be fleeting. Another day at most. Any more would likely destroy what was left of her self-esteem and render her a gibbering, self-pitying wreck. If she shed any more tears, it would show in her face—while Lady Olivia's fresh face would undoubtedly be strain-free.

She let her maid come in and help her prepare for bed, endured the pain of her hair being bound in the tight rags which kept her trademark ringlets in place, better than any curling irons, and then gratefully sank into bed. Only, sleep proved to be as elusive as a proposal and some time between midnight and dawn, she gave up and took herself back downstairs to warm some milk in the hope it would magically cure the restlessness and provide some respite from her worries.

Insomnia had always been an issue, even before she had taken to wearing the uncomfortable rags in bed. Clarissa had never been one of those people who could simply close her eyes and doze off. Her mind didn't work that way. Usually, it was at its most active as her head hit the pillow, and once she had given every dilemma some serious thought she naturally drifted off. But of course, usually the only dilemmas she had were what gown to wear to the next soirée, what topics of conversation would be the most engaging and what was the best way to tell a story so that she could consign it to memory. Everything had to be consigned to memory because she could hardly write it down.

Literally.

Like so many other talents, writing extended prose was beyond her capabilities. Now her head was filled with a conundrum which wouldn't be solved by a well-cut watered silk or a scandalous discussion about the latest society gossip. Now she had to work out a way to outshine Lady Olivia Spencer and capture her Duke for ever.

Then again, perhaps new gowns *were* the answer. Westbridge was a famous collector of beauty. It had been one of the biggest reasons she had chosen him as a potential husband. His ostentatious Mayfair mansion was crammed to the rafters with exotic objets d'art from around the globe. Ancient Egyptian sarcophagi sat beneath paintings from the Renaissance masters, Roman and Greek pottery adorned the finest Italian sideboards. Even the windows were draped in delicate French lace and the very best silk from the Orient. The mish-mash of styles had never been to Clarissa's liking, but the *ton* lauded him for his magnificent taste. Even the Regent was envious of her Duke's collection of art. She pretended enthusiasm with the same aplomb as she pretended to be so much better than she actually was. But Clarissa could be beautiful, if nothing else, and had ensured she was as beautiful as possible whenever she was in his presence in the hope he would add her to his collection. Fortunately, thus far he hadn't expected her to be anything else, which was just as well. Because there really wasn't anything else she could impress him with.

Unlike her sister, Clarissa's talents were few and the least said about her academic achievements the better. Once upon a time she had desperately wanted to learn, only to discover that she didn't possess the skills necessary to accomplish even that. She was the most unaccomplished *Incomparable* that ever graced the ballrooms of Mayfair, her only talents had always been the ability to charm the birds from the trees and to turn the heads of gentlemen.

She had a pleasing face and figure.

That was all.

A face and a figure which had been on the marriage mart for nearly four long years. If she could go back in time, she would have a stern talk with her younger self, remind her of her limits and tell her that setting her sights on a duke was pure folly. Dukes were fickle and few and far between. She should have married one of the earls or viscounts who had lined up to court her in her first two Seasons, then she would have the title which everyone believed an *Incomparable* deserved, albeit a lesser one. Those peers still had literate servants and paid for tutors. She'd be married, have her own home and probably a child or three already.

Then it wouldn't matter if her figure turned to fat because she desperately wanted to eat and her perfect cheekbones disappeared under plumper, happy, *married* cheeks. Or that she couldn't read any faster now than she did when she had been eight years old, despite her secret love of Mrs Radcliffe's novels, and, although her handwriting was lovely, because Lord knew she had practised it often enough in the private confines of her bedchamber, she couldn't spell to save her life. The letters were always correct, but the order they came in was nonsense. As mistress of her own house, she would issue all her instructions verbally, consign all important facts to her blissfully huge memory and pray that nobody—including that elusive yet-to-be husband—would be any the wiser to the shameful fact that she was on the cusp of being completely illiterate.

Agitated, she sloshed milk in a pan and set it to warm, then decided she was so depressed she deserved something sweet. Since her comeout she had denied herself cakes and biscuits, rarely ate anything covered in her beloved pastry and avoided any food bigger than the palm of her hand in case she gained unattractive weight, but frankly, after the week she'd had, only sugar would do. A quick rifle in the well-stocked pantry provided her with a whole round of crisp short-bread and a jar of strawberry jam. Exactly what she needed.

Despondent, she loaded the whole lot onto a tray and carried it into the drawing room. Sitting cross-legged on the sofa she unashamedly slathered a biscuit in a thick layer of jam, dipped the whole lot in her milk until it went deliciously soft and soggy, then shoved it into her mouth, sighing noisily in joy.

'Oh, you poor thing! Shall we call someone else to help carry you?' She had touched his arm in sympathy, an arm which he had tugged away swiftly as if he had been burned, which in a manner of speaking he had. He'd felt that calculated, flirtatious touch all the way down to his feet and at the roots of his hair. And once again, she had known the powerful effect she had on him. Doubtless it was the same effect she had over all men and to be yet another admirer in that long line made him feel insignificant in the extreme.

'I can manage myself.' Seb had let go of the footman and dragged his broken body up the next step unaided, only to be swamped with dizziness and forced to collapse back against the footman in case he fell. Joe had sprinted up next to him and grabbed his other arm.

'You're not strong enough yet to do this alone.'

'There is no need to be so proud in front of me, Mr Leatham.' That seductive voice again, secure in the knowledge that he had attempted to tackle the stairs alone because she was stood watching him. It was beyond galling.

Hours later it still galled. Those were the last words she'd said to him as she had watched him struggle the rest of the way up, denying him the dignity to fail so abominably at a simple task in private. He loathed being feeble and dependent on others; he had spent the first thirteen years of his life being an inconvenient dependent and had come to hate that state with a passion, but being feeble and so obviously dependent in front of *her* was beyond the pale.

The minx had run rings around him all day and had thoroughly enjoyed seeing him wrestle with embarrassment when his ferocious mask had slipped. He closed his eyes and for the umpteenth time relived some of the more cringeworthy moments of a day stuffed full of them. The way he had stuttered over the questions about a wife, a fiancée or anyone he particularly had his eye on had been awkward in the extreme, but nothing compared to the horrendous way he had blushed when she had noticed he had put a coat on for dinner and then told him he needn't have bothered on her account, *you poor, brave thing*, so it was patently obvious she had known he'd donned the too-tight borrowed coat expressly for her.

His stupid ears had glowed for several minutes afterwards because she had made a point of watching them intently and asking repeatedly if he was hot. Which he was. With shame at his own legendary ineptitude around the fairer sex, while she was undoubtedly the fairest of them all, and for being such an obvious clod in her presence. Even while she was teasing him, his traitorous gaze kept wandering back to her irritatingly perfect face, finest of fine eyes and luscious, vexing mouth. His errant thoughts distinctly carnal, yet his mouth crippled by angry self-consciousness. He'd picked at his food like a bird, despite the fact he was famished, in case he further disgraced himself and dribbled more on his chin. By the end of the interminable meal, his conversation had deteriorated into growled one-word answers.

Yet the Gem still persisted with her questions even as they both sat reading before bedtime.

Mercilessly.

He might currently be a monosyllabic, coarse clod, but even clods had some pride. If he couldn't be erudite, he could at least be fit enough to facilitate his own escape next time he collided with her and climb those damn stairs himself! He would exercise away the weakness in his body and find a way to conquer those stairs… Obviously in secret. Well away from the mocking eyes of the *Incomparable* or his well-meaning hosts. If Bella or Joe caught him exercising before they thought he was ready, they'd put a servant on watch and he'd be chained to the bed for sure. But if he wasn't allowed to move, how the hell was he supposed to build his strength up? They didn't know his limits and, by God, he had a long way to go yet before he reached them!

And thanks to her he was now starving as well as emasculated. Building his strength up required food, which was also down those blasted stairs. Imbued with the outraged strength of the self-righteous and clutching his painful abdomen, Seb gingerly sat up, then slowly twisted his legs from the mattress. He used the nightstand and rested the full weight of his body on his arms to stand up, then panted through the pain as it burned in his gut. He shuffled, rather than walked, to the door, then muttered a frustrated obscenity under his breath. It would take a month of Sundays to get fit at this arduous rate and he was damned if he would lose a month. He needed to push past the pain. Ignore the weakness. Be better than he was, which ironically was the sorry story of his life. Always trying to be better, yet never quite measuring up.

Remarkably, the discomfort lessened as he shuffled along the landing. Clearly moving was warming up those atrophied muscles. They still screamed, but not so much in agony any longer, more just a disgruntled shout. Maybe in a few more minutes, the shouting would become the occasional bellow? He simply had to push himself, just as he always had. Especially when things were at their worst. It never ceased to amaze him what he was truly capable of when he stretched himself to his limits, something he did with surprising regularity thanks to the obstacles life constantly put in his way and because of his stubborn refusal to let others believe he wasn't good enough when he tried to prove to everyone he was. From birth, his betters had always looked down their noses at him, casting unsupported judgements based entirely on prejudice, and he prided himself on always proving them wrong. Seb was as good as anyone. He made sure of it. It was that tenacity that made him a fearless fighter, a logical problem solver and a damned good spy. Only he knew he didn't believe it himself.

The staircase loomed, mocking him. The foul taste of humiliation at having to be supported by two men as they hauled his sorry carcass back up it in front of Lady Clarissa was something Seb never wanted to repeat. *'Oh, you poor, brave thing.'* He bet she never referred to her fancy Duke as a thing. It was an insulting label he never wanted to hear again. Which meant he needed to get up and down those damn stairs himself to be able to safely disappear into the sanctuary of the same bedchamber he had thought a prison only this morning. Safe from *Incomparables* with a warped sense of humour and his own intense and mortifying reaction to them.

He stared at the steps with a heavy heart. They were steep, he knew, and the hard wood jarred his mashed guts with each painful step. There had to be a way of doing it without nearly dying from the effort. Rely on the strength in his arms, perhaps? Lean on the banister a certain way? Whatever it took, he would find a solution tonight and save himself from all potential further embarrassment.

Supporting himself on his good side, Seb gripped the sturdy banister for all he was worth and rested his upper body on it. Only then did he risk lowering one foot down. The movement did something to his torn innards which robbed him of the ability to breathe. It took a full ten seconds before he could lower the other foot, but that hurt less as everything inside lurched to its proper place. Encouraged, he managed another four stairs in much the same manner, then, fearful he was about to pass out, allowed himself five minutes' rest slumped over the wood. After the next four stairs, he was dangerously light-headed and needed to lie down, but as there was now a greater distance upwards than down he decided his best option was to recover on the sofa. Down had to be easier than up. Up, in his current state, might well kill him.

The remaining stairs caused white-hot pain behind his eyes despite the fact he took them slower than the clock hands had moved over dinner and he found himself slumped against the bottom banister for an age before he could even think about moving again, heartily annoyed at himself for biting off far more than he could plainly chew and being goaded by his stubborn pride to do so because of her.

Attempting the stairs had been stupidity incarnate. Something a weakened man with a hole in his chest and a distinct lack of energy should never have attempted alone. Pride had been his sole motivator, just as it always had been when fate thought it was having the last laugh. But pride came before a fall. It was a blasted miracle he hadn't fallen and undone all the good work the doctor had done. The implications didn't bear thinking about. Ripped stitches. Internal bleeding. And all in the middle of the night when there was nobody around to save him. Seb deserved a damn good telling off for being so careless with his life and was likely due one unless he could find the strength to get himself back to his bed before his hosts found out what a blithering idiot he had been or Miss Perfect witnessed this fresh humiliation.

However, returning up Mount Staircase at this very moment was out of the question. The muscles in his arms were shaking from the effort of getting down, acid was roiling in his stomach and his head was all over the place. He needed to sit. Rest. Regroup. The door to the drawing room was ten feet away, yet that ten feet suddenly felt like ten miles now, longer if he hugged the wall rather than went as the crow flies. There seemed little chance he could get there without a wall propping him upright, so he didn't bother trying.

Seb fell against it thankfully and squeezed his eyes shut against the pain, allowing the cold plaster to cool the burning in his back until the dizziness and nausea subsided. From then on, he edged his way along the hallway, shuffling again as that was all he had left in him, until he finally arrived at his destination. In a few steps there was soft upholstery. Nothing else mattered.

Chapter Three

Clarissa yelped as the door slammed suddenly open in the silence, the soggy piece of shortbread falling from her fingers and smearing strawberry jam over the front of her nightgown. Not that Clarissa noticed. She was too busy gaping at the sight of the semi-naked Mr Leatham propped against the frame.

He was wearing breeches and a bandage.

Nothing else.

Her mouth went suddenly dry as her palms became moist. Good gracious, he was so…well built. The soft light from the single candle she had next to her gave his skin a golden hue, the shadows emphasising the powerful muscles in his arms and shoulders. Above and below the bandage wound tight around his middle was a dark dusting of hair over even more muscle. It stopped at the base of the strong neck her eyes appeared unable to move above.

Why would they when his body was so very… manly? All in all, it was possibly the most splendid sight Clarissa had ever witnessed.

'I'm sorry… I didn't mean to frighten you.'

Against her own body's wishes, she tore her gaze away from his chest and only then saw the strained look on his face as he rested against the wood. He was very pale. Clearly struggling to stand. Instinctively she shot off the sofa and went to his aid.

'Oh, Mr Leatham. You poor thing! Here—let me help you.'

'I am not a *thing*, madam, and you would do well to remember it!'

Bravely ignoring his murderous expression, she wrapped one arm about his waist and regretted it instantly. His skin was deliciously warm to the touch. Soft velvet draped over steel. His back was as solid as the rest of him appeared, those strong muscles bunched under her fingers making them tingle in the most peculiar way. Forcing herself to concentrate, she wrapped her other arm carefully around his bare arm to help support him. 'Lean towards me. Let's get you sat down.'

He did as she asked and she felt his muscles quiver as she manoeuvred him carefully towards the sofa, supremely conscious of how large he was in close quarters. Her head barely reached his chin, the hand which had clamped about her wrist dwarfed hers. Its warmth seemed to brand her, searing her skin in a wholly pleasant but completely inappropriate way. Her heart quickened and her body yearned. That was the only way she could think to describe what was happening. She had the strange urge to run her hands all over his torso, just to discover exactly what all those impressive muscles felt like. Clearly eating too much sugar had scrambled her brain because she was not normally so...needy.

Attempting to ignore her unladylike reaction, Clarissa changed position to help him sit, her face now tantalising close to his neck. So close she could see where the pulse beat beneath his ear. Close enough to be aware of the glorious, masculine smell of him. Just soap and clean sheets, yet the heat of his body made those common fragrances heady in a way which caught her by surprise. His ragged breath feathered against her cheek and did strange, alluring things to parts of her body that had no place being excited. Not when the poor man was in agony and she was the only person around to help him.

'Thank you.' His eyes were kind again as he shyly looked away. 'I didn't mean to growl.'

She took a hasty step back, clasping her errant hands primly in front of her because they didn't feel anything like hers any more and she didn't quite know what to do with them. 'Do you want me to fetch help?' Part of her wanted to run away and put some well-needed distance between them. Another part of her scandalously wanted to keep him all to herself. Because he was almost naked and…well…she liked it…and was definitely attracted by the festival of intriguing raw maleness in front of her. And it wasn't just his physique which intrigued her. The gruff, blushing, intuitive Mr Leatham was equally alluring. She had never been so confused about a man in her life. The usual signals were a contradiction. He was outwardly unfriendly and detached, but had kind, soulful eyes when he thought she wasn't looking. He seemed so disapproving of her, yet blushed when she flirted. Each time their eyes had met over dinner, her pulse had fluttered. What was that about, when she was supposed to be mourning the loss of her Duke? The fluttering now was making her jumpy. 'I could wake Joe or Bella.'

He shook his head despite the pain etched on his expression. 'No!' He jabbed the air with his finger, ferocious once again. 'Brandy! Lots of it!'

Clarissa scurried over to the decanter and sloshed as much over her quivering hand as she did in the glass. She pressed it into his, the touch playing yet more havoc with her bouncing nerve endings, holding it steady as he brought it to his mouth and then severing the contact as quickly as she could because her uncharacteristic reaction frightened her.

It wasn't like her to be so flustered around a man. Being a flirt and charming them was probably the only thing she truly excelled at, yet here she was, more flustered than she had ever been in her life. Mr Leatham had managed to make her feel off kilter since the first moment she had laid eyes on him this morning. With his clothes on he was disconcerting. Without them he thoroughly disorientated her. In such close proximity to his breathtaking presence, Clarissa was uncomfortably lost for words.

Mute, she watched him gulp down the brandy, trying to ignore the way his Adam's apple bobbed with each swallow or how his ridiculously broad shoulders rose and fell in time with his laboured breathing. He rested his head on the back of the sofa and closed his eyes, the empty glass still clasped limply in his hand.

'Would you like some more?'

He nodded without opening his eyes and held out the crystal balloon glass. 'Don't be stingy with it.'

Clarissa made sure no part of her hand touched his as she took it, refilled the glass and passed it back. For a moment, she seriously considered pouring herself some to steady her nerves, then decided against it because her wits were scrambled quite enough already. There was no telling what they would do under the influence of fortifying spirits. This time he sipped the brandy more slowly and she was relieved to see the colour begin to return to his face. Only when he had eventually drained the second glass did he open his eyes and look at her.

And, good gracious, did he look at her. His dark eyes slowly raked her body from the face down, then darkened as they laboriously climbed back up to meet hers.

Then he chuckled. The sound more intoxicating than any brandy.

'You look like Medusa.'

The chuckle turned into a laugh which had him wincing as he held his abdomen.

'And is that jam all over your front?'

One hand went to her head and then her bosom ineffectually. 'You caught me by surprise. I dropped my biscuit!' A true gentleman would never have mentioned it. Not outright at any rate. The fact that he had made her feel silly and exposed. 'What do you think you are about, slamming through doors in the dead of night? It's your fault I look a fright.'

He glanced to the stain on her front, then back to her head. 'Then I apologise for frightening you—but that still doesn't explain your hair. What the blazes have you done to it?'

Both hands now shielded the brightly coloured array of rags sticking up from her head, as if covering them now would erase the mortification she'd experienced at having him see them. Attempting haughty indifference, Clarissa returned her hands to her sides. 'The rags set the curls.'

'I knew they weren't natural.' More evidence of his lack of gentlemanly manners.

'No ladies' curls are natural. We all go to bed like this.'

'Why?'

'Because curls are becoming.'

'Ah. I see.' Although he plainly didn't. Still smiling, he leant forward and flicked one of them. 'They look painful. Do they hurt?'

Yes. 'No. I barely notice them.'

'But they are dragging your eyebrows up. You look permanently startled.' His lips twitched again. 'Do you wake up with your face aching?'

'Oh, go ahead. Laugh. Have your fun. I doubt a *mere* farmer from Norfolk would understand the world I live in.'

She had meant to offend him, remind him his manners were sadly lacking and to put him back in his place, yet he didn't appear the slightest bit offended. 'You poor *thing*! I never realised how the other half suffered. I'm curious—without those...' he gestured to her head '...monstrosities, what does your hair really look like?'

'It is as straight as a poker. Just like my sister's.' Why had she confessed that?

'Bella has lovely hair.'

'Yes, of course she does, but…' Having to justify her choice of hairstyle was ridiculous, so she clamped her mouth shut in case she said things she would rather he didn't know. Bella didn't have to be persistently beautiful every waking minute of the day. She had her man. And her enormous brain and copious talents.

'But you are the *Incomparable*, therefore your hair *has* to curl. Your clothes *have* to be perfect. Every *nuanced* movement has to convey your sheer perfection. *A diamond of the first water.*' He wafted his large hand in the air like a ballet dancer. Mocking her. Earlier he could barely string two words together and now suddenly he was capable of the most cruel and cutting insults. More cruel because they were completely accurate. The insufferable, insightful man.

'Go back to planting your turnips!' Clarissa stomped to the door.

'It was turkeys actually, not turnips. But mostly geese, if you must know. Norfolk is famous for its poultry. Every year my grandfather would walk them to London wearing little leather boots to protect their feet. Always made me laugh as a child. Birds in boots.' He said this conversationally, his deep voice slurring slightly. Clarissa turned against her better judgement and saw him slumped a little and smiling soppily. It was the brandy loosening his tongue, she realised. She had given him rather a lot of it. 'Would you read to me? You have a lovely voice.'

'No, I will not.' The suggestion alone had brought out a cold sweat and panic. 'It would be wholly improper.'

'Can you at least pass me the shortbread before you leave? I daren't move and I'm starving.'

Of their own accord, her feet moved to do his bidding. She snatched up what was left of the original biscuit and thrust it at him, only to have him snap it in half and pass a piece right back. 'It was your midnight feast. I'd feel guilty if I ate it all. Does shortbread taste better with jam?' His eyes flicked to the jar.

'Everything tastes better with jam.' To prove her point she dipped the edge of hers in the pot and then held it out for him to do the same. He took a bite, chewed thoughtfully, then nodded.

'You are right. It does. But if you have such a sweet tooth, why did you refuse the trifle at dinner?'

'I didn't feel like trifle.'

'Of course.' He said it with a disbelieving note of sarcasm before taking another bite while those dark eyes scrutinised hers. 'Is he worth it?'

'I'm sorry?'

'Your duke? Is he worth depriving yourself of desserts and trying to sleep with all that nonsense on your head?'

This man was too insightful. 'He's a *duke*.'

'Dukes are merely men in finer waistcoats.'

Clarissa smiled then, she couldn't help it. Like this, a little bit tipsy and suddenly vocal, Mr Leatham was quite charming. 'And there speaks a man with little experience with the breed.'

'I have lots of experience with dukes. My father was one.'

The last bite of biscuit paused midway to her lips. 'You jest!'

'Not at all. My father was a very illustrious duke.' He waved his hand in the air loftily. 'Very well connected at court—although I'm not supposed to talk about it or mention his name alongside mine. It's a big secret. He thought himself most benevolent in quietly acknowledging me behind closed doors and providing for me financially. I received a gentleman's education, I'll have you know. I even went to Cambridge… Never had a seat at his table though. Appearances and all that.'

'You are a…' How did one put it politely?

'By-blow? *Nullius filius?* Illegitimate? Born on the wrong side of the blanket? There are many gentle ways to say *bastard*, my lady—none of them alter the truth.' He toasted her with his glass.

'I have a half-brother who's a duke, too. He's a pompous man. Once called me a "thing", just like you did. *"Get that thing out of my house."* I remember it verbatim because those are the only words he's ever said to me.'

Her cornflower eyes widened and Seb wondered what had possessed him to tell her, until he remembered he had consumed two huge glasses of brandy, in quick succession and on an empty stomach whilst physically as weak as a kitten. He'd never been much of a drinker and thanks to his injury hadn't touched a drop in a month. Was it any wonder the strong spirit had gone straight to his head? 'Sorry. Didn't mean to tell you that. I think those brandies have loosened my tongue. I'm not normally this chatty. Usually I'm shy around females. Painfully shy. I don't suppose a fine lady like yourself would understand what that's like, but aside from my mother I never really knew any women growing up... Why am I admitting that?' It hadn't just loosened his tongue, apparently it had also greased his jaws.

'By the time I was grown I had no clue what women to go for. Being a by-blow you sort of sit on the fence between the two. I am neither a gentleman nor a peasant. I have nothing in common with the uneducated women and I have no experience of the merchant class, so never really understood where a man in my position hunts for women. And so many look down their nose at my situation, it's rather put me off trying. Do you know, I can't even flirt? Never dared try it.' Largely because he didn't want to suffer the inevitable reaction when they learned he was nothing better than a rich man's bastard.

Her multicoloured head leant closer. 'Are you telling me that you have *never*…?' Her words trailed off as her perfect cheeks blushed.

'No! Of course not. There have been a *few* women, but fortunately, every woman has seduced me. Thank goodness. Else I'd be hurtling towards thirty with no experience whatsoever.' Seb started to laugh at his own ineptitude. 'The first time, I was so green I didn't realise what was going on until I found myself in her bedroom. Probably shouldn't have told you that either, but I'm very tired.' He could feel his limbs getting heavier with fatigue and suspected he would sleep like a baby for the rest of the night. Lord, he was exhausted. So weary he could barely see straight. All she had to do was ask and he probably would confess all his secrets.

Yet sat here with her in the candlelight, his tongue blessedly untied for once, admitting to his shameful lineage and his failings had been surprisingly easy. With her hair poking out of her head in rainbow tufts, jam stains on the front of her nightdress and one unnoticed sticky lump glued just above her lip, the Gem didn't seem half as terrifying as she had before. There was something endearingly normal about her now and somehow he found this version far more attractive than he did the other incarnation. This woman was real. Vulnerable and much more accessible. Despite the pull of Morpheus, he wanted to spend more time with her. 'Why do you want to marry a duke? Their privilege and upbringing make them very difficult men.'

She inhaled deeply, then sighed it out, perching herself on the edge of the chair directly opposite him while she considered whether or not to answer. Then she shrugged. 'He's a *duke*.'

'Who clearly makes you miserable.'

'Why do you say that?'

'Because I might be hopeless with women, but I notice things, Gem. Every time his name came up in conversation today, your smile wasn't genuine.' At least the brandy had numbed the pain even though Seb had to concentrate to keep his eyes open.

'Dukes are fickle things.'

'That they are. But they are still men.' And untrustworthy ones at that.

She swayed closer, within arm's reach as she listened intently to his words. With staggering clarity considering his progressively inebriated state, and his increasingly heavy eyelids, he knew she had lost her confidence. Something which was as mind boggling as it was tragic. 'Stop giving him power over you. Don't let his elevated social standing and inflated sense of his own importance diminish what you are.' Wise words he had tried, yet still failed, to live by. His hand stretched out and touched her cheek. It was soft. So soft. Absolute perfection. Her eyes lifted to his and they shared what he thought was a perfect moment. One he ruined with a huge, noisy yawn.

She immediately stood up, her lovely face etched with concern. 'You do look very tired, Mr Leatham. Shall I fetch someone to help you back up to bed?'

He couldn't face stairs. Not yet. And certainly not in front of her. 'I think I'll sleep here.' In case she pushed the point, Seb stretched his long legs along the full length of the sofa and rested his weary head on the arm. It felt exactly like a cloud. 'But I wouldn't say no to a blanket.' His eyes fluttered closed as he heard her moving around to get one, then enjoyed the sensation of her gently draping it over his body and tucking him in. 'Are you sure you won't read to me?'

'Quite sure. Goodnight, Mr Leatham.'

'Goodnight, Gem.'

As she stepped away he grabbed her hand and tugged her closer until she kneeled at his temporary bedside, needing to look at her one last time without the usual awkwardness which always crippled him and wanting to chase away the uncertainty she was trying so desperately to hide. Possessed with a mind of its own, his suddenly bold, drunk index finger traced the shape of her lips.

'You are a beautiful woman, Gem. The most beautiful woman I have ever seen. You are sharp and funny and hugely entertaining.' He probably shouldn't have confessed that truth either, knowing she'd likely use it against him in the morning when the Dutch courage had worn off and he was back to being shy again, but right now he didn't care. 'Any man, even a duke, would be lucky to have you. Don't forget that. If he cannot see all the wonderful things you are, then he is also a fool and doesn't deserve you.'

The sunny smile which blossomed on her face had a similar effect to the brandy, making him glad he was lying down. 'Thank you, Mr Leatham.' She stroked his whiskers with her palm, then stood and blew out the candle, plunging the room into darkness. 'I shall try to remember that.'

The last thing Seb heard was the quiet swish of her nightgown as she left the room. But when he woke to bright daylight and the bustling noise of household activity, the Gem, her ridiculous hair rags and the carriage she had come in were gone.

Chapter Four

~~~~~~~~~~

London, six weeks later...

Lord Fennimore's message had come in the middle of the night, summoning all the King's Elite to his study immediately. Seb arrived at the same moment his friend Flint did and the pair of them were none the wiser as to why. Another man was sat alone next to Fennimore's desk. Tall and blond, he introduced himself as Hadleigh, treated them both to a very firm handshake and explained he had been appointed the Crown Prosecutor for their particular case, although why they needed a lawyer when they had no new or living suspects at present was a mystery. The last had been ruthlessly murdered by the same man who had shot Seb before meeting his own maker. Since then, all the leads in the Boss's extensive smuggling network had led to nothing but dead ends.

'There has been a development.' Never one

for preamble, their superior stalked into the room and handed out three sheets of foolscap. 'We have intercepted a message which gives us two new names. If they are to be believed, then it seems the Earl of Camborne apparently controls the operation in Cornwall and Devon, and Viscount Penhurst holds sway over the Sussex coastline. It is the first credible lead we have received since our recent obliteration of the Thames contingent and I am inclined to take it seriously. It makes sense they would divert his entire operation to the south. Whilst it's a longer journey across the Channel, it's also sparsely patrolled by the Excise Men. Certainly, the amounts of contraband do not appear to have diminished in the last two months and, as we've long suspected, the Boss has merely adjusted his supply chain to accommodate the loss of the estuary route. There is also mounting evidence that the majority of proceeds are still headed to Napoleon's supporters. The message was signed Jessamine—a common enough French name—but makes mention of the Comte de St-Aubin-de-Scellon who conveniently happens to be one of the most sycophantic of Bonaparte's cronies. Such a link is too coincidental not to be of grave cause for concern. It also suggests that St-Aubin is keen to raise the amount of barrels of brandy that are entering the country illegally, when the black market is already flooded with them. The amounts of money involved do not bear thinking about, but if he is successful they are certainly enough to raise an army.'

'It's a big risk taking the word of one intercepted message.' Flint said exactly what Seb was thinking. A smuggler's word could rarely be trusted, even in a coded note. Yet they also knew the Boss used members of the British aristocracy to sell on the cargoes. Seb's gut instinct told him there was no smoke without fire and these two peers definitely needed investigating.

'Perhaps—but early intelligence suggests the information is sound. Certainly, both Camborne and Penhurst have recently enjoyed a significant lift in their previously ailing fortunes, both are well connected and both have estates which abut the shoreline.'

'I agree. There are too many coincidences for us to ignore it.' And Seb was chomping at the bit to get back in the field now that he was as fit as a fiddle. 'I can have my men tracking the beaches by tomorrow night.' Already his mind was racing through the logistics. Two simultaneous missions left the King's Elite spread very thin.

'I know Camborne. Our fathers were friends,' said Flint, all business.

'Which is exactly why I'm sending you home to *rusticate* in Cornwall. Infiltrate his circle and learn the lay of the land.' Fennimore turned abruptly to Seb. 'And I want you to befriend Penhurst.'

Seb commanded the Invisibles. Highly skilled operatives who lived in the shadows and watched. He preferred to blend in and never stand out. Never, ever stand out. 'I don't befriend people.'

'This time you do.'

'With all due respect, sir, Warriner is back from his honeymoon in three weeks. Wouldn't it be better to wait for him? We have always worked to our own strengths. You, yourself, selected us based on them and he's the one with the talent for befriending.' Jake Warriner oozed charm and enjoyed society. Basically, he was the exact opposite of Seb. 'Meanwhile, I can lay the groundwork. Infiltrate his staff.'

'I'm well aware of his areas of expertise, Leatham, but we don't have three weeks. Penhurst is hosting a house party for his friends in less than a fortnight and I need you to be there. It's too good an opportunity to miss. You can poke around the grounds and pay close attention to the man and his comings and goings. Your particular area of expertise.'

Lord Fennimore had clearly gone mad. 'And how exactly am I supposed to befriend a total stranger and secure an invitation to his house in just two weeks?' They all knew Seb had no standing in the *ton*. He'd always avoided it, for obvious reasons. He was a completely unknown entity and blissfully content to remain so. Stepping foot into the same elevated ranks as his father would make Seb uneasy. He hated the nagging doubts that went alongside not being born good enough and really didn't need a reminder of his place in the world. He felt his hand automatically trace the scar on his cheek, the reward he had received the last time he'd openly set foot in Mayfair. Since that day, he had remained resolutely in the shadows where he belonged. 'I know no one.'

'Which makes you perfect for the mission. One thing we do know about the Boss is he likes his minions to recruit like-minded fellows into his network. He relies on that ready and waiting line of succession to slot in when the others fall by the wayside.' A very polite way of saying those that displeased the as-yet-unidentified master of the dangerous organised smuggling ring, or had ceased to be useful to him, tended to wind up dead. 'We've created an alias for you. Lord Sebastian Millcroft—originally from Lancashire because we all know few in society venture further north than is absolutely necessary and there won't be enough time to check your credentials. But even if they have knowledge of the area, your family were minor gentry at most. You emigrated with them to the Antipodes as a babe, where they promptly died and left you to flounder by yourself. Only recently are you returned to English soil, your pockets stuffed with the huge fortune you have made on the other side of the globe from slightly dubious means, seeking interesting investment opportunities now that you are finally home.' Fennimore pulled open the drawer in his desk and withdrew a pile of books. 'Reading material to aid you in embellishing your new history.'

Seb stared at them with distaste. Not so much because of the reading, but because what Fennimore was proposing involved socialising. With peers. And ladies. Lots of ladies. He'd much rather be shot again. 'But, sir…'

Fennimore held up his hand. 'You make your first appearance in society tonight. As the honoured guest of the Earl of Upminster. He has been briefed on your mission and will give credence to your new identity. Penhurst will be in attendance and Upminster will introduce you. From there, it will be down to you. I trust you to do your duty and get into the man's house!'

Seb looked to Flint for support, but his friend merely grinned. 'I wish I could be there to see it.' Because they both knew it would be carnage.

'Hadleigh here has been drafted in so that we can act swiftly if and when the pair of you gather enough evidence for their arrests. We don't want either to invoke Privilege of Peerage and avoid trial. As soon as we have proof of treason, Hadleigh will race through impeachment proceedings and have them stripped of their titles. Time is of the essence here, gentleman. If we work fast, we could make some serious inroads into the Boss's supply lines. They have no idea we have intercepted the message. Within a few hours of receiving it, it arrived safely at its destination with the recipient none the wiser. As far as Penhurst and Camborne are concerned, it's business as usual. For now, we watch and we wait. When we take them down, I want it to hurt the Boss significantly. I don't want one packet or twenty. I want to obliterate his stronghold in the south just as we did the Thames. In the meantime, Hadleigh will assist me in scrutinising all aspects of their lives here in town and see if we can find out how they are moving the money while my two best men discover exactly how they make it.'

Seb didn't share his superior's faith in his abilities. 'Perhaps there is another way I can get inside Penhurst's house. Big estates always need workers. That is how I've always operated before.' Playing the servant was much more Seb's style. Working men, their aspirations and their mindset, he understood. Aristocrats, in the main, were a complete mystery.

'Jobs for your Invisibles, Leatham. I need my most trusted field agents shadowing the ringleaders.'

'But I don't have anything to wear!' Had that pathetic sentence just come out of his mouth? Judging by the bark of laughter from his supposed friend on his right, it had. As excuses went, even forlorn, last-hope excuses, Seb was prepared to acknowledge that one had been pretty dire. The King's Elite had all been meticulously selected for their resourcefulness and adaptability. Two attributes he had always possessed in spades. As did his superior.

Lord Fennimore pinned him with an icy glare that would curdle milk. 'Your attire has been taken care of. I assumed your measurements are much the same as they were last December when we had that footman's uniform made for you and your fancy wardrobe should be winging its way to your new lodgings as we speak.'

'New lodgings?' Things were going from bad to worse. Seb liked his secluded little apartment in Cheapside, sandwiched between the rich and poor of London. It was the perfect place to blend in and to escape from his work. Like him, it fitted somewhere in between both classes so he didn't have to pretend to be one or the other. Which he wasn't and never would be. Unease began to churn away in his belly. With his background, surely Lord Fennimore wouldn't…

'Of course you have new lodgings! You're supposed to be in possession of a huge fortune. A fortune to lure money-grabbing criminals to crawl out of the woodwork! You have full use of a town house in Grosvenor Square.'

Still Mayfair, but at least not Berkeley Square. That was a little too close to his past for comfort. Then the perfect excuse struck him. 'And what if my dear brother sees me?'

'Thetford? He hasn't clapped eyes on you in what? Fifteen years?' Almost to the day. Seb still remembered his mother being evicted from the hunting lodge on his father's estate just hours after the man had been declared dead. His long and terrifying journey to Mayfair alone to plead for their home. He'd been a boy. Only thirteen. His childhood had come to a shuddering halt soon after, but he had learned a valuable lesson. A man of his status could never trust the aristocracy. 'I doubt he'd know you if you spat in the fool's eye. It's hardly as if you were close. I hate to be callous, Leatham, but with men like that, it is most assuredly a case of out of sight, out of mind. To him you no longer exist. You ceased to exist the day he inherited his title. Besides, he left town yesterday and is not expected back until September. I pride myself in foreseeing every potential complication, Leatham. You know that. Many of the house staff have been replaced with some of your own men as I knew you'd want them close by. I've even made Gray your valet.'

'Why can't Gray be Lord Millcroft?' As a real lord, albeit a disgraced and impoverished one, his second-in-command was much better qualified.'

'Gray doesn't have your years of experience or your level head. This job requires both. It is too important to palm off on a subordinate.' Lord Fennimore wound the wire frames of his reading spectacles around his ears and picked up a piece of paper, his usual signal that the meeting was done. 'Get yourself to Grosvenor Square and begin your preparations, Leatham. And shave off that damn beard. That's an order.'

Sensing his discomfort, Flint patted him on the back. 'This is no different from pretending to be a groom or a docker or a bare-knuckle fighter. You have always been a chameleon, Seb. Once you're wearing the clothes, the character will come to you as it always does. Remember that time you posed as a French Chef de Bataillon? Your accent and manner were so flawless, your new regiment were too scared to question why their previous commanding officer had suddenly disappeared. You did that for three weeks undiscovered! If you can pose as a foreign officer undetected, then an English toff will be child's play. Nobody expects you to be the life and soul. They expect you to be rich and heartless. Your customary silence will be interpreted as haughty disdain. Trust me, you'll be admired for it. Simply stand straight, look down your nose at everyone and be free with your money.'

'It couldn't hurt to make the odd disparaging remark about taxation and the royal family either.' This came from Hadleigh. 'Those scoundrels will lap that up.'

Seb felt sick. Trapped and, for the first time in years, completely out of his depth.

'Why are you all gossiping like old women? We have a job to do.' Fennimore's eyes narrowed. 'Make haste, gentlemen! Your country needs you.'

The Duke of Westbridge's name was pencilled in for the second waltz. The final dance of the evening. Clarissa had made sure of that the moment she had stepped into the ballroom, wearing another of her daring new gowns. Gowns which no fresh-faced debutante would dare wear. Age did have its advantages, and, imbued with her renewed sense of purpose, she was jolly well going to utilise it. The red was bold—purposefully so, because Lady Olivia wore pastels—and enviably stylish and form-fitting. The single red rose woven into her curls was a mischievous touch, because Lady Olivia staunchly wore the family tiara to every event, letting everyone know she came along with plenty of money. The deep-red petals popping against Clarissa's blonde hair gave her an air of casual confidence, which was far more alluring than the call of money—and she thumbed her nose at her Duke and his now staunchly pink weekly bouquets.

Her lack of jewellery continued below her chin. Instead of hiding her skin under chunky necklaces, she now showed more of it. The plain gown was cut low at the front, lower still at the back, and the small capped sleeves hung tantalisingly off her shoulders. Every male head had turned as she had sailed through the door, including her Duke's, yet she had still had to go to him to receive any sort of greeting. That slight grated, but she ignored it because he had wrapped her arm around his possessively and spent several minutes telling her about his week as they stood in full view next to the refreshment table. Even more pleasing, he insisted she accompany him while he went to talk to his cronies, leaving the furious Lady Olivia silently seething on the other side of the dance floor.

As the men excluded her to discuss gentlemanly things, Clarissa happily drifted to the edge of the group to stand with some of their ladies. Lady Penelope, Viscountess Penhurst, was her oldest and dearest friend. They had come out together, then become inseparable. That was before Penny had married and become far too busy with her new life in the country to engage overmuch with society. Clarissa saw her in town maybe two or three times a year now, but regularly visited her in Sussex. They always picked up exactly where they left off. As a married lady, Penny also acted as her friend's chaperon whenever possible, something which gave Clarissa significantly more freedom than she enjoyed with her over-protective parents at home. Freedom she needed to secure her Duke.

'I cannot believe Westbridge has still not offered for you,' Penny said quietly behind her fan. 'The way he has been dragging his feet and flirting with that Spencer chit makes my blood boil.'

It made Clarissa's boil, too. Though the anger felt considerably better than the sadness which she had initially experienced at his indecisiveness. Where the sadness had made her run and hide, the anger spurred her to fight fire with fire. For six weeks, she had waged war against the simpering younger usurper who threatened to ruin her one chance at happiness, outcharming, outflirting and outshining the young woman at every event they attended.

The Duke of Westbridge couldn't ignore her. Clarissa had made sure of that. She was always in his line of sight. Front and centre in his mind. 'When I have him all to myself in a few weeks, I intend to change that.' Out of the bonds of loyalty, Lady Olivia had not received an invitation to Penelope's forthcoming house party, which gave Clarissa five days to force the issue before the

Duke retired to the country for the summer. If the initial gentle hints did not work, she fully intended to issue him with an ultimatum. A stark one. If he failed to put a ring on her finger before he left, then Clarissa was determined to walk away and find another protector to hide her failings behind. An older gentleman or a less impressive younger peer who would be easily impressed by her connections. Unaccomplished *Incomparables* couldn't be choosy. Any husband was better than none and once they were married he'd be stuck with her and duty-bound to keep her secrets.

Obviously, she sincerely hoped it wouldn't come to that. Without the constant physical reminder of the younger *Incomparable*, she planned to reacquaint the Duke with all the reasons why he was first attracted to her—but enough was enough. A stand had to be made for the sake of her own sanity and for her tenuous reputation. If Westbridge didn't want her, then she would have to swiftly find a suitable peer who did. By hook or by crook, she fully intended to be a married woman by Christmas. In the New Year she was twenty-four and the sad shelf of spinsterhood loomed on the horizon. Besides, all this additional effort was wearing her out and her poor nerves were so frayed by the constant and growing fear of her secret being discovered, she was coming to doubt they would ever return to normal.

'About that…' Penelope couldn't meet her eye. 'Penhurst has insisted she come. I had to send Lady Olivia an invitation this morning. I've already received her acceptance.'

The floor suddenly whipped from beneath her feet, all Clarissa could do was gape. 'But you promised, Penny!'

'I know I did and I feel awful, but Westbridge specifically asked my husband to include her and, as his friend, my husband refused to hear my arguments. You know Penhurst can be a beastly tyrant when riled.'

As Clarissa had seen the occasional bruises on her gentle friend's arms which were testament to that fact, she took pity on her. She'd never liked Penhurst, not from the outset, and had cautioned her friend not to accept his proposal all those years ago. As her dear papa had always said, a man who has to resort to raising his hand to a woman was no man and Penny's dictatorial viscount was everything Clarissa despised. A pompous, selfish, nasty bully. On more than one occasion, she had prayed for her friend's early widowhood and would continue to do so until Penhurst was mouldering in the ground. 'It doesn't matter, Penny.' But it did. She would have to rethink all her plans now. 'I know you tried your best and it's nothing catastrophic that cannot be fixed.' The simpering

Lady Olivia might miraculously find her own gentleman in the interim and leave Clarissa's in peace.

'I will still help you.' Her loyal friend threaded one arm tightly through hers. 'I will occupy all Lady Olivia's time and keep her from underfoot. Between the pair of us, we will make Westbridge see sense.' Penny shot daggers at the pouting Olivia. 'Very soon you will be married to the man of your dreams.'

'Penelope!' At the sound of her husband's voice, Penny snapped to attention and turned into the cowering wife again.

'Yes, my dear?' Had an endearment ever sounded so pained?

'Come. I have someone I wish you to meet.' They turned to see the gentlemen part like the Dead Sea, revealing the Earl of Upminster and a very familiar face. Gone was the beard and the pale complexion. A scar she had not seen before marred his cheek, but bizarrely the imperfection gave him an air of the dangerous and intrepid in this room full of cosseted peers. In his expertly tailored coat and impeccable sage-silk waistcoat, which perfectly set off his broad shoulders and strong arms, Mr Leatham looked positively splendid. Clarissa smiled warmly only to see his face blank and cold. His eyes though, issued a stark, urgent message she didn't quite understand.

'Allow me to introduce you to Lord Millcroft.'

'Lord Millcroft?'

Instantly he surged forward and took her hand, ignoring the other ladies and the correct protocol. He squeezed it tightly and stared imploringly into her eyes as he kissed the back of her glove. The thin layer of fabric made no difference because she still felt his touch everywhere just as she had the last time. As before, a simple touch was positively thrilling—but then she had seen him wearing only his breeches and that splendid sight had rather clouded her judgement.

'Lord Sebastian Millcroft. Lately of the Antipodes. I am delighted to make your acquaintance, Miss…?'

Chapter Five

For the last seven hours, and after giving himself a very stern talking to, Seb had been centring himself. It was a process he often did when assuming the persona of someone else and one which was usually successful. As someone else, he could hide behind a veneer. Within his mind he constructed the character, the way they thought, spoke, their particular idiosyncrasies. The layers which created a believable cover and separated the shy by-blow from Norfolk from the mission at hand.

Lord Millcroft was aloof, arrogant and judgemental. He was a man's man, preferring to talk business or discuss the brash and bawdy things gentlemen did when gathered together behind closed doors. Millcroft was a man who preferred to play cards or drink or socialise with other men in the sanctuary of White's or Brooks's. Seb had no problem with any of those things because they also served to disguise his awkward shyness around the fairer sex. A shyness which never plagued him around men, where his fierce pride came to the fore. In his head, no matter who they were, he strove to be their equal even if he didn't always feel it. Therefore, he would work to that strength and try to ignore the swathes of ladies at the same events. Lord Millcroft wasn't on the hunt for a wife, he was an eager investor on the lookout for ways to swell his fortunes, so it stood to reason he would have no interest in the ladies whatsoever.

It was a canny plan and would cover his shyness perfectly. By the time his preparations were done, he was quietly confident he could pull this charade off just as he had countless others beforehand and had stridden into the Earl of Upminster's ballroom radiating haughty indifference with the very best of them.

He'd had a little moment when he had first encountered the crowd. It was not the crush which bothered him, more the unpalatable fact that this was a *social* occasion, filled with those who had been born to consider themselves better than most and his sort especially, and that Seb would actually have to take some part in the *socialising* rather than merely watch it from a distance. After he had given himself another stern talking to and noticed that many of the gentlemen paid scant attention to the ladies anyway, the flapping eagles in his stomach became sparrows.

Upminster introduced him to several people as they made slow progress around the room and Seb responded in character. He engaged with the men and simply nodded politely to the ladies. The convoluted preamble served to further calm his nerves, to the extent that the sparrows were mere butterflies by the time he met Viscount Penhurst and his circle of friends. He greeted them as equals, bowing only slightly lower to the Duke in the party on principle, and happily engaged in the sort of male-orientated conversation he had planned meticulously for.

Icy calm.

Calculated.

Completely in control.

Then he'd spied her next to Penhurst's wife and those lofty plans flew out of the window. Instead of avoiding the women altogether, he'd had to think on his feet and fast. Rather than treating Gem with the haughty indifference he had practised in front of the mirror, he had rushed at her like a man recently speared deep by Cupid's arrow. He'd grabbed her hand, gazed up at her beseechingly and, to all intents and purposes, declared to the entire ballroom he was suddenly, openly smitten and eager to get better acquainted with a woman he had technically only laid eyes on a few seconds before.

Besotted and desperate to woo! Two states which were as far away from where Seb felt comfortable as it was humanly possible to be. He was also fearful of her potential reaction to his blatant lie and furious at himself and his superior for this potentially calamitous oversight. Fennimore should never have put him in this position! A stable, a garden, the kitchens, even the sewers were better places for his covert talents and dubious lineage. In this kaleidoscope of genteel poppycock he was seriously out of his depth, especially if he now had to play the role of ardent suitor.

'Lady Clarissa Beaumont.' She inclined her head graciously. 'I am intrigued to meet *you*, my lord. And so fresh from the *Antipodes*, too. I look forward to hearing all about it. They sound like such a fascinating place…when the furthest I have been is *Norfolk*.'

As barbs went, hers were perfect. Much like her. Tonight she was stunning. So stunning the flapping eagles returned with a vengeance and pecked at his heart. She stepped back and Seb was aware of her eyes on him as he was introduced to Penhurst's wife. At least it appeared she had given him a grace period before she turned him over to the wolves, yet the very real possibility only served to make his pulse race faster than it already had been before he had set eyes on her. The hours he'd spent rehearsing had been wiped the second he had and he'd very nearly broken character and fled. Already the tips of his ears felt warm; his tongue threatened to fail at any moment and he had no idea now how the mysterious Lord Millcroft would continue to behave because he didn't *know* this character at all. Seb would have to make it up as he went along.

Not his strong suit as the bullet hole could attest.

This was a complication neither he nor the wily Fennimore had foreseen. The rest of society might well have never seen him, his dreadful brother might not recognise him, but the Gem had tormented his thoughts ever since he'd met her, teased him and seen him half-naked, drunk and slurring just a few short weeks before. One wrong word and his mission was over before it had started; worse, it might encourage Penhurst and Camborne to cover their tracks and warn the Boss that the King's Elite were on his tail. The combination of inwardly dying from mortification, the purely male and visceral reaction at seeing her again and the very real fear he had just seriously jeopardised the whole investigation in the process caused him actual physical pain. His damn heart was clattering so fast it was jarring his recently healed bullet hole and the acid churning in his stomach was so potent it would dissolve iron nails.

He needed to get her alone. Lord only knew what he would tell her, but somehow he would ensure her silence.

He had to.

'Did I mention that Millcroft here is on the hunt for suitable investment opportunities?' Upminster was playing his part perfectly and it nudged Seb to do the same. For the time being he was impotent to do anything else.

'He is?' Penhurst replied with an air of boredom. 'What types of investment?'

'Whichever yields the most coin in the shortest time, my lord.' Seb offered the man a knowing smile. 'I am a man with little patience for the long term.'

Penhurst's thin lip curled. 'A speculator, then?'

'If that is the polite terms for a man who enjoys making money, then, yes, I am—and proudly so. Although I know here in town most people are squeamish about admitting to it, especially as land is considered to be the foundation of good society. But as I have no land, and have never been particularly good, I make no excuses for funding my lifestyle through canny investments. I *do* have a nose for those—alongside a taste for the finer things in life.'

'A nose! By Jove, that he does!' Upminster

slapped him on the back. 'I doubt there are many men who could make such a fortune in that home of convicts and ne'er-do-wells at the bottom of the world, but Millcroft has managed it. If reports from the governor are to be believed, he went from nothing to becoming the richest man in New South Wales in less than a decade. *That* is no mean feat, sir!'

'Hardly nothing, my lord. I still had my wits and my keen eye for profit.' Seb's eyes could not resist quickly flicking to hers, trying to ignore the fact that the Duke of Westbridge had taken her arm proprietorially and the jolt of raw jealousy that hardened his own jaw at the sight. 'The spirit of entrepreneurship thrives in the Antipodes. Alongside the ne'er-do-wells.'

The next ten minutes were spent in much the same manner. Seb and Upminster continued baiting the hook for Penhurst, who did his best to seem uninterested, but asked the pertinent questions one would expect from a fishing expedition. Penhurst was trying to subtly gauge his measure and Seb was dismissively flippant in his answers, making sure the corrupt viscount was left in no doubt that all he cared about was increasing his fortune. Because it was a conversation between men, the ladies had moved to the periphery and Gem stayed close to her Duke, hanging on the fellow's every word adoringly, although her eyes frequently wandered to Seb and held, their message obvious. She was biding her time, but still expecting an explanation. Once or twice, Westbridge caught her staring and scowled. She didn't appear to notice.

It went without saying he hated Westbridge on sight. He was exactly the kind of pompous windbag Seb had pictured when she had first mentioned him. Fashionably dressed, the evening waistcoat in a garish turquoise silk, his hair pomaded to sit just so above his regal, straight eyebrows and his cravat secured with a pin tipped with an emerald the size of a quail's egg. Looking at everything and everyone down the slope of his long, narrow nose, he was the epitome of the superior aristocrat—stand-offish, self-important, supremely confident in his wealth and standing to the extent his eyes never met any of those he considered beneath him.

All show and no substance.

But a duke.

Penhurst was a different kettle of fish but equally as dislikeable. The way he had clicked his fingers to summon his wife, followed by the nervous way she snapped to attention, told Seb a great deal. When you closely watched human interactions from the shadows, you grew to recognise certain emotions fast. The Viscountess

Penhurst was frightened of her husband. Her husband, on the other hand, was largely indifferent and cold towards her. Theirs was no marriage made in heaven. A detail which he would store away in case it became useful, alongside the fortuitous knowledge that it appeared Lady Clarissa Beaumont also happened to be more than an acquaintance to the nervous viscountess. Perhaps another avenue into Penhurst's circle if he needed one? And if he could get her to go along with his lies... But would she, seeing as Penhurst and her hidebound Duke were old friends? Perhaps even business associates?

Like her Duke, Penhurst, too, wore his title like a badge, but as a mere viscount came significantly lower in the pecking order and therefore had less scope to blithely ignore those in the room as Gem's Duke did. However, his guarded eyes were everywhere, assessing. Currently they were quietly watching Seb, which he assumed was a good thing now that their brief business discussion was concluded and he was quietly pleased with the job he had done under the strained and unexpected circumstances. It showed Penhurst was intrigued enough to want to know more, but was nowhere near ready to reveal his hand. This next part, the dance that Lord Fennimore hoped would lead to overtures, would be tricky. Push too hard and the hatches would be battened. Fail to push and Seb would be easily forgotten. It was a delicate balance and one for which he would need all his wits about him to achieve. The nagging fear about Lady Clarissa blowing his cover wide open needed to be dealt with swiftly, yet to do it he would need to get her alone.

Fortunately, Seb didn't have to wait long. Another young lady with a head of blonde, tight-corkscrew ringlets sailed over, her destination obviously the Duke. He watched Gem's arm tighten around Westbridge's, but upon seeing the younger chit, the Duke immediately extricated himself from her grip and her smile was suddenly as brittle as spun sugar. Not close enough to hear the exchange, Seb watched the other woman tap her dance card and the Duke step forward to take her arm instead, the *Incomparable* he had just abandoned clearly already forgotten.

As the pair headed towards the dance floor, the younger girl—because she was far too young, in Seb's humble opinion, to be considered a woman yet—looked back and shot Clarissa a triumphant smile before literally hanging on the windbag as they walked away.

When those around her stopped watching, the false smile slipped off Clarissa's lovely face and she appeared rattled. Deflated even, until her slim shoulders stiffened and she elegantly inhaled a very deep breath. Then she swiftly turned on her heel. Seb saw a flash of red disappear towards the refreshment table with more haste than was necessary and deftly followed. Away from her friends, they could talk—if he could get his tongue to untangle long enough to string coherent sentences together. Of all the women he had to run into, all the unforeseen complications, why did it have to be her? And why did she have to look so damn beautiful tonight that she took his breath away?

She sensed him before he had chance to speak and turned just her face to look at him. '*Lord Millcroft*. What a surprise.'

'We need to talk. Privately.'

'I dare say we do. Do you waltz?'

'After a fashion.' At least Flint and Warriner had attempted to teach him the dance when they were all at Cambridge together, in the faint hope he would pluck up the courage to ask a woman to dance with him one day. From memory, he recalled it mostly involved turning and counting to three while avoiding looking at his masculine partner's grinning face.

'Splendid. You can begin explaining yourself the moment we reach the floor.'

Seb held out his arm and she laid hers upon it, the odd sensation her touch created joined all the other unwelcome and swirling emotions currently cluttering his mind and putting him off his game. Fear, awkwardness, determination, sprinkled with a touch of jealousy and a generous pinch of wholly inappropriate lust. How the hell was he supposed to do his job with all that going on? She twirled gracefully to face him and curtsied and he just about remembered to bow, then he slid his farmer's hand around her waist and instantly felt hot.

All at sea.

Her significantly smaller palm slipped into his and she gazed up at him, smiling. Or at least her mouth was smiling. Those fine eyes of hers were shooting poison darts. Even so, his poor heart began to race and his mouth became dry, so dry he feared he'd be unable to speak should he attempt to. He began to silently count the beat in his head—one, two, three...one, two three—as they began to move in the hope that it would calm him.

'Which are you—a Leatham or a Millcroft?' Straight to the point. No nonsense. No time to pause and think. Seb missed a step as he considered lying, then thought better of it. Gem was a sharp one and because she knew some of the truth, he would undoubtedly make a huge hash of it.

'Leatham. You know I am a Leatham. But for the foreseeable future I must be Millcroft.' Whispering and counting was a challenge, too. There was absolutely no chance of achieving anything vaguely resembling calm within. He was simultaneously hot and cold. Terrified and overwhelmed. All the people, petticoats and the oppressive heat of the dance floor seemed to be closing in on him. Fennimore should never have put him in this position. Less than half an hour in and the stench of failure hung putrid in the air. He could barely dance and the scant bit of socialising he had done already, combined with the presence of the distracting woman in his arms, was giving him palpitations.

'I am not in the mood for mysterious! What is going on?'

'Trust me when I tell you it's probably best if you don't know.'

'Yet you expect me to allow you to perpetrate this falsehood in front of my friends! To what end?'

'It is a matter of national importance.'

'Really? Do I look as though I was born yesterday?'

She looked beautiful. Smelled beautiful. If he'd known how to flirt Seb would have told her so. Instead he manoeuvred them clumsily towards an alcove, then dragged her by the arm behind a potted palm. For several long moments she stood waiting, her arms crossed bossily over her chest and her scarlet-shod foot tapping impatiently while Seb breathed deeply, considering all his options.

Pretty soon he realised they all boiled down to one. Either she trusted him or she didn't. If she didn't, he was doomed anyway. If by some miracle she did, then it would only come about with the truth—or at least as much of the truth as he dared tell her without compromising the rest of the investigation.

'I work for his Majesty's government. With both the Home and Foreign Office. I am covertly investigating a dangerous smuggling ring which has infiltrated the highest echelons of society. They are a dangerous gang, with significant resources. Many men have died already trying to infiltrate their ranks, so I must insist that you cannot breathe a word of what I am telling you to anyone.'

'Covert?' She blinked and moved her face closer to his. 'Are you telling me you are a spy?'

'Yes.'

'I don't believe you!'

'Why do you think I got shot saving that school mistress? Do you think such things happen in everyday life? The man who fired the bullet was one of the smugglers!'

Her mouth opened, then promptly closed again as she considered the validity of his claim. 'You're a spy?' This time she sounded less dismissive, her gaze boring into his searching for the truth.

'I am one of the King's Elite.'

'I've never heard of such an organisation!'

'Precisely. That's because we operate under the utmost secrecy. But I can assure you we exist. Lord Upminster works at the Foreign Office—he can corroborate my story should you require it—but I am begging you to keep my true identity a secret from your friends. It really is a matter of national importance.'

Forgetting her usually impeccable posture, she leaned her back against the enormous mock-Grecian pot and shook her head. 'I really can't take it in. *You* are suddenly a spy, as well as a duke's son and a poultry farmer?'

'Hardly suddenly. I've been one for several years.' Seven to be precise. 'And it was my grandfather who was the poultry farmer. I was recruited straight out of Cambridge because my superior noticed I had a talent for blending in.'

'Blending in. Here?' Her eyes travelled the length of him, taking in the fine clothes, the diamond cravat pin, then focused on his face. They both knew the exterior was merely window dressing and that the blood that pumped through his veins was more red than blue. 'But you professed to be *shy*.'

There was no point in denying it, not since he had already confessed as much, although he was still horrified that he had also drunkenly enlightened her to the sad truth of his sporadic and dismal love life coupled with his inability to flirt! What a prize-winning, pathetic fool he must have sounded. 'Normally I work in the background, but with Jake on his honeymoon I've been drafted very much into the fore. Against my will, I might add.' Why Seb felt the need to add that he wasn't certain, but for some reason his mind kept wandering back to the girl in the multicoloured hair rags and jam stains on her nightdress that he had been happily confessing all to. Perhaps because he found that incarnation less intimidating than the sophisticated society lady in front of him. Or perhaps it was because Gem was the closest thing to a safe harbour he had in the uncharted waters of society and he was grateful he had a friend. Not that he knew she *was* a friend yet.

'Jake Warriner? Brother to my sister's husband? He's a spy, too?' Before he answered she shook her head again. 'I suppose it makes sense. You were both there that day—and it was his bullet that killed your assailant... Good gracious. It never occurred to me.' The expression of awe and wonder swiftly changed to a frown as the cogs in her clever mind began to turn. 'The highest echelons? You suspect someone *here* of being part of this dangerous gang? Who?'

Your paramour's old schoolfriend—not that Seb could tell her that part if he wanted her silence. 'At this time, I have no certain idea of his identity. As Lord Millcroft, I hope to find out— although I'm hardly lord material. Why my superior sent me on this mission is a mystery. This is not my world...' What had possessed him to admit to that? And to her? 'I can never find the right words at the best of times. Here I fear I am doomed.' Good grief—why did the damning words suddenly keep coming? Yet more seemed to be lining up behind, condemning him to further cloddishness in front of the most beautiful woman he had ever seen. And all apparently without the excuse of bullet wounds and brandy because in his mind was the girl in rags, the one he miraculously felt like himself with. 'I shall say the wrong thing or, worse, *not* say anything at all. As usual. And everyone here will realise I am a fraud just as you do. I should be guarding something or sneaking around somewhere. Listening and watching. Two things I am exceedingly good at. What I am not good at is…this!' He gestured to his evening clothes and then the whole ballroom. 'But my purpose here genuinely is a matter of national importance, a mission I was entrusted with and I am single-handedly about to ruin it with my woeful social skills. Months of hard work, the lives of many good men, all wasted while I fail abysmally at being a lord. I have never felt so out of my depth before.' Seb's stupid heart was racing again and a cold trickle of sweat was making its way down his spine. Less than one hour in, his plan was shot to pieces and for the first time in his long and successful career with the King's Elite, failure seemed inevitable.

Her face softened and she touched his arm. Seb felt the affectionate gesture all the way down to his toes. 'Don't worry. You didn't seem out of your depth in the slightest. Truth be told, had I not known you were the shy Mr Leatham from Norfolk, I would have been none the wiser. You seemed supremely confident and added just the right splash of aloofness to give the intriguing Millcroft exciting gravitas. You also look the part. Very debonair and handsome. Dashing even. For a fraud, you play a lord very well.'

Dashing? Handsome? Him? 'Hardly. Have you not seen the scar?'

'I have.' He stiffened as she reached out her hand and traced one finger down its ugly length. 'It gives you an air of the dangerous. The ladies love a dangerous fellow. Didn't you see them all watching you? Wondering in what exciting and adventurous circumstances you acquired it?' Her hand dropped and she smiled. 'How did you get it, by the way? Seeing as we both know you've never set foot in the Antipodes.'

'An accident.' Seb had accidentally assumed his half-brother had a heart and a conscience, but like his father before him and all persons of his ilk he considered the low-born disposable. 'Caused by my own stupidity. Nothing exciting or adventurous in the slightest.'

'Well, I like it. You wouldn't be half as hand-some without it.'

Lost for an appropriate response which wouldn't start him blushing, Seb avoided her eyes and, in doing so, in his peripheral vision he saw her Duke skirting the edge of the dance floor, clearly searching for her now that the waltz was done. He tugged her further into the alcove. 'West-bridge is looking for you.'

'He is?' The information seemed to please her, but royally ruined the tender moment they had just shared, cruelly reminding him that for all her compliments she had her eyes on another man. One in possession of a real and grand title, whose blood ran as blue as the Nile. She glanced over Seb's shoulder with a calculated smile. 'I can't see him. How can you be sure?'

'Because I'm a spy. We all have eyes in the back of our heads.'

She giggled without her usual practised ar-tifice, the intimate and earthy sound doing un-mentionable things to his unmentionables. 'Then I shall let him miss me for a few minutes. I dare say a bit of jealousy will do him good.' She could now see the Duke and watched his frantic search with amusement for several long moments. She was still smiling smugly when her gaze returned triumphantly to Seb. It grated. 'Mr Leatham, I have suddenly had a positively brilliant idea...'

Chapter Six

~~~~~~~~~~

Clarissa was still patting herself on the back two days later. Proposing she and Seb should team up had been a masterstroke of pure genius because it served two purposes. Firstly, with her on his arm in the crowded ballroom she consoled herself that his short crisis of confidence was banished away. He was immediately accepted by a great many there because they all knew Clarissa had exceptional taste in people as well as everything else. Next to her, he practised the ever-so-slightly aloof bemusement which suited him down to the ground. Where his society manner faltered, usually when surrounded by a great many curious ladies, she blithely filled in the silent void and openly confided to those eager women what a delicious and intriguing new gentleman he was.

Her talent for story-telling meant his stark, fictional past was now brilliantly embellished with scintillating details. How he once accepted a challenge to race around the streets of Sydney in a cart because he was bored, outrunning a racing curricle with his superior driving skills. How he once sailed to the savage wilds of Tasmania on the hunt for the legendary 'tiger', travelled miles inland until he found a whole pack of them and then left them all gloriously alive because he only wanted to pet one. And her personal favourite, because on the first telling his cheeks had pinkened, how he was the most sought-after bachelor in the whole of New South Wales on account of both his impressive fortune and his scandalous reputation as a ladies' man. Although, she had cautioned, giggling behind her fan as the women cast him questioning and flirtatious glances, to be bestowed with his favour was a very rare honour because he had grown quite particular. Well, it didn't hurt to reinforce her own attractiveness whilst painting him the charming catch. That mysterious Lord Millcroft was a very discerning gentleman after all.

For over an hour she had remained his companion, until he had been invited to join Penhurst in the card room. Watching him emerge near the end of the evening, standing tall and proud and quietly pleased with himself, gave Clarissa a huge sense of achievement. Aside from helping the British government in its quest to rid England of a gang of dangerous smugglers, which she couldn't deny held tremendous appeal, it was warming to see him in his element. The casual way he had ensconced himself with the men of her circle, the subtle techniques he used to draw information out of them and the way he not only melded to become one of them, but also provided a stark yardstick for comparison, was fascinating. Against him, his raw physicality, excellent features and both his real and fictional achievements, Seb quite outshone all the other men. On more than one occasion, Clarissa had had to remind herself to glance at Westbridge, whom she had quite forgotten in Seb's significantly more impressive shadow.

Which, of course, did wonders for the second benefit of aligning herself with the enigmatic, new Lord Millcroft. Poor Westbridge was beside himself with jealousy! Even when Lady Olivia and her ambitious mother encircled him like ravenous vultures, her Duke watched Clarissa and Seb like a hawk. Only once Seb was safely dispatched to the gaming tables did she return to the Duke, just in time for their waltz. He had been both aggrieved and relieved, dancing so stiffly he might as well have had broom handles inserted down his sleeves and trouser legs. To further vex her Duke, because frankly he deserved it, she danced with a faraway, wistful smile on her face. A smile meant solely for Lord Millcroft. Only part of which was truly forced. There was something about Seb that made her feel all warm inside.

* * *

The following morning, Clarissa had awoken to two bouquets. A huge and satisfying basket of crimson roses from Westbridge and a charming bunch of pale-pink peonies and forget-me-nots from Seb, whose posy she much preferred because he had taken the trouble to handwrite the note. Like the man, the words were brief, and blessedly Clarissa was able to read them in less than a minute—which certainly made a change, boosted her confidence and significantly buoyed her mood further.

Dear Gem,
Thank you.
S.

The fact that he had chosen simple in-season cottage flowers from his own garden over showy, forced, ostentation said a great deal about the man. His flowers were more personal. He could very well have picked them himself. A detail she had happily shared with all and sundry on Rotten Row that same afternoon. As an added bonus, the symbolism of the forget-me-nots was not lost on anyone, meaning the gossip that the illustrious Duke of Westbridge had a rival spread like wildfire.

Tonight, there would be more than Westbridge's eyes following them and Clarissa couldn't wait to get to the ballroom. A few more weeks of this and she would safely be hiding behind the title of duchess before August—unless her Duke combusted with jealousy beforehand and procured a special licence.

'The Penhurst carriage is here, my lady.'

Clarissa stood and gave her appearance one last look in the mirror. The sky blue was a statement. It matched those forget-me-nots on her nightstand and the single stem woven in her hair. The colour brightened her eyes and the tight bodice displayed just enough cleavage to suggest that she possessed more bosom than she actually owned, while the translucent layers of contrasting pale-blue and cobalt silk chiffon draped around the skirt gave the gown a graceful movement which would look marvellous as she danced. It went without saying that she would grant Seb the first waltz, something she was rather looking forward to, making Westbridge jealously wait for the second from the wings.

Dancing with Seb had been...well, rather memorable actually. Beneath her fingers his broad frame was as solid and impressive as it had seemed when encased in just a bandage. The soft press of his hand above her waist, his other engulfing hers, had made her feel delicate. His shy glances and adorable, honest awkwardness when they were alone in the alcove had made her feel special. Knowing his background and his true purpose made him much more exciting than anyone else in the crowded ballroom. All in all, Seb was thoroughly delightful.

With a start, she realised she had butterflies in her stomach and her hands went to her midriff to calm them. As a young debutante, such nerves had been commonplace, but now in her fourth Season, she couldn't remember the last time she had been so excited about attending a ball. No doubt, these were because she was making progress with her Duke. It felt good giving him a taste of his own medicine. However, assisting a dashing spy held a different appeal, especially as only she *really* knew Seb. The real man. The mysterious Lord Millcroft was appealing—but the tips of his ears didn't blush nor did his eyes shyly dip after holding hers for any length of time. These were tiny truths which he only shared with her. And which apparently made those butterflies dance a jig. They continued to flap until she was seated in the carriage.

'Will Lord Millcroft be in attendance tonight?'

Surprised that Penhurst had bothered to ask her a question when he usually ignored her and Penny as they travelled, Clarissa forgot to be nonchalant. 'Yes, he is. Why do you ask?'

'No reason, other than the fact that he seems to have made quite the impression on people in such a short space of time. I noticed you spent a great deal of time conversing with him the other evening.'

'He is an interesting gentleman.'

'Wealthy, if the talk about him is to be believed. Keen to invest it, too.' Penhurst was examining his nails as he said this, attempting to pass off the comments as small talk—but as he never made small talk with her, something about it didn't sit right.

'Apparently so.'

'Did he elaborate to you on those plans? Give any clue as to what sort of venture he wanted pursue?'

'Not really. Gentlemen don't tend to discuss business with ladies. Why didn't you ask him yourself?'

'Because it only just occurred to me.' His unnaturally bland expression said differently. 'The fellow makes me curious, although that should hardly be a surprise when he has suddenly materialised out of the blue and one considers his background. I wonder what manner of business accrued him that fortune? New South Wales is the home of convicts, which does make one wonder if Lord Millcroft's extensive fortune was built on ill-gotten gains. I thought he hinted as much the other evening, didn't you?'

'Are you suggesting Lord Millcroft's interests are not above board? He hardly seems the type.' Although Seb would be pleased that people viewed him with those suspicions. A pious, incorruptible man would hardly flush out the criminals he had been tasked to catch.

'I wouldn't dream of it. I'm sure all his past dealings have been wholly proper and any suggestion to the contrary is merely gossip.'

'There is already gossip?' How splendid. She couldn't wait to tell Seb he had already made the exact impression he wanted.

'I happened to like the fellow. As I said, I am merely curious—as I would be of any newcomer into our ranks. Although I do think you should be the one to ask him—it was obvious he was enamoured of you. If anyone can prise his darkest secrets from him, I am in no doubt it will be you.'

'You want me to ask him if he is a trickster?' A decidedly odd request. 'I'm sure that will go down very well!'

Penhurst smiled, then turned his head to stare out of the window. 'Of course not. I am merely suggesting that if anything interesting comes up in conversation then you should subtly delve a bit deeper and share your findings with us. Your dearest friends. We all enjoy a bit of gossip now and then.'

This claim, from a man who rarely deigned to speak to her, was laughable. Yet true to form, he was already displaying all the signs of his usual aloofness, rudely presenting his back to both Clarissa and his wife signalling he was done with the conversation because he found the sight of the familiar streets of Mayfair more diverting than he did them. But then again, he found everything more diverting than poor Penny. Clarissa's mind was whirring. Penhurst had been uncharacteristically civil and interested. The timing surely wasn't coincidental?

She tried to banish the thought as soon as it entered her mind, but Seb's talk about smugglers infiltrating the highest echelons of society had coloured her thoughts and, despite knowing she was being ridiculously fanciful, her suspicions were aroused. Penhurst was a foul individual with dubious morals. He dallied openly with several mistresses here in town while poor Penny lived mostly alone on his Sussex estate with their young son. While she was sure her friend knew of his infidelity, because *everyone* knew of his infidelity, they had never discussed it. Nor had they ever discussed the bruises which marred her skin or the lack of sparkle in her dear friend's eyes since she had become the viscount's wife two years ago. As awful as it was, just as Clarissa had cautioned before the wedding, Penhurst had been a fortune hunter and his interest in his bride had been purely financial. Once he had control of that impressive dowry, he had immediately stopped being the ardent suitor. The switch had been abrupt and cold. Instantaneous. To such an extent, a very different viscount had walked out of the church from the amiable groom who had arrived. Was it too fanciful to believe that vile, selfish, money-grabbing man was capable of aiding smugglers for his own gain as well as being a callous bully? Probably. But since meeting a genuine spy, something she had never expected to happen in her wildest dreams, Clarissa couldn't help wondering why Penhurst was suddenly keen to hear gossip. And from her. His suddenly *dearest* friend.

Seb was nowhere to be seen in the ballroom, but Westbridge was front and centre as always. Disloyally, the first word which popped into her head was *peacock* and she quickly banished that, too. As a duke, he was bound to stand out and as others sought his favour there was no point hiding in the alcove. She had never hidden there either through choice for much the same reasons, so she could hardly castigate Westbridge for doing the same. Although alcoves now certainly had their charm, especially as she had come to realise they were exciting places to be. In the right company.

Handsome, tough, brave and endearingly shy spies hid in the shadows.

Her eyes did a quick sweep of the secluded corners for Seb and when she drew a blank, Clarissa allowed her feet to take her on a course towards her would-be fiancé. Her Duke smiled appreciatively as she approached and lingered over kissing her hand. She willed herself to feel the same peculiar heated fizzle she had with her spy and experienced a moment of disappointment when nothing happened.

'Will you grant me the first waltz?'

It was progress, although nowhere near the level of possessiveness she needed to evoke. A truly besotted man would insist on both waltzes. Every waltz from this point forward. Till death do us part. 'Alas, I have already promised that honour to Lord Millcroft.' If he ever turned up. 'But the second is yours. As always.' She enjoyed the satisfaction of seeing his expression cloud with jealousy. Barely two days in and her new plan was working wonders and for the first time in weeks, she was enjoying being at a function. 'Talking of Lord Millcroft—have you seen him?' Clarissa let her gaze wander on purpose; letting her Duke know that he wasn't the sole occupant of her thoughts.

'No. And nor do I want to. He is too brash for my liking. Too confident for a man of his rank.'

Brash and confident. Seb would be pleased to hear those back-handed compliments and she swelled with pride knowing she'd had a hand in his spectacular performance. 'Do you think so?

Personally, I found him most charming.' Clarissa would ask Penny to invite Seb to the Penhurst house party. This very moment. His presence would drive her poor Duke mad. 'If you will excuse me...' She didn't bother waiting to see if he minded and went off to corner her.

Penny was with a gaggle of married ladies at the refreshment table, and happily agreed to include Seb in the entertainments because she still felt guilty at having to invite Clarissa's nemesis. Now all she had to do was find a way to convince the man to take five days out of hunting down his dangerous smugglers in the highest echelons of society and accompany her on a trip to Sussex.

Seb tossed the third ruined cravat on the small pile on the floor and snapped his fingers impatiently for another. Gray tutted and passed him one. 'Please let me do that. I've never seen a man make such a ham-fisted mess of dressing before.'

'I can tie a damn cravat!' A plain, no-nonsense, no-fuss cravat. The frothy concoctions fools like the Duke of Westbridge sported were apparently beyond him. He pulled one end too tight and the starched linen instantly crumpled in a ruined knot. If Gem preferred frills, he would suffer frills. 'Hell's teeth!'

A withering sigh came from the mattress where the second-in-command of the Invisibles was lounging, dressed as a coachman. 'You are well past fashionably late...'

'I know the blasted time, Gray!'

His friend uncrossed his long legs and rose from his comfortable position with an air of exasperation. 'For once in your life, accept some help. What is it that you are trying to achieve?'

'Something fancy.' He'd be mocked senseless if he admitted he didn't know the actual name of the knot he was trying to duplicate. 'Fitting for a ballroom.'

Gray snapped open another overly starched neckcloth and Seb lifted his chin to suffer the indignity of being dandified by his subordinate. When he had finished, Gray stepped back to admire his work, then nodded, gesturing to the mirror. 'You'll do.'

The simple knot in the reflection filled him with rage. 'What's fancy about that? Any idiot can tie a plain cravat.'

'But only a real man can carry it off with such casual elegance. Up against that foppish Duke your lady-love prefers, you will appear superior. A man with your savage maleness shouldn't try to curb it with frills. Be manly. Ooze confidence in your ability to thrash the life out of every other fellow in the ballroom. Trust me, Seb—less is always more. Especially where the ladies are concerned.

For once, instead of trying to blend in, stand out. Your lady-love won't know what's hit her.'

'She's not my lady-love!'

'I thought the ruse was that Lady Clarissa was supposed to be more enamoured of you than her Duke?' Gray's eyes were twinkling with mischief and Seb knew he had been royally tricked into revealing more to his wily friend than he had intended.

'Ah, yes. Of course. That blasted tie has put me off my game.' That tie and that woman. The one he absolutely had a soft spot for. A foolish waste of his time when his attention was better served elsewhere. As if she would miraculously toss away a duke for a knave. A fortune. A mansion. High status. It would be laughable if it wasn't tragic. 'Perhaps I *should* allow you to be my valet? I need a clear head, not one blighted by cravats.'

'Yes, *my lord.*' Gray grinned, dipped his eyes and bowed. 'I live to serve. Now, get in the damned coach.'

Taking a carriage the few yards between Grosvenor and Berkeley Square struck Seb as a ridiculous waste of time when he could have walked it quicker. The long line of waiting conveyances spilled so far outwards that it took a good twenty minutes to be deposited at the Bulphan town house. However, as this was how things were done he suffered it and used it as an opportunity to go through tonight's plan with Gray.

Six Invisibles would be mingling with the other waiting drivers and groomsmen in the crowded mews, tasked with targeting the Penhurst staff. The long wait, camaraderie, raucous games of cards or dice and the fortifying nips of the rum each of his men carried had proved time and again an excellent source of information. For some peculiar reason, the aristocrats these people served assumed that because they were seen but not heard, their servants couldn't hear.

As they pulled up outside, Gray leaned forward, straightened Seb's lapels, then slapped him on the shoulder. 'Good luck.'

It was the aloof Lord Millcroft who stepped out.

Chapter Seven

Being late, the ballroom was so crowded the heat hit him straight away, closely followed by the noise. A legion of the primping *ton* certainly made a racket. The sweet smell of pomade and a plethora of ladies' perfumes hung heavy in the air. As one of the footmen carrying laden trays of champagne he would be able to move around as he pleased. As Lord Millcroft, the mysterious new lord who had once wrestled a crocodile and emerged with just the scar on his cheek, he had become an instant spectacle. Ladies turned and smiled at him, some blatantly batting their eyelashes behind their fans. Gentlemen paused their conversations to introduce themselves and shake his hand. Within minutes he was surrounded and bombarded with questions, turning the social event into the Spanish Inquisition. As much as he hated it, he knew he had Gem to thank for his sudden popularity and outright acceptance into this strange world. So far, she had been an asset and one he needed. Right this minute, before he become completely overwhelmed.

Then, like an angel from the heavens she appeared at his elbow, her arm possessively weaving through his. 'There you are—you naughty man! You begged me for the waltz and then you turn up barely before it starts. If you weren't so fascinating and handsome, I'd give it to someone else. Please excuse us, everyone. I shall return him to you soon.' She skilfully manoeuvred Seb away from his inquisitors and artfully, yet politely, dodged anyone else who stepped in their way, tossing greetings and compliments around like confetti. All Seb had to do was incline his head and attempt to look superior. Something which was much easier to do with her on his arm— because he felt superior. He was with the loveliest woman in the room.

In no time, they reached the dance floor and she dipped into a curtsy.

'I thought you weren't coming.'

She moved into his arms. The second her hand touched his, his body responded inappropriately. So much for keeping a clear head, although at least his blasted nerves weren't jangling. Another odd but welcome effect she now had on him. Despite being a stunningly beautiful member of the very sex he was shy around, Gem was also his anchor in these uncharted waters. Bathed in her confidence, Lord Millcroft emerged easily. Seb even felt like a peer. 'I thought it was fashionable to be late.'

'As frustrating as it was to wait for you, I have to concede it was a clever move. There was a *will he, won't he* air of anticipation as people awaited your arrival.'

'No doubt embellished by your good self.' He found himself smiling down at her and waited for the inevitable blush to singe his ears. For once, it didn't come. A peculiar, yet perplexing blessing.

'Of course I embellished it! Did you know that you own an opal mine?'

'I do?'

'Yes. I'm wearing the one you sent me this morning.' His eyes dropped to first her neck, then her décolleté and his breath caught. Good Lord, she filled out her dress well. 'Not there, silly.' There was laughter in her voice as if she knew exactly what he had been staring at and was quite used to it. 'It's in my hair.'

The jewelled pin was subtle but very pretty and sat amongst a sprig of real blue flowers. One fat opal was surrounded by tiny diamonds. There were three smaller opals on filigree stems resembling feathers dotted with even smaller diamonds. 'I have excellent taste.'

'Expensive, too, which adds to the fable. My

parents gave it to me as a birthday present last summer and fortunately I hadn't worn it before tonight—but it goes with the gown. Blue to match your forget-me-nots.' She patted her hair again and he realised they were his flowers nestling amongst her golden curls. Curls that had sported an expensive hothouse rose at the last ball. 'A very original choice of flower.'

The tips of his ears did redden then because she probably realised he had clumsily picked the damn flowers himself from his borrowed garden and sent them before he realised *Incomparables* like Gem usually received only the most exquisite blooms. Clueless, he'd felt immensely smug for re-membering that a gentleman should send flowers in the first place. The peonies had looked lovely, but he'd picked the silly forget-me-nots because they were the exact shade of her eyes. It was only when Gray mentioned he knew a man in Covent Garden who could supply long-stemmed red roses all year round that he learned he'd made a mis-take, but by the then the inferior bunch had been sent and it was too late to stop them.

'Yes. Sorry about those. I've never sent a woman flowers before. I'll ensure you receive proper ones tomorrow.'

'Don't you dare! I loved those flowers. The simplicity was heart-felt, which is always a nice touch. The choice of blooms inspired. Forget-me-nots. How utterly romantic. The other ladies have been sighing over your thoughtfulness. Besides, they make my bedchamber smell lovely when I retire for the evening. Did you know forget-me-nots are only fragrant at night?' He didn't, but the thought of his flowers sat next to her bed filled him with irrational joy which was swiftly snatched away. 'Westbridge is watching us! My, that scowl is tremendous.'

'Splendid.' Seb was not going to talk about dukes. 'I thought I would drop in a few little hints about Millcroft's dubious relationship with the law tonight over cards. Moan about the English levels of taxation. How high they are. How much of a scandal it is that the Crown should skim all the cream off the top of a man's investments.'

Her eyes moved back to hold his. 'I suppose a man who loathes paying his taxes is easier to corrupt. Is that the sort of bait you usually use to lure criminals?'

'It's a delicate process. Blab too much and they become suspicious. As people become familiar with you, feel comfortable and relaxed in your presence, their guard comes down. Little nuggets sprinkled here and there blended into normal conversation. The upstanding fellows all gripe about taxation, too—but that's where their rebellion starts and finishes. A good moan amongst their brethren and they feel purged. However, for those seeking partners in crime, those casual asides, peppered with the odd suggestion that this or that was acquired on the sly, form a trail of crumbs to follow. Bait is a good choice of word. Dangle enough bait or just the right bait on your hook, and the wrong'uns bite.'

'How can you tell they are tempted?' Her head had tilted to one side as she stared deep into his eyes. The position made her ringlets bounce and shimmer beneath the chandelier as he twirled her.

'Curiosity. It is the most unsubtle human failing. The odd pertinent question means nothing. Many over a short period of time set off alarm bells. Why would they ask so much…unless they were interested?'

'I see.' When she frowned she had a dimple on one cheek. Just the one. A charming and minuscule imperfection when one compared the whole, but, like the hair rags and her love of sugar, very appealing. 'And where do you wish to go fishing tonight, my lord? Is there anyone particular you would like me to introduce you to?'

'For now, I think it's best I stick with Viscount Penhurst's circle.'

'Penhurst?' There was that frown again. It flitted across her lovely face before she covered it with a shrug. 'Why?'

'Well… I know them.' And she was a family friend who would react badly to the real truth. 'I

think Penhurst is my best chance of getting invited
to the card tables. Don't you? We both know that
is where the men talk business. Once there, I can
naturally join any conversation. Or simply watch.
I am a spy after all. We are notoriously good at
watching.' And perhaps he was over-egging it because he suddenly realised he did not feel comfortable lying to her. Odd, when lying was what he did
as a matter of course. Lying to Gem left a bitter
taste in the mouth and was becoming harder and
harder to do convincingly after all of her help—
and because he really liked her. Probably a great
deal more than he should for the sake of his own
sanity. 'In the meantime, why don't you introduce
me to them?' She followed his gaze to the crowd
of brash bachelors scanning the eligible ladies.
He already knew all their names and knew they
were merely fortune hunters. His Invisibles were
tremendously thorough whenever they started a
new mission. A pile of damning biographies grew
daily on the desk of his new study. Once he put
names to the faces, Seb could reel off all manner
of titbits about each one. Debts. Mistresses. Dubious connections.

Penhurst's was one of the most damning of all.
The man flitted from mistress to mistress without
a second glance. He was ruthless to those poor
misguided women, treating them more like used
handkerchiefs than human beings. He once had

nine thousand pounds' worth of debt which he paid with his wife's dowry and then gambled with impunity, racking up more. Penhurst liked the infamous hells. The most secret ones in the roughest parts of the city where the women were loose and the absinthe flowed freely. The sort of places where entire fortunes could be lost in a single night. An expensive habit which he was funding from somewhere.

'As you wish. But first...' She wiggled her eyebrows and tugged him towards the alcove to hide behind a pillar. Seb forgot to breathe when she daintily hoisted her skirt up a few inches, giving him a very tantalising glimpse of her ankles and calves while she rummaged for something out of his eye line. Her eyes were dancing with amusement when she finally produced a small silver hip flask and winked. 'Brandy. I know a little nip of this banishes that shyness and I believe you'll have greater success smiling rather than scowling at people and scaring them away.' She unscrewed the top and passed it to him. 'Drink up, Lord Millcroft. Let's go and catch some smugglers.'

For the next hour, Seb said little and almost had fun. Fortunately, Gem talked enough for the both of them and did it with such witty aplomb, crediting him for all the funny stories she came out with, to such an extent he was subjected to a great deal of back-slapping from the other gentle-men while barely uttering a word. His unexpected partner had more talent for charming people than any person he had ever known. If he could bottle it and sell it, he'd make a fortune. But the way her eyes trailed after her Duke certainly took the edge off his good mood. Watching them dim as West-bridge found Lady Olivia Spencer and proceeded to dance both the hole in the wall and the subse-quent cotillion with the girl tugged at his heart-strings. Why she wanted that Duke was beyond him, but he had agreed to help her make the idiot jealous in return for her assistance so he had to play his part willingly. Even if it infuriated him.

At Gem's insistence, they rejoined the Pen-hurst party much sooner than Seb had expected and she remained at his side, chatting while her eyes searched the crowds for signs of the fool she had set her cap for. Nobody else noticed. Half the ballroom were too busy watching Clarissa and Seb with barely concealed interest. The viscount himself was one of them. He smiled in greeting.

'Will you be joining us for cards tonight, Mill-croft?'

Seb suppressed the triumphant relief at being asked. Penhurst would have no respect for him if he appeared too eager. 'Perhaps. Will it be worth my while?' The last time, they had played hazard for an eye-watering pot of money.

'Were the stakes not high enough for you?'

'I like a quick and healthy return. The healthier the better.'

'Seb is a tremendous risk-taker. Did you know, in Sydney he owned his own gaming house?' Gem smiled up at him adoringly, knowing full well she was baiting his hook with a juicy, fat worm, but completely unaware that it was destined for her friend's cheek. 'Quite a scandalous one by all accounts.'

Penhurst's eyebrows lifted. 'Hardly a gentleman's investment.'

'Gentlemen are thin on the ground in Sydney. Those that are there tend to stick close to the Governor in case they are tainted by the rest of the population. I preferred to spend my time with men who thought like me…and of course, as the owner, even if I lost a hand or two, I never really lost, if you get my meaning.' He tapped his nose. 'The house always wins. Not to mention, they paid over the odds for my *inferior* port and brandy. As an investment, a gaming hell proved to be very fruitful. I'm already in negotiations with several establishments here in the capital. As I said—I enjoy a quick return.'

'Here, such things would be frowned upon.' But the viscount wasn't frowning. Far from it in fact. He had sidled up to Seb like a confidant.

'By whom? The lofty peers who cling to the old

ideas of commerce? Those blinkered fools who pay ridiculous taxes and believe the future lies in land, in farming and in crops? I dare say Mayfair is filled with nobles whose coffers diminish year by year while they lament the old days, when wheat and rents were all it took to rake in the coin.' Seb allowed himself a wry smile as he shook his head. 'The world is changing, my lord. The new money—the *smart money*—is not shackled by such prejudices and I can assure you they are positively raking it in. Enterprise and imaginative investment are the future. You mark my words. While the old guard are tightening their belts and burning tallow instead of beeswax, I shall be sat in my well-lit gaming house counting my money. If that means I am no gentleman, I am surprisingly comfortable with that.'

'You speak a lot of sense, Millcroft. A lot of sense. But what made you leave the Antipodes? It sounds like you were doing well.'

'I was. I was trotting along quite nicely. But Sydney is a small city and the opportunities to grow my investment were limited. Here, the potential to grow is more than a hundredfold. I make no apology for being ambitious.'

'And nor should you. Your entrepreneurial attitude does you credit. I should be very interested to learn about your plans. Why don't we continue this conversation away from the masses over a glass of our host's finest brandy and a spirited game of hazard?'

Seb enjoyed the rush of euphoria at his success. 'An excellent idea.' Out of the corner of his eye he spied Westbridge crossing the crowded ballroom towards them at the same moment he felt Gem release her hold on his arm just as the orchestra was preparing to play the second waltz. Like a fool, Gem stood anticipating the Duke's arrival like the prodigal son. The euphoria instantly turned to bitter disappointment. It was bad enough watching her pine for the fool, but he was damned if he was going to watch her entwined in his arms. With a wry smile he didn't feel, Seb turned back to Penhurst. 'I've had about as much of this ballroom as I can stomach for one evening. In the absence of a decent hell, thank heavens for hazard.'

Chapter Eight

〜〜〜〜

Seb's invitation to the Penhurst house party miraculously arrived the next day and without Clarissa having to ask him to attend or even mention it, he had confirmed he would be there. She knew this because Penny had sent a note across Berkeley Square immediately. The next week positively shot by as she made her preparations, buoyed with a fresh optimism which had been missing since Lady Olivia had elbowed her way into Westbridge's affections. Her Duke certainly appeared significantly more interested in her since Seb had commandeered her. In the two balls and one night at the opera since, the pair of them had been as thick as thieves. Lord Millcroft always had the first waltz and had brought her refreshments and dominated the interval at the opera, and poor Westbridge had been obviously furious at both while sticking to them like glue until Seb had been dragged away by Penhurst.

She always missed him when he was gone. Being with Seb, having a purpose beyond simply looking pretty, was the most fun she had had in years. For the first time since being declared an *Incomparable*, Clarissa felt important. Vital even. It didn't matter that she excelled in very little, because the things she did excel at were exactly the things which helped him to do what he needed to do. How many other ladies got to help the government? And whilst that lofty achievement gave her a deep sense of worth, so, too, did being there for him.

Watching Seb work was fascinating. He was so subtle and sharp. Those dark eyes of his everywhere, noticing everything. His memory for names and details was staggering, surpassing her own, but when she asked him how he remembered so much information he simply shrugged and said, 'I'm a spy.' As if that was explanation enough.

She wished she could see him in action in the card room. Amongst men he didn't suffer from the awkwardness which still plagued him—even with her. It was lessened now, although while Millcroft was mysterious and aloof, in the few snatched minutes they had shared where he was just Seb his intelligent eyes still struggled to meet hers and he still blushed occasionally and became tongue-tied and gruff. Knowing the real him was a delicious secret and one she selfishly did not want to share. She hoped they would have ample opportunity to spend more time alone at the house party. Clarissa desperately wanted to know more about him. The real him that only she saw.

According to Penny, Westbridge had been very put out to learn of Seb's inclusion in the house party and had done his best to get Penhurst to rescind the invitation, fortunately all to no avail as Penny's foul husband was quite taken with his new friend. Whilst she was pleased for Seb, she was also very satisfied with the way things were going. Now, instead of being on the back foot, Clarissa would cheerfully stride into Penhurst Hall, safe in the knowledge that her other *suitor* would be there, too.

Seven days of excitement.

The carriage wheels couldn't turn fast enough.

Once she was presentable, of course. They had stopped at an inn half an hour away from the Sussex estate so that Clarissa could fix the damage caused by hours of travelling. It was a habit she had begun during her first Season to ensure she never arrived anywhere looking anything other than her best. Something Westbridge would expect in his future duchess. Thanks to the dire state of the road to Eastbourne, her dress was crumpled, her perfume was stale and her ringlets were sadly wilting. This quaint little inn a few miles away from the main road was a regular stopping point on her jaunts to Penny's. She had lost count of how many visits she had enjoyed here and always booked the same cheerful, sunny room well in advance of every Penhurst party. The curling irons were already in the fire and she was stripped down to her chemise after washing with her favourite French soap while her maid was brushing her hair before restyling it.

The innkeeper's wife knocked on the door and stepped inside. 'There is a visitor for you, my lady.' Impossible—aside from the coachmen, nobody knew she was here. 'He's waiting in the taproom.'

'He?'

'A Lord Millcroft.' An expensive calling card was thrust into Clarissa's hand. 'He says he has urgent things to discuss with you.'

How did Seb know she was here? 'Tell him I will be down as soon as I can.' Which would be at least an hour in her current state of dishabille.

'I don't have time to wait.' His deep voice from behind the door brooked no argument, the sound of it sending tingles down her spine regardless. 'This will only take a few minutes, Gem.'

She knew he would expect to be invited in and she also knew that he wouldn't be here unless it was of national importance—but, really! She looked a fright. 'I'm not dressed.'

'Then put on a robe.'

He'd already seen her hair in rags, so loose and virtually straight was an improvement, but allowing him to see her lacking her usual refinement made her feel uncomfortable. Clarissa didn't want him to remember the rag incident and had paid more attention to her appearance since knowing Seb would see it. She grabbed her silk dressing gown and shoved her arms in the sleeves. Pulling the belt into a tight knot, she grabbed all her hair in her hand and twisted it to drape over one shoulder in what she hoped was a becoming manner before pinching some colour into her cheeks. 'Very well. Come in.'

The innkeeper's wife opened the door and Seb filled the frame. He had a habit of filling doorframes and, wearing a greatcoat, he left little daylight to seep around his imposing silhouette. He stood stiffly for a moment, then in two long strides he was stood before her, his eyes flicking to her maid warily. Clarissa recognised he wanted privacy. 'You might as well have my dress pressed now, Agnes. You can fix my hair in a few minutes when his lordship has gone.'

The young woman hesitated at the lack of propriety, then bobbed a curtsy as she glared at Seb. 'I shall be less than ten minutes, my lady. Or sooner.' She snatched up the fresh travelling dress from the top of Clarissa's trunk and marched out, still glaring at him. When she was gone he raked a hand through his hair and offered Clarissa a small smile.

'Your maid thinks I have come to ruin you.'

'She is blissfully unaware of your lack of seduction skills.' Although, all windswept from his ride and struggling to meet her gaze, he managed to seduce her regardless. Her fingers wanted to smooth his mussed hair and touch his face, a scandalous thought whilst only a single layer of thin silk separated her gauzy shift from his gaze. 'How did you know I was here?'

He shrugged and took in the unfamiliar room, the cooling water in the washbowl, the tangled pile of hair pins on the dressing table, the glowing irons in the fire. Anywhere but at her. 'I'm a spy. Where else would you be?'

'I mean seriously...'

'Oh, all right—I had one of my men track you. I knew you would stop at an inn close to our destination.' The smile turned into a smug grin as his eyes finally locked with hers. 'Nobody looks as good as you do after hours of travel without a stop to make urgent repairs.' Sometimes his astuteness was galling. This man would *never* forget the rag incident.

'Why the urgency to speak to me?'

'That fool Westbridge hasn't left us alone all week and I needed to ask you about the guest list.'

'Whatever for?'

'Correct me if I'm wrong, but Penhurst Hall is going to be crammed to the rafters with society, is it not? What if one of the bounders I'm seeking is in attendance?' So that was why he'd readily accepted Penny's invitation. A tiny part of her had hoped he had jumped at the chance of spending a week with her. He pulled a folded document from a pocket inside his coat and held it out. 'What can you tell me about the people on that list.'

Clarissa allowed a mask of boredom to conceal her utter terror at being asked to read when there were no other diversions in the room to plead as an excuse. Instead of taking it, she picked up her brush and began to drag it purposefully through her hair. 'It will be mostly the usual bunch.'

'Who are?'

'Penhurst's horrid friends.' She felt her nose wrinkle in distaste as she listed them. Penhurst gallivanted about with a very dubious group of gentlemen who drank too much and disgraced their wives just as he did poor Penny. One or two made her flesh crawl, although thankfully they tended to hole up together with the host and do their own thing. 'Acquaintances from town. Some family. He also likes to surprise us with an illustrious peer. He spends weeks courting them and then parades those daft enough to fall for his flattery around his house like a trophy, hoping to impress us and, no doubt, to soak up some of that power to inflate his own sense of worth. He's foisted some dreadful bores on us whose only redeeming features are their ancient and impressive titles.' Saying that made her fleetingly think of Westbridge before she uncomfortably quashed it. 'If he has found another new friend to fawn over, then he will keep it a surprise until they arrive. It makes him feel superior. Thankfully, a great many of those men and the hyenas he surrounds himself with disappear swiftly to do who knows what with Penhurst, so we were spared the pleasure of their company for most of the week.' Now that she considered it, there was every chance one of those awful men could be involved in something illegal. The vile viscount needed to choose better friends.

'You do not approve of Penny's husband?'

'What is there to approve of? You are the spy. What are your impressions of him?'

'Honestly…slimy. Cold. Selfish.' In the absence of any other chairs, he tossed his hat on the mattress and sat down next to it, looking delightfully awkward still clutching the dreaded sheet of foolscap. 'What specifically do you disapprove of?'

'The way he treats Penny.' Clarissa didn't need to think about it. 'I have long suspected he is violent towards her.'

She watched Seb's jaw harden as he scowled

and liked him more for that unguarded response. 'Knowing that makes it harder to befriend him… but he serves his purpose.' He seemed momentarily irritated with himself for saying that, but covered it quickly, yet the fact that he obviously disliked everything about Penny's husband made Seb rise higher in her estimation. 'Tell me more about his cronies.'

Clarissa reeled off what she knew. Being Seb, he had no need of notes and tucked each piece of information away in his clever mind, almost as if he was fully aware of the men and their backgrounds. His questions, when he rarely interrupted her to ask one, were very specific. As if he already knew most of the 'usual crowd' of debauched gentlemen, he asked her a few pertinent details about each one. Purported names of mistresses, rumoured vices and scandals. Debts. Topics she had never openly gossiped about with a man or with the ladies without a fan or a cup of tea strategically placed in front of her face. He apologised before broaching the subject of Penhurst's many infidelities because he knew she loved Penny.

'He has a new mistress, I believe. But then he has so many it's hard to keep track. A French woman.'

Seb's ears had pricked up at that. 'French?'

'Yes. She is apparently some sort of opera

singer or actress. A woman involved in entertaining. I overheard him bragging about her a few weeks ago when I was last at Penhurst Hall.' Along with an eye-opening and graphic account of what he had done to the poor woman when she had invited him into her bed. No matter how open she was being with Seb, there was no way she would be able to share those details. It was all too depraved.

'None of my men has heard anything about it.'

'That is good to know. I am hugely protective of poor Penny and would never cause her embarrassment by spreading such stories.' Although why would Seb's men be investigating Penhurst? 'I am suffered at the house party because I am Penny's only friend and I dare say the silly label of *Incomparable* helps, too—but while she has a friend with her he can stay at the card tables or do whatever it is that he does with the majority of his time till Lord knows when in the small hours. Penhurst prefers the company of his cronies. Even at home.'

'Is that fool Westbridge one of his cronies, too?'

Whilst Seb had no regard for her friend's odious husband, he obviously had a special well of deep loathing for her Duke. A loathing which sounded delightfully territorial. 'Westbridge was at Oxford with Penhurst. Their acquaintance is old, but they are not particularly close any more.'

Her Duke held most people at arm's length, in-cluding her. 'He has little interest in gambling and drinking, thank goodness, therefore he doesn't see Penhurst in quite the same depraved light as the rest of us.' To do that he would have to take an interest in another person other than himself. Where had that disloyal thought come from? 'But then as Westbridge is *a duke*, Penhurst is mindful not to show him the true extent of his debauchery either. He mostly flatters him. Having Westbridge as a friend enhances his own standing in the *ton* and Westbridge can be relied upon to attend re-gardless of who else has been invited. Everyone wants *a duke* on their guest list.'

At the mention of the word 'duke', Seb had be-come most belligerent. 'Of course they do. The ad-dition of a duke makes any gathering a resounding success, even if they are fools like yours.'

'Westbridge isn't a fool, he's...' Self-absorbed, fickle, nowhere near as broad, strong, considerate and impressive as the man sat on the bed in front of her. 'He's simply being a duke, Seb. He is ac-tually rather pleasant when you get to know him.'

'And you know him well?'

'I do as a matter of fact. Westbridge is a re-nowned connoisseur. His collections of art and furniture are the finest in Europe. The Regent himself is envious of the Duke's array of Old Mas-ters.' Something he informed her repeatedly.

'Oh, he's a *connoisseur*. That is excellent news.'

'There is nothing wrong with liking beautiful things. Not that you'd understand. But those of us who know him well appreciate his superior taste and faultless eye.' Clarissa was relying on it because like his collection of Ancient Egyptian relics she was all style over substance.

'I can see you know him *far better* than most.' His head tilted enquiringly and he folded his arms across the very chest she had just been contemplating. 'I suppose that is why you do not have leave to call him by his Christian name.'

Her mouth opened and then closed. 'His Christian name is Albert.'

'Yet I have never heard you refer to him as anything other than Westbridge. The Duke or *your Grace*.'

Because Seb was right, damn him, her Duke had never invited her to dispense with the formalities. 'I'm not particularly fond of the name Albert.'

This appeared to amuse him. 'Will you call him Westbridge after you are married as well?'

Probably. 'That is none of your business.'

'How romantic.'

Westbridge wasn't romantic. He wasn't the slightest bit affectionate or even humorous. Devoid of all passion aside from that of collecting the unattainable. 'I am not looking for romance.' She was looking for a well-fortified battlement to hide behind. They didn't come much stronger than a dukedom.

'Or love by the sounds of it. Duchesses clearly need neither. But they are *duchesses*.'

When he put it like that her future sounded miserable. Seb didn't understand that being a duchess would be the single greatest accomplishment for the least accomplished lady ever born. The unique achievement only *Incomparables* hoped for. Not just an advantageous marriage and a secure future, but the most advantageous of marriages. The most secure future. An impenetrable layer of protection against the judgement of all which would render her dirty secret a secret for ever. Clarissa had been a slave to that goal for the last two Seasons. Something the intuitive man before her obviously thought was shallow—because it was shallow, but then so was she. Girls who couldn't paint or embroider, girls who couldn't play an instrument or spell or read a sentence without laboriously trailing her finger beneath it lacked hidden depths. She would be a good wife and a good mother, a flawless decoration, content to live in her illustrious husband's protective shadow.

Her self-absorbed, formal, passionless and fickle husband's illustrious shadow.

'Thank goodness you are beautiful else the *connoisseur* might have missed you. What an asset you will be to his exemplary collection. Unless he decides to add that simpering Olivia to his display case instead. Which I suppose is why you are here. Are you trying to improve on perfection by outshining her from the second you arrive?'

'I'm sure the simpering Lady Olivia is doing much the same thing in another inn close by.'

The overloud cough outside signalled the return of her maid and thankfully the end of this uncomfortable line of questioning. When he forgot to be shy, his astute and painful honesty could be brutal. Agnes marched through the door, carrying her mistress's freshly pressed new travelling dress aloft, and scowled at the sight of Seb sat on the bed to such an extent he stood. 'I'd best be on my way. Will you read this list and appraise me of any details we might have missed later?' He was back to not meeting her eyes and that was just dandy because she would rather die than let him see how much his insightful observations had bothered her.

'Yes.' If she started to read it today she might reach the end of the list by tomorrow. Or the next day. Just thinking about it made the letters swim and dance before her eyes and her tummy churn with the constant fear of discovery. In case he saw it, Clarissa turned her back to him as he walked to the door, both miffed at him and miffed at herself because she knew the source of her irritation was merely his accurate assessment of her situation. This week now couldn't pass quickly enough.

Chapter Nine

Thanks to the continual arrival of the other guests and the assumption that everyone would need to rest before dinner, Seb was able to freely ride around the grounds of Penhurst Hall unfettered. The house sat high on the South Downs, surrounded by a good mile of rolling pasture before it came to a sudden halt at the steep cliffs which bordered the sea. Those cliffs petered out as they ran down towards Birling Gap—an infamous beach for smugglers of old and one which was now patrolled by the Excise Men. Knowing how stretched that service was, it wasn't out of the realms of fantasy to imagine the smugglers he was seeking sailing their boats into this secluded little stretch of beach and then hauling their contraband up the shortest wall of the cliff. But then they could do much the same along the steepest walls. The Boss headed a wily and resourceful operation, therefore a steep cliff face was hardly an insurmountable obstacle and less likely to be monitored by the Excise Men. His men were paid well to risk their lives.

But so were Seb's.

Somewhere in this vast expanse of grass and sheep were two of his Invisibles. Another four were moored offshore in the Channel in a fishing boat. More were dotted along the length of coastline, watching and waiting. Gray was inside the house, ingratiating himself with the servants and mapping the hall while others manned all the possible roads where a cart laden with illegal French brandy might travel. If Penhurst was indeed in league with England's most dangerous gang of smugglers, and used this land to commit his treason, then the King's Elite would see it. But catching the boots on the ground was not the point of this mission. Those men could be replaced easily enough. They needed to catch Penhurst and the other leaders, and destroy the foundations of their organisation completely, which meant that Seb had to thoroughly infiltrate the core or find enough damning evidence to ensure there was no reasonable doubt as to their guilt.

Viscount Penhurst was intrigued at this stage, nothing more. Each time they met he subtly tested Seb's supposed morals again and again, and each time Seb dripped in more detail to make the man believe they were kindred spirits. The fact that

Penhurst made his blood boil over the simplest things was something Seb was trained to disguise, yet the more he got to know him, the harder it was not to slam his fist into the man's face. The viscount had little respect for anything except his own pleasures and spending money. He treated his servants like dirt, his wife worse and had a warped, depraved sense of humour which his hideous cronies shared. The stories they told about the perversions they subjected their mistresses to turned his stomach and set his mind wandering to places he didn't want to contemplate—not when his mother had been a mistress to a powerful man all her adult life. She had loved his father. Seb didn't fool himself his father had loved her back.

But for those powerful men, like his dear papa, their attitude to their mistresses was commercial and detached. They paid good money to keep the woman in luxury, therefore it was their due to be reimbursed for their investment in other ways. Seb likened it to being press-ganged into the navy. If you took the shilling, you accepted the consequences and did what you were told. Even if that meant debasing yourself. Once they had served their purpose or their owner became bored, they were cast aside without a second thought. Peers like Penhurst didn't hear the word *no*. Had Seb's father abused his mother like that? He sincerely hoped not, but the man had certainly not honoured her with a second thought.

Tonight, no doubt, and over the coming days he would have to listen to more poison. For the sake of King and country he would force himself to laugh alongside them, slap them on the back and congratulate them on their prowess. So far he hadn't been able to bring himself to invent the sick lies which would convince them that he had committed similar atrocities against a woman. Pretty soon he might have to, unless Penhurst revealed his hand and invited Seb completely into his debauched world. Just thinking about it made him feel strangely violated. Success in this case had a definite drawback.

Two if he included watching Gem pursue her Duke.

That was equally unpalatable.

With a frustrated sigh he turned his horse back towards the house. He had avoided her when she had finally arrived a few hours ago, disgusted at her single-minded determination to become a duchess and his own inability not to care about it.

He had known that when he had agreed to her suggestion. Known it as she had escorted him around those ballrooms, ensured he was not only accepted but welcomed into the ranks of high society, helped him with his awkwardness and his mission. Known it as he had held her in his arms and danced with her. *Incomparables* weren't for bastards. He and she lived in two very different worlds. Despite that, Gem had come to mean more to him than a means to an end. Much more. His heart wept that she would sell herself so short and accept Westbridge's shoddy treatment. All to be a duchess.

If that was what her heart desired, exactly how was Seb to compete?

Perhaps if he had not been so inept with the opposite sex he could seduce her…her blithe denunciation of his lack of seduction skills earlier had hurt. Those words had collided with another unstoppable surge of lust brought about by the sight of her with her hair down in that revealing silk robe, the fabric almost fluid as it moulded against the mounds of her unbound breasts. It had been a wholly unnecessary diversion borne out of a desire to have her to himself one last time before they embarked on a week of hideous socialising. Seb had justified it to Gray as a need to pick her brain about the guests, knowing full well he could just as easily steal her for a few minutes at the house and talk to her then. But at the house would be her damn Duke and Seb was completely, pathetically smitten.

His normally strategic thoughts were constantly broken by images of her, encroaching on his waking mind and laying siege to his night-time dreams. Again this morning he had awoken hot and hard, wanting, the tangled sheets coiled around his body a testament to his restless sleep. Seeing her in the flesh had been paramount. True to form, the moment he had walked into that bedchamber he had been struck once again by the sheer beauty of Gem in her natural state. Her golden hair was indeed straight. The few kinks created by the previous style made it shimmer in the morning sunshine streaming through the window, the usually short, tight ringlets which framed her face hung as loose tendrils past her jaw, softer and more enticing. His fingers had yearned to reach out and touch one close to her freshly washed cheek. That Gem, the real one, was the true diamond. So precious and unique, no other woman could hold a candle to her. Seb was coming to suspect no other woman ever would hold a candle to her in his eyes.

Talk about barking up the wrong tree. Lady Clarissa Beaumont had swiftly, and obliviously, doused his ardour with a bucket of ice water with her talk of her supercilious Duke and Seb had left her in a foul mood, rightly miffed at her desire to become a duchess above all else and at himself for feeling heartbroken because of it.

For a man who found himself so clumsy and clunky around the fairer sex, why had his foolish heart lent itself to her—the fairest of them all?

This blasted week couldn't pass quickly enough. Seb had to endure seven days of torture. Less if he could link Penhurst to the Boss sooner.

Less was always more.

Back in his cramped allocated bedchamber, irritatingly in the front of the house facing the lane and not the cliffs, Seb tried to ignore his simmering anger as they swapped what he had learned since arriving. His second-in-command had hit brick walls amongst the viscount's servants. They were fearful, distrusting of strangers and some were downright menacing. Things that all encouragingly pointed to secrets, but made the task in hand harder to do. The best lead they had was still Penhurst himself. A long night of work loomed in front of him.

Gray made himself comfortable on Seb's bed and watched him shave and wriggle into the ridiculously stiff evening clothes, rising only to assist him with the dreaded cravat.

'What knot am I tying tonight? Might I suggest the Trone d'Amour? It's excellent symbolism. The mention of love in the title will send your rival mad.'

'No stupid dandified knots. I'm done with them.' Complicated and frothy confections were for pompous windbags like Westbridge. Seb snatched the pristine strip of white linen out of his friend's hands and proceeded to tie the damn knot himself. 'And if you think I'm stepping out-side this room in that waistcoat…' He glared at the garish monstrosity covered in embroidered peacock feathers with outright distaste. 'You have another think coming!'

'Waistcoats are always bolder for evening wear.'

'I will suffer colours, but not a kaleidoscope.'

Gray gave a good-natured shrug and grabbed another two out of the closet. 'How about peacock blue to match you lady love's eyes? She likes blue, doesn't she?'

'Give me the red.' There would be no more attempting to please Gem with daft wardrobe choices. From now on, Seb was going to focus on his mission. What she chose to do was her own business. Now that he was here as a guest, there was no reason why they needed to continue to work together. She could chase her Duke with impunity while Seb got briskly on with what he had been sent here to do. He needed neither the distraction nor the heartache. Let her have her blue-blooded Duke! 'How do I look?'

'Furious. Burning with jealousy and border-line scary.'

'Go to hell!' He heard Gray's receding laugh-ter as he slammed the door and stalked down the landing.

The drawing room was crammed full of the

twenty or so guests Seb would spend the week with. He was on nodding terms with three-quarters of them now and found his head bobbing like a woodpecker's as he navigated his way to the trio of men stood at the fireplace while pretending he had not noticed the temptress sat holding court on the sofa. In his peripheral vision he saw her try to catch his eye and set his jaw stubbornly in case his traitorous neck turned her way. A passing footmen with a tray laden with champagne provided an excellent excuse to pick up his pace and put distance between them. With a glass in his hand and an ache in his teeth Seb forced a sociable smile, ready to work. 'Good evening, gentlemen.' A misnomer. These two men were the most debauched of Penhurst's cronies.

'Evening, Millcroft. I hope you came with a purse full of money. The cards this week promise to be exciting. Too bad there isn't a game tonight.' Viscount Regis. Ailing lands, yet interestingly a no longer ailing fortune. Enjoyed tying his mistress up. 'This evening we must all suffer the rest of the company, but tomorrow...' He grinned, displaying a row of crooked yellow teeth which matched his hideous mustard waistcoat. 'Tomorrow is ours.'

'Hear, hear.' Lord Gaines, second son of the Marquess of Rochford and fond of very high, very shiny tasselled Hessians, looked like a weasel and acted like one. His role in this motley group was ostensibly that of sycophant, but he had the ear of Penhurst. Seb had witnessed the pair whispering when they thought no one was looking. If Penhurst was in cahoots with anyone, it was Gaines. 'Tonight we are stuck with the ladies, although I wouldn't mind being stuck with yours, Millcroft. Eh?' Gaines winked, then moulded a female figure in the air with his hands which made the other laugh. 'I'd pay good money to get my hands on her bountiful charms.' The urge to break the weasel's long, narrow nose almost got the better of Seb.

'I doubt he needs to pay, do you, Millcroft?' Regis slapped him on the back. 'Not when the pastry is already headed this way. Act nonchalant, my dear fellow. Treat them mean and keep them keen and you'll bed her before this week is done.' Another back slap followed by conspiratorial chortling. Seb's returning laughter sounded too boisterous and false to his own ears as she came up alongside.

'Hello.'

'Well, *hello* to you, too.' The weasel stepped forward and kissed her hand. His eyes latched themselves on to Gem's cleavage. 'You look delightful this evening, Lady Clarissa.'

'Indeed she does.' Despite being thoroughly annoyed at her, the urge to protect her from these men was overwhelming and Seb found himself reaching for the hand and purposefully extricating it from Lord Gaines's grip to wrap it around his. He was seriously tempted to take off his coat and drape it around her bared shoulders. The glamorous coral gown, although not overly revealing by *ton*nish standards, was too daring for Penhurst's friends. 'I would be honoured if you would take a turn about the room with me, my lady.'

'I believe I should like that very much, my lord.'

Chapter Ten

'Were you purposely ignoring me?'

'No. Why would I do that?' As he wasn't looking at her it was difficult to ascertain if he was telling the truth. 'What can you tell me about this house?'

That it was little better than a prison for poor Penny. Desolate and miles from anywhere. 'Oh, dear. How very boring—but if you insist. The original building is medieval and now forms the central entranceway. The giant fireplace there is fourteenth century. The east and west wings were both built by the third Viscount Penhurst nearly a century ago to double the number of bedrooms and add the ballroom.'

'Impressive, although the bedrooms are less so. There is barely enough room to swing a cat in the one I have been given.'

Clarissa couldn't help but smile at his dismissive tone. Overt displays of wealth and status really didn't affect him in quite the same way they did most people. 'I think you will find the same in most great houses. They tend to compromise on size of bedchambers to ensure an adequate number of guest rooms for events just like this. Poor you, though I pity that cat more.' Some unexplained force made her run her palm greedily along the shape of his bicep before she stopped herself. 'As I am a long-standing friend, Penny always puts me in one of the huge rooms at the back on the family floor. Aside from a magnificent and decadent amount of space I also get a splendid view of the sea—or at least I would if I had remembered to pack my opera glasses.'

Seb's face turned for the first time since they had started their slow perambulation, his deadpan expression betrayed by his eyes. 'I have a telescope.'

'Who brings a telescope to a house party?'

'A spy.' His voice had dropped to an amused whisper that sent goosebumps rising all over her neck. 'We always come prepared for every eventuality.' He tugged her to follow him to the emptier end of the room. 'Have you ever ventured down to the cellars?'

'I have never had cause to.'

He looked oddly disappointed. 'Then I don't suppose you know if there are any tunnels or secret entrances?'

Tunnels and secret entrances? She was beginning to suspect the mysterious Lord Millcroft might not have come here strictly on the off chance. 'You mean like smugglers' tunnels? *Here?*'

He shrugged and stared off into the distance as if checking they were not being watched. 'Merely out of interest. Not so long ago this coastline would have been a hive of smuggling activity. Many buildings along these cliffs have a hidden warren of caves beneath them, most of which would have been used to hide contraband from the authorities. It can't hurt to investigate them if they exist—to see if they collide with other old tunnels. I'm a spy, remember. Being nosy goes with the territory.'

Clarissa was getting a decidedly uneasy feeling, like an itch which refused to be scratched. Her own voice dropped to a conspiratorial hiss. 'Do you suspect Penhurst?'

'No.' He appeared uncomfortable at the suggestion. 'Of course I don't. But he runs with a very dubious crowd, don't you agree, Gem? Men I notice *you* dislike with a vengeance. I would be remiss in my duty if I didn't explore every suspicion or suspicious person. Viscount Regis, for example—where does his money come from? He's never short of it, yet his estate has been on the verge of ruin for years. Gaines is another one. His reckless spending does not bear any resemblance to his small allowance and lack of property.'

'Perhaps they make their money through gambling. All of Penhurst's set practically live in the hells.' As did he. Penny's dowry must surely have been spent long ago on her husband's hedonistic lifestyle? Her eyes scanned the room critically as if seeing it properly for the first time. Had it been so luxurious when Penny had been a new bride? The paintings certainly had been dirtier, the gilt on their frames dulled by years of neglect. There had been a distinct lack of the valuable antiques one would expect to find in a house of this age. The furnishings then had been old and outdated. Clumsy, uncomfortable Tudor and Stuart relics which had disappeared in the last few years to be replaced with sumptuous chairs and sofas covered in fashionable, plush brocade. Her friend's dowry had been good, but nowhere near that good. Was this the fortuitous result of gambling? Hardly.

Seb touched her arm and smiled as if he could read her mind and found her vivid leap of imagination funny. 'Most money is made through speculation nowadays, not that pure-bred aristocrats would ever admit to such a thing. Only upstarts like Millcroft or new money brag about such investments. Please take my questions at face value. I have been doing this job for so many years now, I ask them as a matter of course, even when there is no cause to do so. Besides, we both know I am useless at making small talk. Even with you.'

He swiftly changed the subject, but the seeds of doubt had been sown and consequently Clarissa's mind was racing, not helped by the fact that Seb was behaving differently. He was more distant, more the invented Lord Millcroft than the man she knew, and that change also bothered her. The last time she had seen the real Seb had been at the inn this morning, and the more she thought about it, the more she believed the switch of persona had also happened in that hired room. The endearing and awkward ally had walked in and his brash alter-ego had strode out. She missed the real Seb. Missed the way that man made her feel.

Penhurst wandered over with Penny in tow and was soon followed by Westbridge, who had extricated his arm from Lady Olivia's to come to Clarissa. What began as a group chat soon petered into just Clarissa and her Duke as first Seb, then the others drifted away.

'I am not sure I approve of Millcroft.' Westbridge sounded gloriously churlish. 'People are beginning to talk about the pair of you.'

'They are?' How splendid. 'Pray, what do they say?'

'That he is sweet on you.' The idea made her pulse flutter.

'Lord Millcroft is very sweet.'

'Sweet?' An unattractive blood vessel pulsed near his eye as he scowled. 'The man is a crook. And a disrespectful one at that. Did you not see the half-hearted attempt at a bow he welcomed me with?' She had, although the slight incline of Seb's dark head hardly constituted a bow by any definition, more an acknowledgement they co-existed on the same planet. 'It shows scant regard for the proper formalities.'

'Conversely, that is one of the things I like about him the most. Seb is *delightfully* informal.' Westbridge never would have called unannounced at her bedchamber or discussed scandalous things with her. He mostly discussed himself. And largely with himself. All Clarissa had to do was nod at the right time.

'Seb!' The pulsing vessel went into a gallop as his face contorted. 'You scarcely know the fellow and yet he has given you leave to call him by his name and not his full name either! Please tell me you have not been so silly as to grant him the same privilege? Tell me he doesn't call you Clarissa, my lady.'

'He doesn't.' Westbridge sagged with relief. 'He calls me Gem—because in his eyes I am as precious as a diamond.' Or at least that was why she hoped he called her by the pet name. He could just as easily see her as a big joke. The girl in rags with jam on her nightdress. 'I rather like it.' While he was consumed with jealousy, now might be a good time to push him. 'In fact, I wouldn't mind if you started to drop the formalities, as well. Would you call me simply Clarissa?'

This concession seemed to placate him because he nodded, the irritating blood vessel calmed to the occasional twitch. 'I should be honoured to.'

She let the silence hang for a few moments, waiting for him to ask her to call him Albert, but he didn't. Pride prevented her from asking him to extend the courtesy, so she tried a different tack to test the waters. 'How was your journey here, *your Grace*?'

'Tolerable. The state of the lanes across the South Downs leaves a lot to be desired. Penhurst should see to that. One of the first things I did when I inherited the dukedom was to have the lanes approaching my estate cobbled and lined with becoming trees. It is important to give off the correct impression, don't you think?' Typically, he failed to notice the brittle smile she offered in reply, largely because he was back to talking about himself.

Her hosts had sat her nowhere near either Seb or Westbridge at dinner. As soon as the meal was over the men retired for port and cigars and had remained retired for over two hours now. Clarissa kept herself entertained by chatting to whichever ladies took her fancy until somebody suggested they all read aloud a play that one of them had brought with her. Most of the ladies, including Penny, clambered for a part, which left Clarissa at a bit of a loss. Obviously, she declined her proffered part. Trying to read alone was struggle enough, doing it in front of this gaggle of judgemental females would be a catastrophe. Instead, she took herself to the other end of the room where she could see down the hallway and pretended to read a book that someone else had left lying around while counting the seconds till the gentlemen reappeared. From the noisy laughter coming from the billiard room, that was likely to be some way off.

She was just about to call it a night when she saw a familiar shape moving on stealthy feet further down the hallway until he disappeared around the corner. The way Seb kept checking left and right piqued her interest. He was working.

Quietly and with the minimum of fuss, Clarissa slid the book to the arm of the chair and slipped casually from the room. The door to the billiard room was open a crack, so she quickly darted past in case she was seen and followed Seb around the corner. The hall beyond was empty, the lights dim. She checked the deserted ballroom and the small library, then stopped dead outside the only other door in this lesser-used wing—Penhurst's study.

As it was a room she had never entered—why would she?—Clarissa pressed her ear to the wood to listen. If Seb had been invited by their host and she suddenly barged in, it would look very odd and probably compromise Seb's mission. After a full minute of hearing nothing, she turned the handle and stepped inside.

The room was dark and a little ominous. The ancient wood panelling made the night blacker, while the ghostly shapes created by the weak moonlight added to the eerie feel. It smelled of too much stale tobacco and hard spirits, causing her nose to wrinkle at the acrid scent. The involuntary shiver made her wrap her arms around her middle and all at once Clarissa was scared.

'Seb?' She whispered his name, wondering where else he could possibly be, yet was still startled when his shadowy form emerged from his hiding place behind the curtain.

'What are you doing here?'

'I could ask you the same thing.' The fact that he, too, was whispering spoke volumes. 'Why are you creeping about Penhurst's study in the dark?'

He stared back blandly. It was all the confirmation she needed. 'You *do* suspect Penhurst!' Shocked, Clarissa leaned against a plinth, gripping the shamelessly naked statue of Aphrodite that stood upon it. 'You lied to me!'

'I didn't lie.' He raked a frustrated hand through

his hair as she gaped at him for the falsehood. The only saving grace was that his expression was wretched. 'All right, I did once or twice... I tried not to lie... I hated lying to *you*... But you have to understand this is my job. I was sent here on a specific mission. An important mission. Out of necessity, the line between deception and truth has to be blurred.'

'Oh, my goodness! Poor Penny...'

'You cannot breathe a word of this to your friend.' He rushed forward and his hands came to rest on her arms, his eyes more serious and steely than she had ever seen them. Leatham the fearless spy, not the man who couldn't flirt.

'But...' His fingers came up and covered her lips and his tone was urgent. Determined. Almost ruthless.

'There can be no buts. If my mission causes you a conflict of interest, then I will have you removed and returned to your sister's tonight. Under guard. I've lost enough men to this murderous gang and I won't willingly lose another.' As if seeing his hands for the first time he suddenly let go of her and took a step back. 'I'm sorry about your friend. I like Penny a great deal and I am certain she is innocent of any of this—but Penhurst reeks of guilt and it is my mission to prove it. These are not nice men, Gem. They are cutthroats and Penhurst is one of them. Our intelligence suggests he now runs the entire distribution network here in the south-east. And we are talking thousands of barrels of illegal French brandy. Thousands.'

'Penhurst is a smuggler? You are sure of it? Is it such a dreadful crime to evade paying the duty?'

'I'm afraid it gets worse. This gang are not your run-of-the-mill smugglers out to make fast money. The profit from their huge empire goes directly to the supporters of Napoleon. We believe they are trying to raise an army to continue what he started. An army destined for here. Anyone who supports it in any way is a traitor to the Crown.'

Her mind scrabbled to take it all in. Question after question popped into her thoughts like champagne bubbles, each bursting and drifting away as another more pressing one hurried behind so quickly that her lips failed to form a single word. It was all so surreal, yet the more she thought about it, also alarmingly possible. Penhurst was a monster with the morals of an alley cat. Cold, spiteful, selfish and thoroughly debauched. Clarissa had never liked him. If she was being brutally honest with herself, she hated him and all his odious friends. Always had. Was that hatred clouding her judgement? Was he capable of being in league with smugglers to feather his own nest? He was certainly greedy. He had spent Penny's dowry like water and quickly, too. Yet there had been a significant uplift in his fortunes since. These frequent, decadent house parties were merely the tip of the iceberg as far as his spending was concerned. This house and their Mayfair town house were now stuffed to the rafters with the latest furnishings, tawdry new gilt had been applied to every frame and chair leg. Penhurst's wardrobe alone must have cost a king's ransom. Even the bronze Aphrodite, bared bosoms jutting on her silly plinth, was a flagrant ostentation. So many things were falling into place because they suddenly made perfect sense.

Penhurst had a fortune and, unless he had made some very clever investments with Penny's dowry, there was no other explanation for its sudden appearance. But was he capable of treason? Was he that greedy? That wicked? Was there the slimmest chance Seb was completely wrong? Deep in her bones she feared she knew the answer.

'I won't say anything.' Not yet at least. Defending a traitor was indefensible no matter who he was married to. There would be no need for guards to ensure her silence, her fear for her friend was enough. Penny didn't need to know about these outrageous allegations while Seb and the British government had no evidence to prove it. She could protect her from that at least. When the time came, *if* the time came, Clarissa would bend over backwards to save her friend. How? She didn't yet know, but she would find a way to protect Penny even if all she could do was give her enough warning to hide in exile before the scandal blew wide open.

Poor Penny.

The initial chill upon entering the room permeated her entire body, she felt dangerously light-headed and nauseous, and found herself rushing to the window to open it, leaning heavily on the sill as she gulped in cleansing breaths. Seb had known this all along and used her to infiltrate Penhurst's circle. More things slotted into place as she remembered they had renewed their acquaintance when Penhurst had introduced them after he in turn had been introduced to the mysterious lord fresh from the Antipodes by the Earl of Upminster. A man who was so high up in the Foreign Office he had the ear of the King. Everyone knew that.

Seb had confessed to being a spy and admitted he was seeking high-ranking aristocrats involved in the crime—but all along he had known who the aristocrat was and she had helped to thrust him into Penhurst's circle, unwittingly putting her dearest friend's very existence in jeopardy as a result. Knowing he was forbidden to tell her more than his mission allowed didn't make his betrayal any easier to bear. Because right now she did feel betrayed, and frightened. So very frightened. 'What happens next?'

He came to stand beside her and, to his credit, looked as wretched about the whole sorry situation as she felt. 'At the moment all we have are well-grounded suspicions. It is my job to find enough evidence to arrest him and, by default, every minion who works under him.'

'And if you get enough evidence?'

He stared down at the floor for a few moments, then his dark eyes slowly rose to meet hers. Unwavering but unapologetic. 'That is for the law to decide. I just catch them.'

For years, Clarissa had wished for a way for Penny to be free of her husband, but not like this. The danger, the scandal, the ramifications of treason did not bear thinking about. Like all traitors, Penhurst would hang. 'What about Penny?'

'I will do whatever I can to protect her if she is innocent.' His eyes dipped back to the floor and she realised he had no choice. For King and country he would have to do whatever was necessary.

'Then I will help you.' Because somebody needed to be wholly on Penny's side and Clarissa would do whatever was necessary for her friend, as well. She could do that better working with the King's Elite than banished to her sister's under house arrest.

Her answer surprised him and for the longest time he searched her face. 'You have done enough.

All I require now is your silence. It is better if I do this next part alone…'

'I'm not suggesting I tackle any smugglers. I am not that foolhardy, but I can still be an asset to you socially—unless you lied to me about that, as well.' If he had, if the real Seb was not the awkward, insightful and honourable man she had believed him to be, then her heart would be broken in two.

'I am not that good a liar. You saw the real me before all this started, otherwise you would still be none the wiser.' He said this with the calm confidence of a man who lived in the shadows and dealt with this sort of thing as a matter of course. Perhaps he was truly shy. And perhaps he wasn't. Clarissa really didn't know this man stood before her at all.

The noisy sound of male voices in the hallway beyond signalled the end of the billiards as one by one they tumbled out of the door. Both held their breath as the voices receded back in the direction of the drawing room. Clarissa was about to speak when he stayed her with his hand. Only then did she hear the soft sound of approaching footsteps on the carpet outside. Footsteps his trained ear had been supremely aware of. Good heavens, she was out of her depth.

'I'm not drinking any more of that cheap muck.'

The slurring voice of Lord Regis punctuated the strained silence. 'Gives me wind.'

'There's cognac in the decanter. Port, too.' At the sound of Penhurst's voice, both Seb and Clarissa's eyes shot to the crystal set on his desk complete with three glasses. Three, not one. In a few moments they would be caught snooping and then heaven only knew what would happen.

Seb gestured to the still-open window and Clarissa shook her head. Even if she could get to it in time, he would still be discovered and then all the trust he had built up with their vile host would be gone. There had to be a more satisfactory way of explaining their unauthorised presence here. In the dark.

Only one sprang to mind. Before she thought better of it, she lunged and grabbed him by the lapels and then pushed him back onto the shiny new chesterfield before quickly scrambling onto his lap. For good measure, she tugged one sleeve to hang off her shoulder while grabbing frantically for the hair comb which held the bulk of her coiffure in place. She felt Seb's sharp intake of breath as the door knob began to turn and pressed her lips soundly against his.

Chapter Eleven

An illicit tryst was a brilliant idea, a perfectly plausible and simple solution when he was over-complicating things yet again. Seb managed to think all this before all rational thought evaporated in the intense heat of the moment. To Clarissa it would seem as if he played his part well, when in reality plunging his fingers into her hair and tumbling her to lie beneath him had been as necessary as breathing. She felt so good in his arms, utter perfection. She curled both hers around his neck, her body softening in surrender as she sighed into his mouth. That was all it took to send him over the edge. His pent-up lust and yearning exploded as he hungrily kissed her, fired hotter by the passionate, earthy way she kissed him back. Seb didn't need to fake the carnal groan which vibrated in his throat or the rampant need which instantly surged though his body to settle in his groin. Just the taste of her lips and tongue released them and he was powerless to hold back.

Seb filled his hands with her curves, running his flat palm along the side of her silk-covered ribs, her waist, hips. The burning desire to cup the breasts which were pressing insistently against his chest was overwhelming, so he allowed himself to kiss her neck and collarbone, drowning in the intoxicating smell of her perfume on the bared skin above the low neckline of her gown instead before returning like a starving man to her mouth. Almost as an aside, he became aware of the candlelight from the hallway bathing them in a revealing glow and didn't care because her hands had snaked between the fabric of his jacket and shirt and her nails were raking over his back. In seconds, what had started as a ruse had become very real to him, mirroring his fevered dreams and he never wanted the miraculous, heady experience to end.

'I say, Millcroft. Bravo!'

At the sound of Lord Gaines's voice, Seb reluctantly tore his mouth from hers and the pair of them did an excellent job of appearing mortified. Gem wrestled with the misplaced sleeve of her dress because the laces had somehow come loose during their embrace, her eyes wide and a fat coil of tousled hair trailing from her cheek to below the wonderfully pert breast straining against the top of her gown. A breast which had been squashed against his chest just a few moments ago. He didn't need to pretend to be a gentleman by trying to shield her, because the primal need to hide her bared skin from the unworthy eyes of those men kicked in before he realised it made being caught *in flagrante* more convincing. 'You don't waste any time, do you?'

Lord Regis leered openly at her. 'Now I know why you crept out of the billiards room, you dog— you had better things to pot!'

The cronies laughed bawdily at their own inappropriate humour and nudged one another, shamefully ignorant of how they might be hurting Gem's feelings at being spoken about as if she were both deaf, mute and inconsequential. Only their host didn't join in. Penhurst's eyes took in the scene with barely disguised interest and finally locked with Seb's as a slow smile spread up his face.

'Are we interrupting something?'

Seb forced himself to stare back smugly. 'I'd say you *interrupted* something, wouldn't you?' It sickened him to smile back. Sickened him to treat Gem with such an outright lack of respect, but that was what these men would expect and he hoped she would understand it was what he had to do. 'And you continue to be an interruption. Be good fellows and disappear. *Clearly* I'm not done.'

Gem stood, playing the part of an affronted

woman well—or he hoped she was acting. The last thing he wanted to do was treat her like an object as her idiot Duke or these filthy rogues did. She made a pitiful mewling sound as her hands flapped around her mouth and the still-displaced, sadly wilting sleeve, then picked up her dishevelled skirts and dashed from the room.

'It appears you are done now, old chap.' Gaines feigned a sympathetic frown and then shuffled towards the decanter on the desk. He sloshed a generous splash of brandy into the glass, took a huge gulp and belched. 'I knew she'd be a feisty one… I like a feisty one.' He placed his hand on the bronze buttocks of Aphrodite and bucked his hips for the entertainment of the others, then winked at Seb. 'Never mind, Millcroft. The week is young and there will be ample opportunities to get your leg over. Especially as she was obviously desperate for it.'

Seb's stomach was churning with disgust. His fists wanted to pummel Gaines. 'What can I say? I'm irresistible to the ladies. Always have been. It's a curse. But who am I to deny them their pleasure?'

'Westbridge is my friend.'

Penhurst was testing him, Seb knew it just as surely as he knew the callous viscount was as guilty as sin of everything they suspected. All the scoundrel cared about was himself. Men like that had a warped sense of what the word *friendship* meant. Seb made a show of adjusting his clothing and tightening his cravat. Only when his cuffs were in their correct place did he deign to answer. 'Westbridge is a damn fool. If he'd romanced the girl properly, then she wouldn't be so welcoming of my advances. Instead he plays her off against the Spencer chit right in front of her pretty nose and is oblivious of her needs. Beautiful women like that *need* to be adored. It's what they live for. I'd be a fool not to enjoy a bit of *adoring* if it's there presented on a platter. And believe me, it is very much on the platter and I am no fool. I do hope it's not going to be a problem between us.' Finally he stood and simply stared as he awaited the viscount's judgement, showing him he neither cared about his opinion nor was remorseful for ravishing a lady right under his roof.

In the end, Penhurst shrugged, unoffended. 'I can't say I blame you. I wouldn't mind taking the chit for a ride myself.' He would pay for that comment. 'Once you've done the deed, we'll expect details, Millcroft. All the explicit details.' He would pay for that one, too.

'A gentleman never tells.' Seb winked conspiratorially. 'But as you know, I am no gentleman.' Idly he picked up one of the empty crystal glasses and held it out towards Gaines. 'Seeing as you've royally spoiled my fun for this evening,

the very least you could do is share that cognac.'
When some was offered to him, he swirled it in
his glass and took a sip, then sighed at the taste.
'Smuggled?'

'Of course. How did you know?'

'Because the best brandy always is. Like
women, the forbidden is always sweeter.' He
downed the glass and held it out for more. He
needed something to steady his nerves enough
to do his duty after the most earth-shattering kiss
of his life.

Nearly two hours later, Seb found his way to
Gem's bedchamber and gently tapped on the door.
'Are you awake?' To his surprise, the door opened
swiftly and she stood before him dressed in another diaphanous and flimsy robe, that beautiful honey-gold hair draped over one shoulder in
a thick plait and her trademark ringlets almost
completely gone. She ushered him in with a flick
of her hand and then closed it swiftly.

'Did they believe us?' She wasn't offended—
he instinctively exhaled as that huge weight lifted
off his mind—however, she didn't appear very
happy. She had worry lines between her brows
and a tightness about her mouth that he had put
there and was desperate to erase.

'Completely. I've been tasked with thoroughly

ruining you and reporting back all the tawdry details.'

'Do gentlemen always discuss those things?'

'None of them are gentlemen.' His eyes dropped to her lips and he immediately remembered the taste of them. How he had crushed his own against them as his hands had taken liberties. To avoid them he looked down at the floor and felt the tips of his ears warm. 'Neither was I. I'm sorry if it offended you… The kiss, I mean… I went too far.'

'Offended? How could I be offended by something I started? And if you went too far, then so did I. If you want to know the honest truth, it was all rather exciting.'

Hope blossomed in his heart and he risked gazing at her face. 'Really?' To think that she had felt it, too, that weird, passionate, overwhelming, intoxicating sense of rightness. That she had enjoyed his kisses…

'Yes! To know I was helping the government made me feel a bit like a spy, too. That *frisson* of danger and the knowledge it was for justice was thrilling.' The flame of forlorn hope cruelly snuffed, he simply nodded and hoped the sound of his grinding teeth was inaudible. 'But it's tinged with regret. I feel awful for Penny and dreadful for keeping it from her.'

'I'm sorry about that—but for now it has to be that way.'

Her shoulders slumped as she sighed, but he saw the resignation on her face. She would maintain her silence. For now. 'Did you learn anything new after I left you?'

Where to start? He learned he wanted to tear Gaines and Penhurst limb from limb. Learned that a kiss could mean the world and alter it completely. Learned that his feelings for Gem were real and visceral and bordering on the forever kind. Now, thanks to her profound uninterest in the effect of his kisses, he was more convinced than before that his stupid heart was destined to be broken by the ethereal creature stood before him. 'Not really. Aside from the fact that Lord Gaines belches far too frequently for my liking.'

He moved to look out of the window rather than continue to yearn for what he couldn't have. In the distance the moon glinted off the sea and he realised she had an even better view of the coastline than she had claimed. A clear and unencumbered view. Perhaps she needed spectacles. In spectacles, hair rags and covered in jam, perhaps he stood a better chance? 'I'm edging closer into their circle. I can feel that. You should probably know I went along with all their bawdy talk.' It was another apology. Talking about her like an object didn't sit right and Seb needed to at least clear that part of his conscience.

'Very wise. They will afford us more privacy if they believe we are indulging our passions.'

Our passions. If only.

'That's what I thought. I need to sound like one of them, so if I do say something completely insulting within your earshot, please remember it's not the real me talking. It's Millcroft.' A man he was coming to dislike.

'No offence will be taken.' She dropped her bottom unceremoniously to rest on the mattress, blissfully unaware that the sight of her looking so beautiful and tempting was pure torture. 'Will they tell Westbridge?'

'As they have all made separate wagers with me as to the speed at which I ruin you, I sincerely doubt it. Penhurst seemed delighted by my shocking morals.' And more delighted at the prospect of hearing Seb describe every inch of Gem's naked body. 'Promise me you will never get caught alone with him.' Now that the viscount assumed she was game, Seb wouldn't put it past him to chance his arm.

She shuddered and shook her head. 'I've always avoided being alone with Penhurst and his horrid friends. They all eye me like a cake in a baker's window. Always have.' And they would pay for that, too. 'But let's not talk about them. After I left you I did a bit of exploring of my own. I had never noticed that the footmen appear to be standing guard. There is one posted on every door to the outside.'

'Only at night. But then, no smuggler worth his salt would dare to be out during the day.'

'How did you already know that when this is your first night here?'

Gray had already appraised him of as much and his Invisibles had been watching the house for days.

'I'm a spy.'

'You say that a lot, as if it explains your omnipotent knowledge of everything.'

'If I knew everything, then Penhurst would already be in chains.' He saw her expression cloud with worry again and wished he hadn't been so blunt. 'Try not to fret about Penny. The King's Elite is run by Lord Fennimore. He is ridiculously well connected and resourceful. I'm sure he will help your friend once this is all over. Perhaps we could set her up with a new identity? A fresh start. One where her horrible husband never existed.'

'Do you really think he would help?'

Her lovely eyes had brightened. 'I'm certain of it.' And now Seb was making promises he couldn't keep. If the viscountess was complicit in her husband's treachery then she would have to stand trial, too. His gut told him this was unlikely.

Poor Penny mostly resembled a frightened deer around her spouse and Penhurst held all women in little regard so it was doubtful he would confide in one—even if she was his wife. But occasionally people surprised him. The image Penny projected to the world might well be as false as Lord Millcroft's.

Gem reached out and took his hand, clasping it tightly between both of hers as she stared up at him in grateful adoration, yet oblivious to how much that simple touch was playing havoc with his conscience, his body and his heart. 'Oh, that would be wonderful, Seb. Thank you.'

Uncomfortable, he gently tugged his hand away and went back to his safe spot by the window. Her touch made him want more than usual and he was still stunned at the power of one kiss. 'This room sits between the French doors and the side door to the kitchen?' The only two back entrances on to the garden on the west wing of the house. Both of which were guarded at this time of night. All the routes outside were guarded at night. Getting outside unseen would require some covert manoeuvring.

'It does. Why?'

'The dense bit of shrubbery below makes this an ideal escape route to go snooping around after dark.'

'We are two floors up...do you have wings now, too?'

'Spies don't need wings.'

'Ah.' She smiled and his foolish heart soared again at the sight, supremely pleased that he had distracted her from her worries. 'I suppose you are now going to ask if you can borrow my bedchamber from time to time?'

'Actually, I was going to ask if I could borrow it indefinitely. Your view is perfect and I look out on to the drive.'

'Won't my moving arouse Penhurst's suspicions? Or are you scandalously suggesting we share?' The purposefully flirtatious look set his cheeks burning and she giggled, then stopped abruptly to stare at him like a specimen. 'You really are shy, aren't you? I had wondered if that, too, was a one of the convenient tools in your spying arsenal.'

'No. It's all natural.' Seb found himself shaking his head at his own ineptitude until he plucked up the courage to meet her eyes again. Once he did, bizarrely he felt less awkward and realised he was becoming more at ease in her company than he ever had been with a woman before. But then Gem knew more about him than he allowed most people to know so he supposed it was to be expected. 'And you wouldn't have to move. I shall avail myself of your window once a night and climb back in at dawn.' Where he would have to see her rumpled with sleep. The image of her sprawled across the same mattress she was sat on rooted itself in his mind and refused to leave it, except in his mind the nightgown was gone, her golden hair was fanned out over the pillow and her lips were deliciously swollen again from his kisses. For his own sanity, it was time to leave. 'Goodnight, Gem. I shall see you tomorrow. For croquet, I believe.'

'Amongst other things. There will be tennis and bowls, too. Then riding late afternoon. The Penhursts always plan a packed itinerary. Or at least Penny does. He normally sleeps till three after *his* night before. Keeping busy takes her mind off whatever her foul husband is doing when all the decent people go to bed. I suppose you will be privy to that debauchery, too.'

'Out of necessity, not choice.' His fingers grazed the door knob and he had the sudden urge to clarify. 'I'm afraid you truly did meet the true Seb Leatham at your sister's house last March. Socially awkward and desperately camouflaging it with hostility, or else he blushes profusely and cannot converse at all. A poultry farmer's by-blow grandson. A man who prefers to blend into the background or hide in the shadows. An all-round forgettable fellow by and large.'

Her brows furrowed as she scrutinised him

again and he let her. Seb understood her trust in him was severely damaged and would take time to rebuild. As a rule, nobody appreciated being lied to. After an eternity she sighed.

'Believe me, you are hardly forgettable, Seb. I sincerely doubt I shall ever forget you.'

As compliments went, he made the snap decision to take that one at face value and treasure it for ever. Further embellishment would likely ruin it, catastrophically, just as the real reason for her excitement at his kiss had bludgeoned a corner of his heart which would likely never repair. 'Sleep tight, Gem. Treat yourself to a night off those rags.'

'And appear tomorrow without my customary ringlets? I'd sooner be seen with jam smeared all over my front.' The shared laughter felt honest and intimate. If nothing else a tenuous friendship was blossoming between them. One where they could both be themselves. He could be awkward rather than gruff and she could be less than perfect—although still sheer perfection in his eyes. 'Tell me—if you are going to be around all day for the entertainments, talk bawdy with Penhurst's cronies all evening and then be out all night doing Lord knows what, when do you plan to sleep?'

'I'm a spy.' He found himself grinning as she rolled her eyes. 'Spies never sleep.

Chapter Twelve

The day dragged interminably, and, thanks to a distinct lack of sleep, Clarissa was struggling to function before dinner and found herself constantly mulling. She sipped her ratafia listlessly and stared out through the French doors, allowing the ladies' conversation to waft over her. It wasn't as if she would miss anything. With Penny, the Viscountess Regis and Gaines's poor wife, the conversation always followed a depressingly similar pattern. Over-bright smiles, safe and banal topics which avoided any mention of their miserable lives with their self-absorbed and neglectful husbands. The three of them, all similar in age to Clarissa, more brittle and ground down with each passing year of marital bliss. Hollow shells of the women they had been just a few short years ago. A stark warning of the perils of marrying the wrong man.

She stifled a yawn and took another sip in the

hope it might miraculously restore her vitality else she'd look as battle-weary as her companions. Last night, her overactive mind made sleep impossible and she had lain on the soft eiderdown and simply stared listlessly at the ceiling until the sun rose. Hardly a surprise when her mind had been positively reeling. Was still reeling, if the truth be told. The revelations about Penhurst had whipped the floor from beneath her feet. The loyalty and worry for her friend made her hope Seb was wrong. Clarissa desperately wanted to believe Penhurst wouldn't be involved in something so dreadful. Yet the more she thought about, the more she noticed and the more plausible the unthinkable became.

Something was very wrong in this house. The servants were too guarded, Penhurst's fortunes were undoubtedly much improved and there were sentries on the doors when the house retired for bed.

Poor Penny.

Once again her eyes drifted to her friend and she was swamped with both pity and the crushing guilt at keeping what she knew a secret from her. More guilt came from the genuine feeling of euphoria at being involved in something so exciting. Dangerous yet worthy. Purposeful. Something other than being the flawless *Incomparable*, fearing her lack of attributes would imminently be discovered. Each emotion kept flitting around her head alongside the certainty that, for now, she was doing the right thing in assisting Seb by keeping quiet. For both Penny and him. What else could she do under the bizarre set of circumstances?

Not for the first time, Clarissa wished she had not followed Seb into the study last night. Ignorance was bliss. This knowledge was torture. Behaving like nothing was amiss was so hard, when everything was now amiss and in more ways than one.

Her thoughts about Seb were less decisive, yet creating more than their fair share of her current confusion. The man was indeed a bit of a mystery…and he wasn't. She both understood him and didn't. She trusted *shy* Seb implicitly because whilst the sometimes stilted, charming comments and occasional jerky self-conscious mannerisms could be all affectation, there was no way he could fake the frequent blushes which seemed to plague him at the oddest moments. Clarissa knew this because she had regularly tried to muster a becoming blush to charm the gentlemen of the *ton* over the years and had never managed to achieve one unless there was genuine cause for embarrassment. In fact, she blushed so infrequently that only Seb had seen one in the last Season or more, and at the time she had looked like Medusa and had been so horrified she had smeared jam down her front.

Besides, his blushes clearly irritated him because he got a particular look of exasperation alongside one, as if he was inwardly chiding himself for being such a fool. Something she also sympathised with, thanks to her own incompetence at nearly everything bar being pretty and charming.

However Seb the spy—or his construction Lord Millcroft—was a wholly different kettle of fish. She was in two minds as to whether she should trust this incarnation. His icy determination to have her removed if she attempted to compromise his mission, the canny way he assessed people and stored information in his clever mind, the smooth and calculated way he could lie convincingly to do his job—well, those were things which she admired, but they also scared her. And whichever of those two contrasting Sebs had kissed her...

Her body spontaneously heated and hummed at the thought of it.

That man was deadly.

She scanned the drawing room again, looking for him, and sighed because he still wasn't there. His absence was worrying because whatever he was doing it was probably dangerous. Not being able to see that danger, or be there to warn him of the perils, was awful. The constant, frantic worrying was draining, yet while the dratted man had been physically missing for the best part of the day he was vividly present in her mind. Largely thanks to last night. One minute she had acted on impulse to prevent their imminent discovery and the next she had melted into a boneless, wanton puddle of nerve endings beneath him, everything else a distant memory.

Who knew kissing felt like that?

Her control had certainly evaporated with Seb. In that brief few seconds—*minutes?*—of their kiss it was as if a hidden fuse had been lit within her, driving her to behave in a manner she had never behaved in before. She had not only welcomed his hands on her body, but tried to angle her breasts towards them, arching her greedy hips against him and clawing like a bitch in heat.

And that body!

Her hands had wandered wilfully of their own accord over his shoulders and back, far too eager to explore, and were in the midst of hauling up his clothing so she could feel his muscles and his skin unencumbered by annoyances like jackets, waistcoats and warm linen shirts when he tore his mouth from hers. For a split second, she almost pulled him back on top of her so that they could continue what they had started. In that unexpected, passionate moment she had wanted him naked; had wanted to be naked for him. Thank heavens she had a ready excuse to explain away her reactions, else he would think her a scandal. Young unmarried ladies didn't moan for or paw

and grope gentlemen. Most married ladies probably didn't either. Her eyes slanted to Penny. Did
poor Penny feel such passion for her traitorous
husband? Probably not. Her friend had always
been very proper.

With Seb, Clarissa had never been so unmind-
ful of propriety before. One kiss had ignited the
desire she had not known she was capable of and
enlightened her body to needs she hadn't known
she needed. If that hadn't been enough wanton-
ness for one day, her body deemed it necessary
to relive it even now. Her breasts and lips tingled, calling for his touch, her mind plagued
with images of Seb, especially the glorious sight
of his dark eyes almost black in the moonlight.
Darkened with what she sincerely hoped was his
matching need for her. Could that, too, be faked
or was it like a blush? She didn't know, but wished
she did. To think her explosive reaction had been
one-sided was mortifying.

He'd apologised later, of course, when he had
sought her out in her bedchamber and she had
brushed the incident aside—but those dark eyes
had seemed wounded that she had done so and
she had rejoiced to see that there, as well. If he
had kissed her again, in that precise moment she
would have let him. If he miraculously appeared
ardent at her bedchamber later and demanded to
finish what they had started, Clarissa was honest

enough with herself to acknowledge she would throw caution to the wind and succumb once more. Gladly. Simply for the sake of her screaming, constantly heavy and aroused bosoms and the rampant, newly awakened need which refused to go away.

Her guilty gaze wandered to Westbridge, who was holding court at the fireplace, the limpet Olivia at his arm, hanging on his every word as if it was interesting. Part of her felt a rush of pity for the girl, as feigning interest in that quarter was exhausting. The Duke's self-absorbed conversation could be a trifle repetitive which often made it as dull as dishwater. There were only so many times one could act intrigued about a discussion of his extensive art collection, or his latest expensive deliveries from his tailor... Good Lord! Was that lace on his cuffs? Why had she never noticed that affectation before? Like their host's impressive displays of his new wealth, was this yet another thing she was only just seeing? Had Westbridge always worn lace? She had never seen lace on her spy. Seb didn't do lace on anything, but then Seb was a man of adventure and intrigue, whereas Westbridge was a duke. Dukes and spies were cut from very different cloth, one clearly lacy and one not, so it was grossly unfair of her to compare them.

But she seemed unable to stop, almost as if she

was now searching for faults in Westbridge to justify her new obsession with Seb. She watched Westbridge move to reach for more brandy and found herself scrutinising his arms for muscles. Another unfair comparison. Why would Westbridge have cause for muscles? He'd probably never done a day's work in his entire life. Yet Clarissa now knew she had a penchant for them. A needy, scandalous, wanton penchant for them. Perhaps, after they were married and she and Westbridge shared intimacies, she would close her eyes and picture Seb's muscles and imagine it was his big body covering hers...

Good heavens!

Yet another reason why she wasn't really duchess material. Unaccomplished, academically challenged, borderline illiterate and now an outright wanton who lusted after another man. Was it that much of a surprise her Duke was looking elsewhere? He was seeking a duchess beyond reproach and Clarissa had worked hard for two years to convince him she was such a candidate. She needed to banish all thoughts of the passionate interlude she'd shared with Seb from her mind for ever for the sake of the security of her marriage.

If Westbridge ever proposed.

Today, without Seb as competition he had been as disinterested and self-absorbed as he always was. No change from that quarter. The archetypal starched and lacy shirt...

Clarissa really needed to stop thinking such rebellious and disloyal thoughts about the man she planned to be engaged to by the end of this week. Thinking about Seb was making her hot and bothered when this airless room was stifling enough. Perhaps concentrating her thoughts on her Duke might restore her temperature to normal?

Although now that she thought about it, with everything else going on she hadn't bothered thinking about Westbridge and Lady Olivia or her plan to win her Duke at all today either, and the young usurper had been clamped to his side like a barnacle since breakfast. Perhaps she had given him *some* consideration over breakfast because she had noticed that much—but then Seb had strolled into the breakfast room looking all manly and commanding and utterly gorgeous and her fizzing nerve endings had developed a mind of their own as she had studied him surreptitiously while she pecked at some dry toast.

He was being Millcroft, as she supposed he would be, but it had been Seb's ears that had reddened slightly when he had lifted his eyes to look at her. The sight of that alone had almost made her sigh aloud. Had she not been sitting, there was a good chance she would have swooned. Her body had heated, distant, shameless parts of her had throbbed with need and her eyes adamantly lingered. In fact, she had been so absorbed by watching him at one point during the meal that she hadn't remembered smearing half a pot of strawberry jam on her unappetising slice and gobbling the whole lot down.

Anyone would think she had designs on him.

Perhaps she did? She felt safe enough to be herself around him—or as much of herself as she dared without confessing how stupid she was. During his drunken confession all those weeks ago, he had mentioned he had nothing in common with the uneducated women of the labouring classes. That comment, just as similar throwaway remarks made by others in the normal run of conversation, had reminded her of all the reasons why she hid her failings and made her feel small and unworthy. That said, she rarely felt small and unworthy around Seb now. Far from it, in fact. Maybe that was part of his magnetic appeal? Clarissa certainly lusted after him. Curiously wanted to see him naked. Completely naked. His dark eyes stormy and intense with passion once again, his big, rough farmer's hands roving over her body, his lips driving her to distraction…

Good gracious.

Frustrated and bothered by the odd direction her imagination was taking her in, Clarissa decided to go splash some water on her flushed face before dinner, vowing to redouble her efforts to woo her Duke as soon as she had finished. She headed towards the retiring room, but heard Penhurst's voice on the landing above. Not wanting to either see him or be forced to converse with him alone, she darted behind a suit of armour. Boots clipped ominously on the marble steps above her head, alerting her to the fact he wasn't alone, and she found herself holding her breath.

'What time are we leaving?' His companion was Lord Gaines. 'I'm as hard as a pike staff just thinking about it.'

'They are expecting us at midnight—but I dare say we can slip out earlier once the port is done. We've been promised some new girls tonight.' Clarissa heard Penhurst rub his hands in anticipation. 'Buxom ones.'

'You requested Celeste, didn't you?'

'Of course I requested Celeste. I know how much you like her.'

'I like the way she plays my flute, Penhurst. That wench has a talented mouth. You should try it. After me, of course. I call dibs on the first round.'

'Unless we share her? Top and tail.'

'Now there's an idea.' Both men chuckled as they passed directly over Clarissa's head and instinctively she clamped a hand over her mouth in case they heard her, her stomach roiling with disgust.

'A message just arrived, my lord.'

The butler's voice made them pause mid-step and wait. Clarissa's heart thumped loudly in her ears as he walked briskly towards them while she pressed her back into the wall and prayed for invisibility. All her senses were heightened. Even the smell of Lord Gaines's usual bay rum cologne was so cloying she wanted to gag.

She heard the faint whisper of paper as he took it. There was a pause, then Gaines grunted in acknowledgement, before Penhurst spoke. 'That will be fine. Make sure they are waiting.'

'Very well, my lord.'

The butler scurried away, but the two men lingered. 'They're early.'

'Only by a few days. It's a small inconvenience, I will grant you, but it doesn't affect tonight.' She heard the sound of Penhurst scrunching the note, then slapping his odious friend on the back. 'Tonight your Celeste will still play her sweet, sweet music.'

To her utter relief, because she feared she was about to turn purple from lack of air, their heels clipped the stairs briskly while they continued their disgusting litany about their plans for Celeste. Only when Clarissa heard the footsteps disappear down the hallway did she risk peeking out from her hiding place to watch their retreating backs. With a casual flick of his wrist, she watched Penhurst toss the ball of paper into the enormous medieval fireplace that dominated the entrance hall.

Chapter Thirteen

Mindful of the busy sounds of food preparation coming from the kitchen close by, Seb quickly surveyed the main servants' corridor. Gray had already thoroughly mapped the whole house and gardens beyond. Whilst he implicitly trusted his friend's work, he still needed to explore it all for himself to consign the layout to memory in case he needed a swift escape route. Like all country houses, there was a warren of narrow corridors and stairs beyond those used by the family. Aristocrats enjoyed the luxury of a house full of servants, but didn't want them getting underfoot. With dinner about to be served, the servants were thin on the ground which meant he could poke around in relative peace.

This corridor was the main artery of the house, with passages linking both the east and west wings, staircases to all floors and down into the cellar. That cavernous space was still a bit of a mystery because someone was constantly on watch within. Gray had attempted to explore it three times over the course of yesterday and given up out of fear of discovery, but it didn't take a genius to know that a guarded cellar was an anomaly. A clear signal that Penhurst was up to no good. Seb crept passed that door without poking his head inside and continued along the route his second had meticulously recorded towards Gem's bedchamber which was on the exact opposite side of the house to his. The safest and cleanest route to the outside and a much less conspicuous one than he had taken last night.

Seb kept half an ear on the goings on behind him, testing each door to see where it led as he moved methodically along the dim hallway. He made a mental note of what was behind each door, comparing them to the map in his hand. The first two were linen closets. The third opened on to a passageway leading to the already noisy drawing room, which in turn had French doors which led out to the garden, meaning it also sat directly under Gem's room two floors above. Was she still in it? Was her maid using irons to curl her beautiful hair into submission before dinner? Unhelpful images of her lounging naked in a bathtub suddenly filled his mind and he banished them with a ruthless shake of his head. Not now. Later, when he was all alone on the dark Sussex Downs watching the water, he would allow those illicit, futile thoughts to creep back in to break the monotony. Until then, he had to remember his mission.

The last door took him up a staircase to another dark corridor where every door led on to a bedchamber. Seb listened carefully for sounds of maids or valets before daring to crack each door open and take inventory of the room beyond to work out which guest was where. Gray had pencilled in a few names, but most were irritatingly blank.

In one, he recognised the garish mustard waistcoat Regis had worn the night before, next to that in a similarly appointed room were a pair of tasselled Hessians exactly like the ones favoured by Lord Gaines. A significantly larger and sumptuous room a few doors down was Westbridge's. Because of his elevated status, the windbag had been given the best room in the house. The opulent selection of waistcoats laid out in readiness on the enormous four-poster bed and ostentatious jewelled cravat pins tossed idly on the dressing table could only belong to Gem's dandy. Because he couldn't help himself, Seb slipped into that room and took a proper look round.

Idly, he picked up the sleeve of a shirt and glared at the deep lace cuff. Seb had never worn lace—in fact, he had noisily drawn the line at lace when his new wardrobe had been delivered and consigned those offending garments to a heap on the floor, but now that he knew Gem liked a man in lace, then perhaps... With a groan he dropped the sleeve and shook his head. Prancing around like a fop was not his style, any more than illegitimate farmers from Norfolk were hers, and besides, he wouldn't give Gray the satisfaction of seeing him relent on the lace. Not when his subordinate was already teasing him mercilessly about his *lady love*.

Seb slipped silently out of the door and then spied into the next. This room was as grand as Westbridge's although Seb could see no signs of occupancy. The bed was made. There were fresh flowers on the windowsill, but not a single personal belonging could be found. Then he noticed the open window where the maids must have opened it to air the bedchamber and realised that Penhurst must be expecting another high-ranking peer—or business associate—who had yet to materialise. For a moment he allowed himself to feel peeved at not being in a room in the same wing as the honoured guests, the true, blue-blooded aristocrats, then shook his head at the absurd turn his thoughts were taking. It was ridiculous to feel slighted when he had a job to do. Just as well. Thanks to Gem's distinct lack of enthusiasm for his kiss, Seb was peeved enough already. Lying on his bed knowing she was nearby would send him mad with longing.

He took the narrow stairs two at a time up to the third floor. Her floor. It was also the family floor. He could hear Penhurst's valet moving around in his room, so tiptoed past to his wife's which was as silent as the grave. Separate bedchambers. Formal and cold.

A damning indictment on the way society marriages worked. Distant and depressing. In many ways it reminded him of his mother's life before his father had died. She had occupied her time with needlework and novels, confined to the hunting lodge while she waited for the man who kept her to appear and make one of his rare and unannounced visits. The man she had loved, but who had not loved her back. She had come to life then, so pathetically grateful for the few crumbs he had thrown her, playing house with a man who only came to slake his lust. Obviously the life of the wives was no better than the mistresses. Both were merely chattels to *great* men like Penhurst. Insignificant.

Why have a wife you didn't want to wake up with? Having seen firsthand how being both used and ignored chipped away at a woman's soul, Seb had always promised himself he would be a good husband if the time came. He wouldn't settle for anything other than the sort of loving union his grandparents had enjoyed. Even in their dotage, his grandfather and grandmother had worked alongside one another, slept in the same bed, shared their meals, their laughter and even their demise together. The impersonal marriages of the aristocracy held no appeal to him. But they did to Gem, probably because she knew no different. Upbringing again. So very different from his lowly origins.

Enough! Seb needed to stop conjuring futile images of them together. He sincerely doubted she suffered from the same misguided malaise and he would not be perennially hopeful like his mother or settle for crumbs.

Yet still he paused outside her door and angrily shook his head at his body's instant reaction to the lingering scent of her perfume. Like that perfume, Gem was nothing more than a transient waft of fragrance in his life. Soon he would move on to the next mission and she would have her own private rooms in her Duke's fancy house. It wouldn't make her happy. Westbridge would be as pompous and unfeeling a husband as he was a suitor and within a year or two of their marriage she would begin to resemble poor Penny.

All very sad. But inevitable.

Not that he would make her happier if fate miraculously made her his wife. Marrying so far beneath her would only serve to make Gem more miserable than being a duchess ever would. With him, she'd be ostracised from the society that adored her and doomed to living the rest of her days observing all she'd once had from the periphery...

Damn and blast! Why did his thoughts keep wandering to the unattainable? Seb had eked out a good life for himself against all the odds. He worked for the Crown. He was respected by his peers. He was solvent and blessedly not beholden to anyone for anything. Instead of wanting more, he should be thankful. Going forward, he would be thankful and certainly wouldn't entertain the pointless yearning any longer. It was just a kiss, for pity's sake! One that she had already forgotten.

The distant chime of the clock reminded him of time. Retracing his steps, he wearily accepted his fate, pasting on Lord Millcroft's cocky aloofness as he strode into the hall once more only to see the woman who haunted his dreams stood anxiously outside the drawing room. Waiting.

His stupid heart hoped it was for him.

'What have I missed?'

The intimate whisper behind her caused goosebumps to erupt all over her body. And a blush. Because she had been thinking about him, alongside worrying and trying to decipher the crumbled missive in her hand. The relief at seeing him safe and sound was palpable. 'Where have you been?'

He motioned to one of the servants' doors with his head. 'In the bowels. Poking around.'

'Did you find anything?'

'Nothing incendiary. The cellars are guarded, but then I expected as much. I know my way around now though, which will make the coming days and nights much easier.' He was staring off into the distance in that quiet, assessing way he had, mentally ticking off all those present in the busy drawing room. She watched his jaw harden as Westbridge turned and eyed them from his position in the room beyond. Seb met his glare dead on. It had the most splendid effect on her Duke. Immediately he went from indifferent to jealous, the persistent Lady Olivia completely forgotten. To see if steam might shoot from the Duke's ears, and because she simply had to touch him, Clarissa threaded her arm possessively through Seb's and led him further into the hallway out of sight.

Once again her nerve endings came alive at the innocent contact. 'I found this. It was delivered to Penhurst less than ten minutes ago.' Although every minute had felt like an hour. 'He threw it in the fire.' She pressed the note into his hand. She had given up trying laboriously to read it because the words made no sense.

'It's from Jessamine!' A name that seemed to

excite him. Then he frowned. *'"Espérance de Dieu".'*

As Seb read with an impeccably convincing accent, she recognised the words to be French, but was still clueless.

'What does it mean?'

'Espérance de Dieu—well, that literally translates to Hope of God, I believe.'

'That's it? That doesn't even make sense.'

'It does to someone.'

'I suspect it did to Penhurst.' Clarissa relayed the pertinent parts of the overheard conversation twice while he grilled her on the details. Like Seb, Clarissa believed the message and the subsequent message back hinted at the imminent but unexpected arrival of the smugglers. When she had finished he reread the note in frustration as he paced towards a candelabrum and held it just above the flame while he scrutinised it.

'What are you doing?'

'Certain invisible inks appear with heat.'

Invisible inks? What a bizarre world he lived in. Curious, Clarissa huddled close and bent her head to watch, immediately becoming distracted by the heady smell that was uniquely Seb. Soap, fresh air and excitement. He was somehow more attractive when he was all the dashing spy. The intensity of his stare as he considered the note, the hard set of his jaw, the way he tapped the missive impatiently against his open palm as he chewed his bottom lip. Lips she wanted to kiss again, just to be sure that last kiss wasn't a fluke and that he did have the capacity to make her melt.

After a minute he huffed when nothing materialised and began to pace again. 'Hope of God? It must be a code of some sort. The last message we intercepted from Jessamine was in code. Maybe the letters correspond to a cypher—but without a key it could take for ever to crack it. Or perhaps it's an anagram?'

'Or simply the name of a ship.' Although that was probably far too simple. Not in a world where invisible inks were commonplace. His mind was like a steel trap, used to solving the most difficult puzzles and hers was…well, frankly substandard. Clarissa couldn't even focus on letters or numbers on a page without them jumbling and spinning. Or concentrate long enough on the problem in hand because her flighty mind was having grossly improper ideas involving his mouth.

He stopped pacing instantly and stared at her. 'You might have it! *Espérance de Dieu* certainly sounds ship-like to me and our viscount is arrogant and ignorant enough to believe he is untouchable. In which case, why bother trying to hide it? You said he blithely tossed it in the fireplace without a backward glance.'

'Surely that is too simplistic. What if one of

the servants saw it and retrieved it just as I did, then gossiped about it? He wouldn't take the risk of throwing it away so carelessly.'

'Have you not seen the servants?'

Now that he came to mention it, they were a dour bunch. The night footmen were menacing, the butler a lurking despot and the maids were afraid of their own shadows. Maybe they didn't dare gossip. 'What if Penny stumbled across it?'

'Penny is as downtrodden, perhaps more so, than the staff. Besides, we know about the smuggling so are immediately suspicious. If she doesn't, then this letter is nonsense.'

'I suppose…'

'There is no suppose about it, Gem. You're a genius!' His boyish grin combined with the nicest comment she had ever had did peculiar things to her insides. Nobody had ever praised her intellect before. Not once. 'Sometimes I overcomplicate things when the simplest solution is staring me right in the face. I'll bet it's a ship. A merchant ship. The Boss does like to hide in plain sight. The Excise Men should be able to tell us if the *Espérance de Dieu* is indeed a boat. I'll set my men on it later tonight when I see them.'

'You are still going out? Can't your valet pass on the message before the house is locked up?'

'The smugglers might arrive tonight.'

'No they won't. Penhurst said it didn't affect their plans for this evening.'

Clarissa didn't like the idea of him risking discovery by sneaking out when it was unnecessary, or at all if she was honest. Dealing with Penhurst's guards or, heaven forbid, smugglers alone didn't bear thinking about. Not when he was the sort of man who threw himself in front of bullets and she was becoming rather attached to him. Perhaps even a tad besotted. Since that fateful kiss, she had floated around on a sensual cloud daydreaming. 'It hardly seems likely anything will occur with them gone all night. Nor would they dare have a shipment of illegal brandy delivered while he has a house full of guests.'

He turned to her then, all serious, and her heart did a little dance in her chest. 'I sincerely doubt he would turn down profit. I am of the firm belief it will be business as usual. Besides, he also instructed the butler to reply with *they* will be waiting. I'll wager he never gets his hands dirty unloading his ill-gotten gains. If there is a tunnel leading to the cellar, then he would definitely feel no compunction to curtail them. Not when the demand for that brandy outstrips supply and the guests in the house would remain completely ignorant of what was going on beneath their feet.' His long legs were already striding to the stairs. 'Make my apologies to our hostess, I might be a few minutes late to dinner while I share all this with Gray. We'll be availing ourselves of your window later.'

'But it is dangerous!' Clarissa's insides were already taut with worry.

He shrugged as if it was no matter. 'I'm a spy. We thrive on danger.'

Chapter Fourteen

Clarissa returned listlessly to her chair with the wives, trying to appear composed, but failing miserably. How could she sound excited about riding tomorrow when Seb was putting himself in harm's way tonight? Damn Penhurst to hell! At the unladylike thought, her eyes came to rest on him coldly. He was stood smiling smugly with his awful friends, the three looking exceptionally pleased with themselves as they listened to Westbridge who was still holding court by the fireplace.

'I see you are staring longingly at Westbridge.' The interruption made her jump. 'He cuts such a fine figure, doesn't he?' Lady Oliva offered her a brittle smile and sat determinedly in the chair next to hers.

It was then Clarissa felt the magnetic pull and just knew he had returned. The room felt warmer. Her eyes drifted to Seb of their own accord and she found herself smiling at his Lord Millcroft persona as he greeted some guests in that imaginary lord's customary arrogant fashion. 'Yes, he does. A very fine figure.' The way Seb's shoulders filled out his black evening coat was really quite something. Although he wore a bandage better...

'We shall be seated next to each other at dinner. I am very much looking forward to it. His Grace is excellent company.'

Gracious—they were supposed to be discussing the same man and Clarissa had momentarily forgotten her Duke once again because Seb was occupying her thoughts. Foolishly, she was giving the horrid Olivia the upper hand. 'Yes, indeed. Dear *Albert* is very diverting.' No, he wasn't, but it would serve the young usurper right to think that she was missing something.

'This morning we took a turn around the gardens together.'

'That's nice.' Good Lord, how had Clarissa missed that?

'Yes, indeed. We have been spending a great deal of time in one another's company since we arrived here in Sussex.'

'Have you? I haven't noticed.' A staggering truth, yet the truth none the less. At this rate, she would have lost the game through her own negligence. It was all well and good being caught up in Seb's mission, but Clarissa had come here with her own. One that was rapidly receding into the mist and which she couldn't appear to muster the energy to retrieve.

'It has been wonderful getting to know him on a deeper level.'

What did that mean? 'That's nice.'

'May I confide in you, Lady Clarissa?' The girl had a calculated gleam in her eyes.

'Of course you may.' Jealousy warred with the overwhelming urge to check on Seb, She could sense him close by. It took a great deal of resolve to stare into her rival's eyes and smile.

'His Grace has implied that he is fond of me.'

Implied? Not a declaration, then. But a worry. Yet another worry when her aching head was full of them. 'Let me guess—he has complimented your beauty?' One of the few things Westbridge ever noticed about a woman.

Lady Olivia pretended to look coy, as if she found such compliments outrageous. 'Not just my beauty, but my grace and innate sense of style.'

The usual, then. 'Try not to read too much into it. Dear *Albert* does tend to flatter the ladies.' Clarissa took a casual sip of her ratafia and acted bored. Tomorrow, she would get up early, have her maid arrange her hair in a very becoming style and squeeze her into one of her specially made new gowns. Gowns which had been copied from the latest Parisienne fashion plates and the most vibrant un-debutante-like silks. They would swiftly remind Westbridge who was the true *Incomparable*.

If she could miraculously muster the energy.

'It is funny that you mention reading—we have discovered a mutual love of the poems of Lord Byron. He has specifically asked me to read some after dinner.'

Clarissa's heart plummeted to her toes just as Westbridge turned towards them. His eyes darted between the pair of them as if he wasn't entirely sure where to look before he hastily turned back to the gentlemen. A telling omen if ever there was one. Her Duke was torn. Her nerves were frazzled. Her old friend and her spy were in jeopardy and she couldn't memorise an entire Byron poem in an evening at such short notice. Such things usually took days to fake. The best Clarissa could muster on the back foot was a particularly salacious passage from Mrs Radcliffe's *The Romance of the Forest* which had been exciting in the extreme and filled with derring-do. That dog-eared favourite novel was hardly of the elevated literary genius of the fêted Byron. Reciting it would make her appear shallow—which of course she was. Olivia had won another round before it had started, making Clarissa's long-hoped-for future less secure. Every day the ground beneath her feet seemed to get less certain. First her Duke and then the revelations about Penhurst, poor Penny…

The warmth of awareness suddenly cut through her despondency and once again of their own accord her eyes sought and locked with Seb's. Clarissa had never experienced such an overwhelming connection with another before. It was as if Seb had read her mind, knew that she had needed his support and was immediately there for her. In his gaze was reassurance. Calm. Amusement at the ridiculousness they both found themselves embroiled in and the people they were forced to endure, things they would deal with together. He believed in her enough to entrust her with his secrets. He believed she was clever and witty and resourceful, because with him she felt she was all those things. Not just a pretty face. But more.

He smiled and she smiled back, because somehow that smile made it all better and allowed herself to bask in the moment. There were more important things to worry about than the usurper. On Clarissa's ever-growing list, Lady Olivia came now close to the bottom. One reading of Byron wouldn't make her a duchess any more than two years of being the flawless *Incomparable* had rewarded Clarissa the same fickle Duke. If that was all he wanted, then she was doomed. Mrs Radcliffe aside, poetry readings and discussion of books were never going to happen with her.

Oddly, that thought didn't panic her as it would have done a few short weeks ago. If anything, it was a minor irritation while Seb's eyes held hers. Perhaps not even minor...

It took a few moments to realise that Westbridge was watching them intently and was not at all happy about it. The two men were inadvertently stood a few feet apart. Westbridge was glaring at Seb, Seb pretending her Duke didn't exist as his gaze remained possessively on her. Drawing her into it until she was in grave danger of sighing and grinning like a besotted fool.

How could a simple look mean so much?

But it did.

It meant everything. There was more than lust and friendship now. Her heart was a little engaged. She knew this because it seemed to swell whenever he was near.

Feeling slightly off-kilter, Clarissa tore her eyes away and took a nervous drink from her glass before turning back to her unwelcome neighbour with an affected bored serenity she didn't feel. 'I'm sorry, Lady Olivia—you were saying?' For good measure she even stifled a yawn and watched Seb grin in her peripheral vision.

For the next five minutes, she nodded blandly as the girl continued to extol Westbridge's virtues and embellish the blossoming relationship between them. This time, instead of feeling envy, she found her mind and her focus drifting idly back to where her Duke and her spy now stood talking to Penhurst and his cronies.

Seeing them side by side, it suddenly struck her that they were much the same height. Up until that precise moment, Seb had always seemed so much taller in her mind, probably because his girth was double that of her Duke. Broader shoulders, more muscle and a significantly sturdier-looking skeleton beneath his sun-burnished skin made Seb an imposing, wholly male presence filled with vigour. Against him, the Duke was rather weedy and pale.

Seb was exciting, enticing and easy to talk to. She found herself being herself more around him than she had ever dared with a man before, while Westbridge was…well, Westbridge. Her eyes didn't feast upon him, she had never had a lustful thought about him ever and, now that her life had suddenly becoming considerably more exciting and meaningful, the illustrious Duke was rather dull, truth be told. Her eyes wandered to his hands and she was alarmed to see how small they were buried amongst the lace. Perhaps that was why his cuffs were always so frothy? Her eyes flicked to Seb's and Clarissa immediately recalled how tremendous those huge, capable, calloused palms had felt on her body—just as Penny announced it was time for dinner.

Like a shot, Lady Oliva jumped up and bounded over to claim Westbridge in case Clarissa got any ideas. Surprisingly she didn't and that in itself was liberating. The Duke took the dolt's arm, but his narrowed eyes remained resolutely on Seb. No doubt to continue to vex him, Seb sauntered over to Clarissa's chair and held out his arm with a devastating, cocky smile which did peculiar things to her insides. 'May I escort you in to dinner, Gem?' His dark eyes were swirling with mischief. It was such an alluring sight she found herself grinning back as she wound her hand affectionately through the crook of his elbow. Then he bent to whisper in her ear and it sent her pulse jumping again as she remembered the feel of his lips on her ears. Her neck. Her collarbone. Her bosom…good gracious!

'Poor you getting stuck with that Spencer chit. I had to sit next to her at breakfast. My, doesn't she love herself? I caught her staring at her reflection in the back of her spoon.'

'In some quarters she is considered very beautiful.' It was a little test to see if Olivia held any appeal with Seb at all and perhaps a pitiful attempt to hear another compliment from him. His compliments made her feel so special.

'She's pretty, I suppose.' His head turned to watch Clarissa's rival sail past with a triumphant expression on her face. 'But I don't like what's beneath.'

'Beneath what?'

'The face, of course. A face that won't last for ever. I mean, how many old people do you look at and think, *He's handsome...she's beautiful*? Old people all look like old people. Age is a good leveller. *Then* the exterior pales into insignificance against what lies beneath the wrinkly and sagging skin and grey crinkly hair.'

Clarissa laughed, she couldn't help it, because Seb always hit the nail on the head and his honesty was refreshing. 'Are you an expert on the aged now?'

'It's basic common sense. By the time you get to that age it's *all* about the character. They are either nice people or they are not. Interesting or dull. Jolly or as sour as lemons. Lady Olivia is destined to be wrinkly, saggy, crinkly like the rest of us. But she will be a nasty, dull and sour old lady. With miserable wrinkles.'

'And what, pray tell, are miserable wrinkles?'

'The sort which come from a lifetime of frowning and looking upon things with disgust.' He pulled a face to demonstrate. 'It trains the skin to set the expression in perpetuity once the bloom of youth has faded. The description says it all—frown lines. Who wants frown lines? Jolly people have happy wrinkles. Laughter lines. They brighten the face even when the face has seen better days.'

Ahead of her, Clarissa could still see the Duke glaring at them—to the barnacle's obvious consternation. 'If he's not careful, Westbridge will have frown lines. I think you've upset him.' And she didn't care. Let the Duke glare. Chatting to her spy was infinitely more diverting.

'Have I?' Seb's dark head turned and he appeared surprised to see Westbridge's hostile expression as he took his place ahead of the other lesser-ranked guests in the queue. 'I hadn't noticed. But, yes. I fear he is another one doomed to age grumpily.'

'It's an interesting theory…'

'It's based on fact. Years of observation actually. My grandparents were happy people right to the last. They were kind and generous and didn't take themselves too seriously. Both were covered in laughter lines.'

'They do sound jolly.'

'They were. And they were devoted to one another. Couldn't bear to be apart. Worked alongside each other and slept on the same mattress till the end. I wasn't the least bit surprised when my grandfather died that my grandmother followed him a week after.'

'That's sad.'

He turned to her then and smiled. 'No, it isn't. Watching her live without him by her side would have been sadder. They wanted to stay together.'

She paused and gazed up at him, surprisingly touched. 'Well, I never! You are a hopeless romantic.' He blushed then. It was as endearing as it was spontaneous. 'But I shan't tell anyone.'

'You can't.' His voice dropped to a whisper for her ears only, the inevitable trail of goosebumps standing to attention at the intimacy. 'Spies are supposed to be ruthless and cold, not sentimental.'

'Nor are they supposed to blush.'

'Indeed. And we both know it doesn't take much to set that off.'

Clarissa giggled and tightened her hand affectionately around his arm, trying to ignore the urge to walk her fingers over his muscles again as she anchored him in place or the way her body awakened at the innocent physical contact. There was nothing innocent about the images suddenly flooding her mind. That flush she had less than half an hour ago returned unabashed. She could already feel it creeping up her neck and threatening to ruin her face. Adoring, flushed faces and needy hands were hugely inappropriate when he had generously come to her aid in the midst of an important mission to save her from Olivia.

At this rate he was going to know she had a bit of a *tendre* for him. A big, obsessive and wholly improper *tendre* indeed. And lust. Lots and lots of lust. Talk of romance had reawakened her desire. So much so, she should change the subject.

'Thank you for just now. You made me feel better about Olivia.'

'You shouldn't let her bother you. She is not in your league. Westbridge must be stupider than I thought to even consider her.' More proof Seb had been trying to uphold his half of their bargain.

'Thank you again. For saying so and for making him jealous with your splendid flirting. It was just what was needed.' At least her voice sounded normal. Just the right amount of playful to go along with the lightened mood, without alerting him to the fact she was suddenly indifferent to the Duke and her rival because her head was filled with thoughts of Seb instead. 'With everything else going on, I have allowed that girl to dominate his time. Perhaps too much. Something you will be pleased to know I intend to remedy tomorrow.' Or the next day.

If she could be bothered.

She felt his arm stiffen beneath hers as his dark eyes hardened. 'I'm glad I could be of service.' But he didn't sound particularly glad. He sounded like Millcroft.

Seb seethed throughout the interminable meal and castigated himself for his own stupidity. Of course she hadn't been gazing at him in adoration. She had been gazing at him in *feigned* adoration because she had wanted to make the windbag jealous. For Seb, the entire drawing room had disappeared as he lost himself in her eyes. One second he had seen her looking bothered by the simpering Lady Olivia and he had offered her a smile of support. Then time stood still as their gazes locked. He hadn't felt the need to blush or break eye contact, because in that transcendent, flawless moment there had been just her and him. Understanding. Affection. The latent heat which had simmered between them when they had kissed. A magical sense of rightness.

Clod! The magical, special, achingly tender moment Seb had experienced was uniquely his.

Now he was invisible as Westbridge dominated her time. The pair had been seated together at dinner and ensconced together now that they were all back in the drawing room for the after-dinner entertainments. Something Seb should have expected because that was the way of things. Currently, she was seated next to her younger rival, both gazing up at the fool while he waxed lyrical about something. Westbridge was always waxing about something. So much so he rarely paused for breath. Even Penhurst couldn't pretend to be riveted by his most illustrious guest's conversation. He had drifted off a good twenty minutes ago for pastures new.

But Gem was still riveted.

Still desperate to be his duchess.

Why did she want to waste her life with a man who never listened? A man so full of his own hot air that he was blissfully ignorant of all others nearby. He hated seeing her reduced to a pathetic dolt, purposefully suppressing her own sharp intelligence and clever wit in deference to that man's overwhelming self-importance.

Seb was tempted to go over there and list all the reasons why he was much better than the pompous fool she had set her sights on. Despite his dubious bloodline, lack of significant fortune and absence of illustrious connections, at least he appreciated the woman beneath the perfect face—despite the fact he had grown to loathe her trademark ringlets. If she were miraculously his wife—a foolish image his mind refused to jettison—he would dig a big hole in the garden and bury her dratted curling irons and ban rags at bedtime. Or better still, distract her so thoroughly at bedtime that she was too exhausted to bother with all that nonsense. Those curls, like the silent, adoring creature sat in that chair, was Westbridge's incarnation of perfection. The woman with poker-straight hair and the smart mouth was his. She could eat biscuits till the cows came home and the pair of them could grow old, plump and wrinkly together. Perhaps he should tell her that and see what she thought about it?

Tell her! As if he could find the words.

Besides, such a declaration would only end in polite rejection. Lady Clarissa Beaumont, earl's daughter and lauded *Incomparable*, was always destined to marry a pure aristocrat. What had he expected? That under these unlikely and fraught circumstances two people who never would have collided under the normal run of things could suddenly overcome all the obvious obstacles and live happily ever after? She might make *him* blissfully happy, but he couldn't make *her* a duchess or erase the dirty stain of his lineage.

She didn't come from his world. She came from the world of titles and privilege, where the measure of the man didn't mean a thing against the rank he was born into. *Thank you for making him jealous with your splendid flirting!* He had been flirting—a milestone in itself—and it had been splendid, and once again his hopes and his heart had been bludgeoned by her thoughtless words. In that moment, that dreadful moment of pain and clarity, he realised he had gone and allowed himself to believe his nocturnal fantasies and fallen a little bit in love with her. Like his naïve mother before him, he had given a chunk of his heart to someone incapable of loving him back.

But unlike his mother he was damned if he would let it define him. If he had fallen for her swiftly, he would damn well fall out of love swiftly, as well. He wanted that chunk of his heart back in his chest where it belonged. Where it would doubtless sit and pine for all that was out of its reach for ever. Clod! He didn't notice Penhurst sidle up next to him until he spoke.

'Oh, dear. I see your quest is not going well.'

Clearly he was displaying all of his jealousy and frustration to the room. It was time to be Millcroft again. 'She will succumb in the end. They always do.' It would be laughable if it wasn't so tragic. All his life he had pitied his mother's poor judge of character, yet now he knew he was no better. Gem was as shallow as she was beautiful. If he was here as plain Seb Leatham, a fatherless nobody, rather than her Duke's rival, Lord Millcroft, he doubted she would be as cordial. 'And if she doesn't, there are plenty more fish in the sea.' Tasteless and dull fish that would never be as perfect in his eyes. Gem had ruined him for all other women.

'I'm glad you said that. I might have just the thing to cheer you up.'

'I'm listening.'

Penhurst touched the side of his nose and winked. 'A select group are taking a little excursion later tonight. There is a seat in my carriage if you want it.'

'That depends on where you are going.' The viscount liked it when Millcroft played hard to get, but already Seb felt sick. Thanks to Gem he knew exactly where they were going and really didn't want to be invited. Not even for King and country.

'We are going to a place where the women are willing and plentiful and rules don't exist.'

Lord save him. This night was rapidly deteriorating into the worst of his life. 'Splendid. What time do we leave?'

Chapter Fifteen

⸙

Penhurst used the journey to quiz Seb about his investment plans and seemed particularly interested in the idea of the gaming hells and his list of contacts within that community. While many of the men Seb claimed acquaintance with were very real and exceedingly dubious, a great many were also fictitious as he found himself imagining how Gem would embellish the story. The viscount's eyes lit up when Seb declared his vow never to pay a penny of tax to the Crown—but he kept his counsel. For now, Lord Millcroft was on trial. Once he had proved himself guilty of all manner of debauchery, then perhaps he would be invited into the inner sanctum. In his experience, all criminals were cautious, but fundamentally greedy. If the right opportunity presented itself, that greed would lead them astray. This outing was another test. As much as he was dreading it, Seb knew this was a significant trial by ordeal.

The brothel was less than ten miles from Pen-hurst Hall, although to all intents and purposes it was just a quaint, stone cottage on the Downs. Inside, it was anything but. Not only was this an out-and-out house of ill repute, it was an expensive one. The madam who owned it was French, as were two of her girls. She greeted Penhurst, Regis and Gaines as old friends, although the lingering, deep and distasteful kiss she bestowed upon the viscount suggested they were more than friends. Was this madam the French mistress Gem had heard him bragging about? Was this painted harlot Jessamine?

The madam eyed Seb with barely disguised interest. 'Who is this?'

'Monique, allow me to introduce you to my friend Lord Millcroft. Another hedonist in search of pleasure.'

'Then he has come to the right place. *Bienvenue.*'

Aside from the disappointment at the incorrect name, there was something off about her accent. *'Vouz avez une maison charmante.'* He kissed her hand so he could watch her face closely and, as he had suspected, she blinked rapidly in confusion before she covered it with a smile. *'Est-ce que la maçonnerie semble médiévale?'*

'Your French is excellent, *monsieur.*'

He'd wager it was better than hers because she

had no clue he had asked if her brickwork was ancient. 'I try—but I am little more than a novice.'
Penhurst didn't appear to notice what was wrong
with the exchange either, which was interesting.
Clearly he had even less French than Madame
Monique. Whoever he worked with higher up in
the Boss's extensive organisation, that person was
most likely as British as this harlot.

'Fortunately, all my girls speak reasonable
English, *monsieur*, but they are all fluent in the
language of love... If you have enough coin, of
course.' She winked saucily, then eyed his fat
purse greedily when he held it aloft and shook it
for effect. Any theories he might have harboured
about this brothel being an intrinsic and vital link
in the smuggling chain quickly evaporated at her
enthusiasm for a few pathetic shillings and he bitterly regretted accepting the viscount's sordid invitation.

'Come, my lord. Let me introduce you to my
girls.' The madam coiled her arm around his
waist, allowing her fingers to stray down his backside. She smelled of too much perfume. Her dress
hardly covered the large breasts fighting to escape
her bodice. 'What do you prefer? Blondes? Bru-
nettes? Perhaps a redhead?'

The only redhead in the room was eyeing him
openly, suggestively licking her red lips as she
thrust out her bountiful chest. Penhurst hadn't lied

about the girls being buxom and willing. A scan of them all draped over furniture or stood preening in front of him so scantily clad filled him with utter dread. Perhaps one of these girls was the mysterious Jessamine?

His head turned towards the sound of a giggle behind him just in time to see Gaines tug one of the girls onto his lap. The woman was already in the process of wriggling out of her bodice so that the weasel's bony hands could grope her charms openly. In the corner, another girl had her hand down Regis's breeches—neither apparently had any shame about such a public display. Seb was doomed if he was expected to perform in public. Not that he had any intention of performing at all if he could help it. He'd been in a few brothels in his time, it came with the territory, but he had always been a spectator up until now.

He turned back to the redhead, only just managing to hold in the gasp of surprise at seeing the wench now completely naked to the waist, and pasted on Millcroft's bored mask as he pretended to survey the goods on sale one more time while he decided. It was then he saw her. Beneath the heavily painted face and revealing, gaudy gown was a girl whose come-hither smile was as false as Millcroft's mask. She was young. Far too young for a place like this. Seb estimated she was barely sixteen—if that. Her eyes were terrified. He sympathised entirely. 'I'll take her.'

Madame Monique snapped her fingers. 'Claudette! Lord Millcroft would like to talk to you.'

The frightened child appeared about to bolt at any moment, yet still managed to undulate towards him with one pale hand resting on her generous hip. Under the rouge she was as white as a sheet. Without saying anything, he took her hand and gently led her to the furthest seat in the room, then, like the vile Gaines, tugged her to perch on his lap because his host was watching him intently. She was as stiff as a board.

'I knew you wouldn't hang about, Millcroft.' Penhurst had draped one arm possessively around the madam. He saluted Seb as the harlot dragged him to the sofa. Neither wasted much time with the preliminaries. Like his minions Regis and Gaines, the viscount was very at home here in this brothel—and very comfortable getting down to business with an audience. It was all so sordid.

Seb let the minutes tick by until the sight of the bucking twin bare arses of Penhurst and Gaines made him feel bilious. There was spectating and then there was voyeurism, and while he was watching them, they were probably watching him.

'Tell me, Claudette, is there somewhere we can be alone?'

'I have a room, sir.' There was more Geordie in her accent than Gallic. 'Shall I take you to it?'

'Yes. A splendid idea. I don't suppose you have any brandy?' It was going to be a very long night.

Clarissa had been doing some thinking, a great deal of thinking as she prowled around her bed-chamber reliving the evening, and had come to two conclusions. One, there could be no doubt about Penhurst's treachery. And two, she was rapidly going off the Duke of Westbridge. The latter might well have something to do with the third conclusion she was wrestling with, which currently lent towards a growing belief that she had a bit of a *thing* for Seb. Outlining exactly what that *thing* was was less tangible because it kept shifting and changing hourly and like a coward she didn't want to think about it properly.

When her cluttered mind did wander down that path, which it did with alarming frequency, Clarissa stubbornly dragged it back. Lust, worry, respect, excitement, ease, admiration, kinship and affection were all fitting definitions for what she felt. A great many words. Words that altogether hinted at something entirely different and altogether scary, because *that word* was one she had never anticipated feeling for any man—including Westbridge.

Her future plans had always revolved around

marrying well and then hiding behind the battle-
ments of her title. It was the one thing she could
excel at, after all, and a good marriage would give
her the social standing which commanded respect
and shielded her from being discovered as nothing more than a pretty face. It was a pragmatic
solution.

Only now, that calculated and impersonal sort
of society marriage had lost some of its appeal and
she blamed Seb for that. All his talk of his besotted, happy grandparents combined with the odd
thoughts she was having about him were making
Clarissa question her plan. The idea of years and
years of marriage to a man who largely talked
about himself was nowhere near as alluring as
years and years with a man who made her body
yearn, who made her smile and feel special and
spoke to her like an equal. Whilst the idea of inevitable wrinkles should be terrifying, when all she
had was her face, the suggestion that those wrinkles would be carved by happiness and laughter
was hugely appealing. There wouldn't be much
laughter with Westbridge. But with Seb…

The tap on the door made her jump. He was
here. Finally. She tightened the sash on her robe,
rearranged her thick bedtime plait to hang over
one shoulder and then arranged herself into an attractive seated pose on the mattress. 'Come in.'

The door opened and a grinning stranger filled

the frame. He bowed as her mouth hung slack. 'Lord Graham Chadwick of the King's Elite at your service, my lady. My friends call me Gray. I am Leatham's replacement for the evening.'

'R-replacement?' Her voice sounded squeaky. Disappointed. So she stood up and tried to appear in control. This man could be lying. 'I have no idea what you are talking about.'

Gray shrugged and deposited a large coil of rope on the floor. He was dressed from head to foot in black. ''Tis I who gets the pleasure of climbing out of your window tonight to watch for smugglers as Seb is otherwise engaged.' Blue eyes twinkled out of a face which appeared to be smeared in boot black.

'Where?'

Another shrug. 'He left in the carriage with Penhurst and his cronies about twenty minutes ago.'

'But where have they gone?'

'To that place you overheard the viscount talking about, my lady. The gentleman in me cannot bring myself to say its name in front of a lady.'

To that den of iniquity she'd heard them talking about? Surely not. Not Seb. Her shy and attractive spy. He wouldn't…would he? Gray saw her outrage and positively beamed.

'Penhurst invited him and Seb couldn't say no, now could he? Duty and all that. Lucky devil.

Meanwhile I get to spend the night sat on a cliff while he gets to…do his best for King and country.' He chuckled and winked. 'This is a difficult job sometimes.'

The pang of jealousy pierced through her outrage and it took all her strength to appear nonplussed as the man she hadn't been sitting up waiting for—the man she hadn't brushed her hair one hundred times for so that it shimmered in the candlelight or wore her best silk nightgown for—secured the rope to a sturdy piece of furniture and quietly lowered it out of the window.

Seb was in a brothel.

That place where the girls were buxom and could *'play the flute'*—although she wasn't altogether sure what that particular analogy meant—whatever Celeste did with her *'talented mouth'* she could be doing it to him! With *his* talented mouth…

'Are you all right, my lady?'

'Yes, of course. Perfectly fine. Splendid, in fact. What time is Mr Leatham expected back?'

'Who knows. Dawn? Lunchtime? Such things can take time.' Gray appeared to be vastly amused. 'I wouldn't wait up. For either him or me. Just leave this window open a crack and I'll sneak in. No doubt considerably earlier than that lucky Lord Millcroft.' He chuckled again as he threw his legs over the ledge, then disappeared over the side.

* * *

Seb did not appear at breakfast. Nor did he take morning tea with everyone in the garden when both Lord Regis and Lord Gaines managed to arrive. Granted, they looked the worse for wear, but at least they managed to make an appearance, which left Clarissa stewing in her own juices and conjuring all sorts of ghastly images in her head.

Was Seb so exhausted by his night that he was still abed? Or worse, was he still there engaging in a whole host of sordid pleasures of the flesh with Penhurst? Were they sharing the same woman? How did two men share the same woman? Exactly how many ladies had Seb been with? Clarissa was incensed and appalled at the thoughts which refused to go away no matter how hard she tried to ignore them.

And it wasn't as if she had anyone she could ask. Gray must have stealthily clambered back in during the single solitary hour she had managed to get some sleep after his dreadful revelation and she hadn't seen him since. Penhurst and his cronies couldn't know that she knew where they had all been and she could hardly ask poor Penny. *Excuse me—but what time did your husband and my spy roll in from their night of debauchery?*

To make matters worse, Westbridge wouldn't leave her alone and had been following her around all morning, which meant by default the limpet Olivia had also been following her around, as well.

Good Lord, the man droned on.

If she had to listen to one more rendition of how the Regent admired his stupid art collection, she would scream. Another thing she was furious at Seb for. Before he crashed into her life and turned it on its head, Clarissa had been perfectly content in Westbridge's company. Had been grateful for it because it singled her out as special and she had hoped it would lead to a permanent arrangement. But now that she had been introduced to the intrigue and excitement of Seb's world, had been more than a pretty face and had learned what passion felt like, the Duke and his privileged but bland existence seemed insipid. It was difficult to be enthusiastic about objets d'art when you were assisting your King and country on a higher purpose. This must be how her sister Bella felt about practising medicine. Feeling useful and needed was intoxicating. Just as Seb was. Dratted man!

'Is everything all right, Clarissa?' Penny's concerned whisper tempered her fury with guilt. How could she selfishly continue to indulge her roiling jealousy when her friend's life was about to be ruined?

'Not really. If you want to know the honest truth, I'm worried about you.'

'Me? Whatever for?'

'You seem unhappy, Penny. With Penhurst.' They had never talked about the state of Penny's marriage. It had always seemed too personal and intrusive to do so. Yet maybe Clarissa was being neglectful by not asking. Her friend stared into her teacup with such an expression of despair, it made Clarissa feel dreadful for not asking beforehand. 'I hate to see how he neglects you.'

'It is the way of things in a marriage.'

Not according to Seb. Or the happy union between Clarissa's parents or that of her sister and her brilliant physician. 'It doesn't have to be.'

'I fear it does for me. The neglect is not so bad. He lives his life and I live mine.'

What did that mean? 'And when he doesn't neglect you?'

'Then I wish I had listened to you all those years ago. You had his measure while my head was turned. But I have made my bed and now I try to make the best of it. These parties help. I get to be with you while he amuses himself with whatever mistress has currently taken his fancy.' At Clarissa's shocked expression, Penny offered her a wry smile. It was achingly sad. 'You don't have to pretend, Clarissa. I realised the sort of man I'd married after I said my vows. He is quite open about his infidelities, especially now that he has his heir, and I find myself selfishly relieved that he goes elsewhere for his pleasures. It is nice to be able to go to bed and not worry if he will honour me with a visit.' Embarrassed at her own candour, Penny sipped her tea and forced a cheerful smile. 'But don't worry about that side of things. Not all men are like Penhurst and I am told that the marriage bed can be quite tolerable with the right sort of husband. Talking of which, Westbridge is taking more notice of you since Lord Millcroft showed up. He has asked me specifically to place you next to him at dinner again. You. Not Lady Olivia. You are making progress on that score. Why, he has been talking to you exclusively for over an hour.' Penny obviously wanted to change the subject.

'Tell me—if by some bizarre turn of fate the opportunity arose for you to escape Penhurst, would you take it?'

'I would grab it with both hands.' Penny's fierceness and lack of hesitation alleviated some of Clarissa's guilt. 'But alas, short of a miracle I fear I am trapped to spend eternity with him.'

'Miracles can happen.'

'Not to me.' The forced cheerful smile was tragic. 'But perhaps to you. I think you will enjoy being the Duchess of Westbridge. Now be a good friend and cheer me up. Tell me all about you and the Duke.'

Like a coward, Clarissa humoured her friend while she kept an eagle eye out for Seb. When

Penhurst shuffled across the lawn looking like a man who had been engaged in vigorous and drunken physical activity all night, and there was still no sign of Seb, Clarissa happily let her anger fester as their hosts chivvied everyone towards the stables to collect the mounts for today's planned ride. She was halfway to the destination when she sensed him, and briefly turned her head to confirm it, only to see him striding across the lawn looking handsome and purposeful. Invigorated by his exercise.

It must have been quite the night indeed!

Clarissa picked up her pace, deciding to ignore him from now until the end of time. How did Penny sound so resigned about Penhurst's infidelities when she was eaten away with bitter jealousy for Seb's? Not that he had been unfaithful in the strictest sense, because they were not a couple and nor would they ever be, but… Good gracious! There were no buts. How could he? It was galling. Infuriating. Humiliating. Beyond the pale…

'Good morning.'

Would spitting in his eye be inappropriate?

'Good *afternoon*.'

'What have I missed?'

'Breakfast and luncheon.' Clarissa stared straight ahead and hurried her pace. They had nothing to say. Nothing.

'I know. I'm starving. And tired. I've only managed to snatch an hour of sleep.' What did he want? Sympathy? Unbelievable. 'But I had an interesting night.'

Insufferable! 'So I gather.'

'Would you mind slowing down? I have things to tell you.'

'And yet I have no desire to hear them. In fact, I have no desire to be within ten miles of you so would you kindly go away!'

'Gem?' He touched her arm and she snatched it back. Lord only knew where those hands had been. Clarissa wanted to cry. The tears were already there, ready to fall.

'I said leave me alone.' Westbridge had stopped pacing ahead to look at them, so for good measure she waved and quickened her step to meet him, leaving her philandering spy behind. Which was exactly where he and all his exciting and intriguing machinations needed to be in all aspects of her life. Clarissa had allowed her head to be turned before and had learned through bitter experience that daring to dream for more than she deserved was always a mistake.

Chapter Sixteen

'Do you want to tell me what the blazes is going on?'

After an hour of trailing after her and watching her alternate between simpering up at the windbag and scowling at Seb as if he were the Devil incarnate, enough was enough. Fortunately, Gem was an atrocious rider and Lady Olivia had finally enticed said windbag to gallop ahead with her to admire the sea view. Clarissa had tried to go after them and made such a hash of it she began to list in her sidesaddle and had to slow down to adjust her seat. Something she was failing at spectacularly.

'Let go of my reins!' She was glaring down her nose at him. The silly little hat which matched her impractical and too-tight blue-velvet riding habit was hanging precariously just above her ear. How typical of her to choose her outfit based solely on aesthetics. It was obvious her corset was laced too tight to allow her to squeeze into the garment. A garment doubtless designed to catch her fickle Duke's eye. Perhaps that fool hadn't noticed how magnificently she filled it. Unfortunately, Seb's entire body had noticed. Even half-hanging from a horse and furious she was a sight for sore eyes.

'I need to speak to you.' And he was damned if he was going to chase her again. Watching that delectable bottom bounce in her saddle was killing him. Clenching the leather tightly in one fist, he nudged his own horse towards a small cluster of trees. They weren't much, but at least they would afford them some privacy from the rest of the group who were still none the wiser the pair of them were no longer following.

Seb still refused to release the reins as he dismounted. Leading her horse towards some low branches and securing them tightly, he held out his arms to help her down to the ground. She ignored them, folded hers across her pert chest and turned her head away like a petulant child. 'I am perfectly capable of getting down myself!'

'Go on then.'

This he had to see. That inappropriate habit hugged her like a second skin, the corset held her upper body rigid and the sidesaddle, with her in it, was slowly slipping further down the horse's back. Seb took himself to lean against the tree trunk and folded his own arms to watch. She twisted to lay her upper body across the horse's neck and began to slither down with her back to him, but then shrieked when her ridiculous skirt caught on the pommel. He took a step forward and she hissed like a cat, 'Stay back! I do not want your grubby hands on my body!'

'My grubby hands?'

'Yes. I know where they have been!'

'I'm sorry?' It was hard to remain stalwartly affronted when gravity and the pommel had left her part suspended from the ground. The toes of one foot had hit terra firma, her other leg dangled suspended at her side while the silly skirt was rucked up to show two shapely silk-clad calves and the taut fabric revealed two perfectly formed buttock cheeks. She started to wriggle as she wrestled with the trapped fabric and Seb found himself simultaneously aroused and amused by the sight. Something had made her lose her temper and she was clearly fuming. At him. Best to get it over with, whatever it was. 'Speak in plain English, Gem, and tell me what grievous crime I am supposed to have committed.'

'There is no supposed about it! Admit it! You spent the night in...in...'

'A brothel?'

'There is no need to sound so smug about it. I know what goes on in those places.'

'You do?' And more importantly why was she angry about it?

'Yes, I know! Gray might have only hinted at the sorts of unspeakable things you were engaged in out of politeness, but believe me, I see nothing noble in your sacrifice for *King* and *country*! It's disgusting. You're disgusting!'

Whilst still not entirely sure quite why she was snarling, but certain that his subordinate had had a hand in it, Seb decided to placate her while he extricated her. Watching that spectacular body jiggling in front of him was giving him all manner of unspeakable ideas. 'Gray likes to amuse himself by elaborating on the truth. Hold still and let me untangle you.' Necessity meant he had to wrap his hands around her waist to reach the pommel. She instantly stiffened at the contact, standing on one leg like an outraged statue in the cage of his arms, the pert peach of a bottom which had taunted him moments ago just inches from his aching groin.

'I suppose you deny doing your *duty*?'

'I suppose that depends of what you mean by duty.'

As the fabric finally gave, she immediately spun around to face him, her blue eyes stormier than any eyes he had ever seen before. Her finger came up and prodded him hard in the chest. 'You allowed a harlot to play your flute!'

The bark of laughter earned him a firm shove,

but he couldn't stop even when she marched away and stood incandescent with rage. 'I don't see what is so funny.'

'Let me get this straight. You are of the belief that I spent the entire night consorting with harlots.' She sniffed in response and looked away again, her arms folded tightly across her chest. 'That is partly true. There were harlots and technically I did spend the night with one.'

Her eyes widened in outrage, causing Seb to laugh again and raise his palms in surrender. 'But no consorting of any sort went on and certainly no *musical* renditions took place. If you want to know all the ugly details, I picked a young girl who looked more terrified than me, had her take me to her room where we proceeded to spend the night discussing how she came to find herself in a bawdy house in Sussex.' He risked taking a few steps forward. 'It was a tragic tale. She had run away from home to escape a drunken father and then fallen on hard times. Last night was her first night as a harlot and, thankfully, it was her last. I gave her enough money to see her right for a few weeks and if she has any sense, she will have met one of my men on the roadside this morning as we arranged and will already be winging her way to London where Lord Fennimore will find her some suitable employment. Penhurst's French mistress isn't French, by the way. She is the owner of the brothel he dragged me to. None of the girls are French and none go by the name Jessamine. Our debauched viscount and his cronies are regulars at the establishment and they took me there as a test. One I am very pleased to say I passed because, like you, they assumed the worst was going on behind those bedchamber doors.'

The stormy expression had now softened to one of relief—but what did that mean? All his instincts told Seb she was jealous. His head wanted to dismiss that futile hope as preposterous. Should he ask her? No. Definitely not. He would combust with embarrassment and shame when she denied it. Then he would still be incarcerated at this blasted house party and forced to suffer for days. 'On the way home, he suggested he might be able to involve me in an investment opportunity which guaranteed me high returns, but might not be strictly legal. He declined to elaborate, but I'm making progress, Gem.'

'That's good.' She was subdued, but no longer angry.

'On a separate note, whilst we are none the wiser as to who the elusive Jessamine might be, Gray did find out about the *Espérance de Dieu*. Look.' Seb took out the information his Invisibles had been given by the Excise Men and passed it to her to read, only to have the paper swatted away.

'Just tell me.'

'You were right—it *is* a ship. A merchant ship which is part of a small but specialised fleet shuttling the finest port from sunny Portugal to the major shipping destinations across Europe. It makes regular stops in Bilbao and Cherbourg, where I'll wager those boats get loaded with our free traders' French brandy before they sail on to Portsmouth. Before which I assume they take a little detour along the Sussex coast to offload the illegal portion of their cargoes right here first.

She still couldn't meet his eye. 'I take it they didn't attempt to offload last night.'

'No. But when they do I'll be there to meet them.'

'Unless you get dragged to Penhurst's brothel again.'

'I shall plead a headache. Now that my favourite harlot has left, I might actually have to *do* my duty for King and country. Which I would hate, by the way. Because I am not that sort of man.' He watched her reaction closely and when he saw no further evidence of any sort of jealousy or relief he realised he had imagined both. Merely the thought of a brothel disgusted her, not the thought of him in it. 'Besides, duty calls me out to the Downs and those ships tonight.'

'And those cut-throat smugglers.'

Seb pressed the paper into her hand. 'There is a list of the most recent dates those ships came into Portsmouth here. I need you to do some subtle digging with Penny to ascertain whether or not Penhurst was at home at those times. Can you do that?'

'Of course I can. Seeing as I'm now a spy, too. A rather good one, I think.'

'You're resourceful, I'll give you that. And you do have excellent instincts, especially on the hoof.'

'We both know you'd be lost without me.'

Sadly true, but thankfully she didn't know in how many ways. 'We should probably head back to the others. Shall I help you or are you perfectly capable yourself?'

Her smile warmed his heart. 'We also both know I can barely move in this silly habit.'

Seb secured her saddle while she stood so close he could smell her perfume. Not what he needed when his mind was valiantly trying not to think about touching her. Once that excuse was gone, he turned awkwardly and attempted to control his suddenly erratic breathing as he placed his hands gently around her waist and she rested hers intimately on his shoulders. He hadn't intended to make eye contact, yet his immediately sought hers and locked. A big mistake. He watched her pupils widen, then lower towards his mouth. The tip of her tongue darted out to moisten her lips, drawing his eyes to them, the air around them seemed to crackle with something heady and potent and of its own accord his head began to dip.

'Lady Clarissa!' Westbridge's voice stopped him in his tracks. 'Is everything all right?'

'My saddle was loose. Lord Millcroft has fixed it.' The sunny smile was now not for Seb, nor did it appear particularly genuine. 'He is just lifting me onto my horse.' Her gaze remained fixed on her waiting Duke as Seb did just that. While she adjusted her position he untied the reins and handed them back to her and for a second their gazes locked again. Gem's expression was perplexed. A little startled. Awkward. As if she had known what he was about to do and was vastly relieved he hadn't. Then she offered him the same disingenuous smile she had shot her Duke before she set her pony after the others and didn't look back.

Dinner was running late because their host had failed to materialise, so Clarissa pasted a smile on her face and hoped she appeared riveted by Westbridge's story rather than occupied with indecision. She blamed the peculiar moment she and Seb had shared earlier before he had lifted her onto her horse. Then their eyes had locked and, for one splendid moment as he held her, she thought he might kiss her.

Had wanted him to kiss her.

She had even licked her lips in anticipation in

the hope he might realise she was not averse to the idea. But Westbridge had arrived, breaking the sultry spell, and denying Clarissa the chance to find out. Seb had appeared flustered as he had hoisted her up into the saddle and then he had stepped briskly away. Since then he had put as much distance between them as he physically could in the confines of the hall. Even now he was at the exact opposite end of the drawing room to her and deftly avoiding her gaze.

Was that shyness or uninterest?

'If you will excuse me for a moment.' The barnacle looked pained as she scurried off in the direction of the retiring room, finally leaving Clarissa alone with her Duke for the first time since their arrival at the house party. The poor thing must be desperate to relieve herself to relinquish her permanent spot at his side. As she watched Olivia go, Clarissa's eyes once again wandered to Seb, willing him to stare back in the hope he would leak one clue as to how he was feeling.

'I am glad she has gone. I have been meaning to speak with you.' Westbridge drew her gaze reluctantly back.

'Really. What about?'

'Us.'

'Us?'

'Yes. I thought we might make things official.' Was that a proposal? Stunned, Clarissa gaped like

a fish. 'I apologise for dragging my feet, but I had
to be sure, you understand. A man in my position must choose carefully. Now that I have, I see
no reason to delay matters longer than necessary.
I've instructed my steward to book St George's
and have the banns read at the end of this week. I
see no reason why we can't get the deed done in
June before the *ton* leave in their droves to rusticate for the summer.'

'The deed?' Why was she not euphoric? Disappointed, definitely. Worryingly nauseous at the
prospect. Desperate to talk to Seb.

'I've also taken the liberty of sending a letter
to your father to discuss the settlements and to
request he organise the wedding breakfast. Obviously, we shall work together with the modiste on
your gown. I have made enquiries with Madame
Devy who I am certain will be delighted to cre-
ate just the right sort of design to befit the occasion. We can announce our engagement tonight.'

Of all the emotions she had expected to feel at
this moment, anger wasn't one of them, yet it was
most certainly the one which had rushed to the
fore. The urge to tell him where he could shove
his lacklustre and arrogant proposal was visceral
even as the sensible voice in her head cautioned
her to choose her words carefully. This was what
she had dreamed of and worked for. Becoming a
duchess would be her greatest achievement in a

life devoid of any. Sensible won, though the words were strained. 'You are assuming I have said yes.'

'Well, of course I am.' He had the audacity to chortle while she wanted to scream.

'Well, I haven't. Yet.' And all at once Clarissa desperately needed to think about it.

Properly.

Good gracious!

There was now so much to think about. This was what she wanted, yet her legs wanted to bolt. Her heart was horrified and her head was in the midst of listing all the reasons why marrying the man of her dreams might well turn into a nightmare. Was this the bridal jitters she had often heard talked about or something more? Jitters would pass. Genuine doubt would not. And why, when her head should be filled with the thoughts of wedding preparations, was Seb all she should suddenly think about? Her eyes flicked to her spy and her heart did a funny little lurch in her ribcage.

Why was that?

Yet the sight of him gave her the confidence to say the words which she never believed she would have reason to say to a *duke* in the history of ever. 'I shall consider your proposal and respond in due course.' As Seb had rightly said, she should trust her excellent instincts and allow them to guide her. Right now they were all over the place and images of Seb were clouding her judgement. Clarissa had allowed herself to be seduced by espionage and spies. If she were completely honest, more a certain spy than the espionage. One she was not entirely sure she was ready to give up.

Good gracious!

'What?' Now Westbridge was gaping like a fish and that unsightly jutting blood vessel was twitching near his eye. It dawned on Clarissa then that she was not the least bit attracted to the man. 'You will respond in due course! What sort of answer is that?'

'The best you will get this evening, your Grace.' And she was going to walk away. To think and ponder, weigh up the pros and the cons and consider her feelings. Unbelievably, she was going to walk away right this second and leave him in the same state of flux he had been perfectly content to leave her in. For two whole years. That knowledge made her giddy with an emotion she couldn't fathom at all. It wasn't outrage or relief. It certainly wasn't fear, nor was it delight. If she was pressed to describe it to anyone, it was a bizarre sense of freedom. One that made her smile at Westbridge in wonder. His insulting, pompous proposal had released her from the constant stress of striving for it.

'Ladies and gentlemen!' Penhurst's loud entrance behind her had her turning towards the door. He was stood with another man. One she knew well and liked less. Another pompous duke. 'Thetford has graced us with his illustrious presence!' The vile viscount looked tremendously pleased with himself as the portly and balding Duke stood smugly at his side. Knowing Seb would be as unimpressed with the surprise guest as she was and keen to let him see she had just had the most marvellous epiphany, she shot him an amused glance only to see his face had blanched of all colour and his fists were clenched tightly at his sides.

Something was very wrong.

'If you will excuse me…' Although she had already marched several feet away from the still stunned Westbridge before she remembered to apologise, her eyes fixed on the man who needed her.

Chapter Seventeen

Seb was torn. One half of him wanted to smash his fist into the smug face of his half-brother and the other wanted to run. Instead he remained rooted to the spot and hoped his legendary talent for blending into the wallpaper would single-handedly save the mission.

He had to think.

He had to remember his training and his higher purpose here today. Had to rise above the volatile emotions which he had long buried and not expected to return. Not here and certainly not now. He had to do what was best for King and country. The scar on his cheek began to hurt, just as it had on that fateful day when his father's acknowledged son had split it open with his riding crop and Seb had realised that he and his mother were truly destitute. Penniless. It hadn't been a misunderstanding, but deliberate. The new Duke's petty revenge on his father.

It had broken his mother.

Killed her soon after.

Indecision turned to white-hot rage and Seb decided to kill his half-brother and to hell with the mission. Today had been fifteen years coming…

He felt her hand on his elbow and allowed her to move him towards another door, ridiculously grateful for her perceptiveness because he was able to draw on her calm strength to control the sleeping monster which had suddenly reawakened. She closed the door behind them and dragged him down the quiet hallway towards an empty room.

Wordlessly, she pushed him into a chair, then poured a glass of brandy which she pushed into his hand. She never said a thing, almost as if she already understood everything, but sat next to him on the arm of the chair and stroked his free hand. The contact and her presence soothed him.

'How did you know?'

'Your reaction. The subtle similarities in both of your features. You have the same dark eyes. A similar nose—but you will be delighted to know you look nothing like him other than that. If you hadn't confessed to being a duke's son, I would be none the wiser.'

'Did he recognise me?'

'Is there a chance he might not?'

A laughable question. Seb and his mother had been disposable. As Lord Fennimore had quite rightly said, his dear brother had probably forgotten he existed soon after he had callously wounded him. 'I was a boy when we last collided—not that we had ever collided much before. I went to him for help and he gave me this instead.' He touched the scar and her fingers immediately followed, tracing the line of it gently before brushing the hair out of his eyes. Without thinking, he leaned against her palm and sighed, trying to control the rapid rise and fall of his chest.

'Do you want to tell me about it?'

To his surprise he did. He wanted to rant and rave and purge the anger. 'We lived in the hunting lodge on Thetford's estate. An open secret, yet detached from both the great house and its tenants. He would come and she would blossom. My mother loved my father. She assumed he loved her back, but even as a child I knew that was wishful thinking. I called him sir in the lodge but instinctively dipped my eyes if I saw him outside. He paid for tutors. He paid for everything. Then he died and we learned that he had made no provision for my mother in his will. She had given him sixteen years and didn't warrant a mention. He left me money in trust to pay for my education when I came of age. Nothing else. That same day the steward came. Ordered us out of our home. After all those years he gave us three days to be off Thetford's land.' Churning it up again brought all those turbulent feelings back. To realise they were still so raw and unresolved was unsettling. Seb didn't recognise himself because it was hard to reconcile the boy with the man he had become. He had thought he had moved on, yet they were one and the same. The fierce independence, the pride, the unacknowledged shame of not being born better, the resourcefulness and the shyness— even the drive to see justice done—all stemmed from those formative years and the consequences of that day.

Gem was still sat comforting him. There was no judgement on her lovely face, only sympathy. Seb took her hand and threaded his fingers through hers, needing the contact. 'My brother was residing in London. He was—*is*—ten years older than me. I took myself there to inform him of the steward's mistake, stupidly believing it *was* a mistake and my father would undoubtedly have issued proper instructions about my mother's future care. Because it never occurred to me that I would not be granted an audience, I rode directly to Berkeley Square from Norfolk, presented myself at his front door and told the butler that his Grace's brother was here to see him. I was sat waiting in his hallway when he came. Two footmen held me down and he beat me senseless, then threw me out on the street. I haven't seen him since.'

'What happened to you and your mother?'

'My grandparents took us in. My mother had been estranged from them since before I was born because they disapproved of her choices. I'm not entirely certain she had bothered to tell them about me until we turned up at the farm, but they welcomed us and gave us a new home. One I loved, but my mother didn't. She never stopped grieving for what happened. It was just shy of two years later that she caught a chill and lost the will to live.' And he was still angry at that, too. That he had not been enough to make her want to stay. 'So there you have it. In a nutshell. Beyond that door is a man I loathe above all others and I have no idea what to do about it.'

'Oh, Seb.' Her arm came around his shoulders and she pulled him close, resting her head on top of his. Inexplicably, her embrace lessened the pain. 'What a conundrum. What do you want to do?'

'Break his neck with my bare hands.'

'Understandable. I sense there is a *but*.'

'But I have an important job to do.'

She inhaled, then exhaled slowly. 'Then you have your answer. As it is highly unlikely from what you have said that he will recognise you, you must be Millcroft until it is safe to be Seb again. Then you can take what action you think fit and I will happily help you. In the meantime, for the mission you must pretend to be cordial and so must I.'

'And if he does recognise me?'

'Between us, we will think of something.'

'You make it sound so simple.'

She stood and shrugged, her smile banishing the last of the murderous thoughts for the time being. 'We are spies, Seb. Nothing is ever simple.'

Clarissa paced the bedchamber floor impatiently, waiting for Seb to come, feeling very daring in the borrowed breeches, shirt and dark coat she had pilfered from a wardrobe. She had no clue as to whether he still intended to go out tonight, but if he was then she was going with him. The idea of Seb in danger without her eyes there, too, to keep him out of harm's way would make sleep impossible, especially after the evening he had endured through no fault of his own. Seeing Seb distraught and briefly panicked had bothered her. It made her feel hugely protective of him. At some point, he had come to mean a great deal to her and she worried about him. Therefore, it stood to reason if she wouldn't be sleeping anyway, she might as well assist him tonight and every night henceforth in all aspects of his mission—because together they were the perfect team.

It was a decision she had made very early in the evening immediately after his confession because it was obvious he was vulnerable and needed looking after. By her. Clarissa had straightened Seb's lapels, neatened his hair again because she couldn't seem to stop touching him, then threaded her arm through his proprietorially. When they emerged back into the drawing room, it was Lord Millcroft and his adoring *Incomparable* that everyone saw.

She stood by his side while he was introduced to Thetford and, while they both inwardly held their breath, they were soon relieved to see not one flicker of recognition in the older half-sibling's eyes. Overall, it had been a brief exchange but the knowledge that Thetford was blessedly ignorant of her spy's real identity seemed to alleviate some of Seb's tension and allowed him to focus during the long dinner to such an extent that before the gentlemen left for their port and cigars, he managed to engage in some small talk with his nemesis.

Clarissa, on the other hand, fretted the entire time he was gone, but she needn't have worried. A surreptitious peek into the billiards room on her way to bed reassured her he was all Millcroft and she felt an inordinate sense of pride in him. There were not many men who could behave with such restraint and grace when under intense pressure. In the presence of two dukes, he stood tall and proud. Just the right amount of arrogance and confidence to convince anyone he was as good, if not better, than the rest of the men assembled. No wonder he excelled at what he did. But he still needed looking after. Especially tonight. Coming face to face with his past had rattled him and only she knew Seb was wearing a carefully constructed mask.

The tap on the door made her breath hitch. 'Who is it?' Her maid would have a fit if she saw her dressed like this. Especially after Agnes had taken half an hour to bind her hair in the rags. Rags which now sat listlessly on her dressing table next to the Mrs Radcliffe novel she had been attempting to read for four months.

'Me.' The deep whisper made those goosebumps appear all over her skin again. The sight of him dressed head to foot in black gave those goosebumps goosebumps. The colour suited him, making him seem more dangerous and sinfully exciting than usual. He closed the door and gaped at her attire.

'What are you wearing?'

To lighten the suddenly tense mood, Clarissa did a little twirl. 'My new spying clothes. Do you like them? I could hardly climb out of the window in layers of petticoats, now could I?'

'You are not going out of the window.' He dropped the heavy rope on the floor and began to secure it to some furniture as if his word was law.

'Yes, I am. You need me.'

'I need you in here, not out there where it is dangerous.' His ferocious scowl could have curdled milk.

'In case it has escaped your notice, it is probably just as dangerous in here as it is out there. What happens if they become suspicious or wonder why you are missing? They will come and find me.'

'Take off those ridiculous clothes and go to bed.'

'If you think I am going to spend the night worrying about you while meekly waiting here after tonight's revelations, then you can think again. Need I remind you that I have saved your mission at least twice that I know of and without me you would still be floundering in a ballroom in Mayfair rather than here in Penhurst's house. You said I am resourceful and have excellent instincts, two things that would come in useful if the unthinkable happens. *You* have had a trying day. Trying days play on the mind and make us miss things. Extra eyes will ensure that doesn't happen. Besides, if you refuse to take me with you, we both know I shall only climb down once you have gone. And then I will be all alone. Wandering the Downs in the dark. Looking for you. Wouldn't you feel better knowing I was with you in the first place?'

She watched his eyes narrow while he thought of a response and decided to deny him the chance. Decisively, Clarissa marched to the window and began to lower the rope outside. His big palms came down and imprisoned her hands. 'I'd feel better knowing that you were safe and sound in here.'

'And what about how I feel? Or does that not matter?'

His mouth opened and she silenced him with her hand. 'I am supremely tired of trying to do what other people want. I'm tired of all the effort it takes to be an *Incomparable*. I'm tired of feigning politeness to the limpet Olivia or Penhurst and his cronies. I'm tired of all of Westbridge's dithering, I'm tired of competing for his affections or being treated like an ornament and I am fed up with taking orders from you.'

He seemed offended to be included in that list. 'I don't give you orders.'

'Yes, you do. In the last few days alone you've ordered me to remain silent, keep secrets and you've threatened to put a guard on me if I disobey. Just then you ordered me to go to bed. Well, understand this—I'm not going to nor am I going to spend more fruitless hours worrying about you in here when I know I can be an asset to you outside.' She snatched her hands from under his and sat on the window sill, feeling righteously indignant. 'You either take me with you or I *will* follow later.'

'I bet you've never even climbed a rope.'

She was winning if that was the best argument he could think of. 'I haven't, but you have. If push comes to shove, then I'm sure you can throw me over those impressive shoulders.'

Chapter Eighteen

The need to be with her overruled everything his head and his training told him. Seb used many excuses to justify it—another pair of eyes, she *was* resourceful, they were only going to be observing—but he knew without a doubt the only reason he had allowed her to come was because he was emotionally unsettled and for some reason Gem's presence made him feel better. Right now he wanted to feel better, not seething or lost in the past.

She had managed to lower herself from the window without needing his help and, after camouflaging the bottom of the rope as best they could in the bushes below, they silently skirted the garden, keeping to the shadows until they were well clear of the house. It was a good mile from Penhurst Hall to the sea across the Downs and one they did uttering few words. Seb was understandably preoccupied, yet she seemed much the same. Maybe it was nerves or fear of what they were doing, but he couldn't shake the thought that there was something else going on in that clever head of hers.

Gem jumped out of her skin when one of his Invisibles stepped out of his hiding place, but to her credit barely a squeak came out of her mouth. 'Good evening, sir. All is quiet now, but there was a flash just up there on the cliff about an hour ago. Nothing since.'

'Where is everyone?'

'There are men posted every half a mile from Birling Gap to Cuckmere Haven. Gray has arrived in Portsmouth and is with the Excise Men ready to board the vessel once she has offloaded.' Assuming that the *Espérance de Dieu* was a smuggling ship, then they needed it to remain one for as long as feasibly possible—albeit with a slightly different crew—to allow the King's Elite to infiltrate the organisation on the Continent before word got out of Penhurst's capture. The ship could lead them to the rotten core of the Boss's organisation.

'You expect them tonight?' Gem's eyes were wide. 'It looks like rain.' An understatement. Such an angry sky suggested a storm.

'We have to expect them every night, but tonight it's cloudy and as there is little moonlight it makes conditions perfect. As long as the weather holds off for a few hours.' He watched her eyes automatically turn towards the ocean and study the black horizon and quite admired the fact she didn't simply take his word for it. Seb double-and triple-checked intelligence, too. Lives depended on accuracy.

Seb listened intently as his man brought him up to speed on everything that had been seen or learned in the days he had been incarcerated with Viscount Penhurst and then relieved him of his post to rest. Taking it in turns to snatch a few hours here and there was how they survived a mission. It was exhausting work and being exposed to the elements for long hours of surveillance wasn't fun. Necessary, but mind numbing.

Gem watched him unravel the large rectangle of oilskin which he had brought and fold it in half before laying it on the ground. 'There you go. Our palatial home for the night.' He lifted one corner to allow her to sandwich herself between the layers. At that moment it dawned on him that he should have brought two. Climbing in beside her would remind him of being in bed. Cosy. Warm. Intimate. He dropped the sheet and sat on the damp ground next to it, rummaging in his bag for his small field telescope to cover the sudden physical discomfort his errant thoughts were creating.

'What happens now?'

'The really exciting part. We get to stare at the sea for two hours.'

'And there I was thinking the life of a spy was glamorous.' Gem adjusted her position, rolling on her front and propping herself up on her elbows, tossing the ridiculously thick, golden plait of hair to one side. 'Pass me that telescope, then.'

He did and smiled as she taught herself how to focus it, scrunching up one eye and unconsciously poking out the tip of her tongue. It was the least *Incomparable* expression he had seen her pull and he found it enchanting. Not as enchanting as the erotic sight of her in the tight breeches which had tormented him as she undulated down the rope above him. Even with the layer of oilskin, that image was seared into his mind for ever. 'What am I looking for?'

'Big moving shadows or the occasional and brief flash of light. They are too experienced to use lanterns, but smuggling vessels communicate with those waiting onshore by using gunpowder. A little burns very brightly for a few scant seconds. If we are lucky, we will see flashes both at sea and somewhere along these cliffs or the beaches below.'

'Like a conversation.'

She caught on quickly, as usual, and that made him smile. 'Exactly. No replying light means something is amiss so the boat will not sail any closer.'

'How did things go with your brother?' The abrupt change of subject didn't surprise him. The spectre of his past had been hovering all evening.

'We were cordial. He's still an arse.'

'Wouldn't it be wonderful if he was involved with Penhurst's treachery and then you would have the pleasure of arresting him.' She shot him a cheeky grin, then went back to her telescope.

'Alas, like your pompous arse, Thetford is merely window dressing. Little trophies of Penhurst's social standing now that he is rich once again.'

Seb was expecting her to correct him and defend her Duke, and when she didn't he couldn't resist another dig. 'Talking of the windbag, he was glaring at me all night. Did the pair of you have words?'

'Why don't you like Westbridge? Specifically, I mean.'

Where to start? The blue blood. The undeserved privilege. The way dukes sneered down their nose at humble bastards. 'You deserve better than him.' Which didn't really answer her question—but as she had asked she deserved his honest appraisal, even though he knew she wouldn't like it. 'The fellow only ever talks about himself. He's detached and self-absorbed. I haven't seen any evidence of either a sense of humour or any compassion. The man is a bore. A fickle, pompous, arrogant fool.'

'You really don't like him, do you?'

'Ultimately, my opinion is of no consequence. It's yours that counts. What do you think of him?' Seb shouldn't have asked that because he didn't want to hear her waxing lyrical about the fool's appeal—although for some reason tonight he kept pushing her to.

'I'm not sure.'

He hadn't expected that answer, nor the expression of confusion on her lovely face. Could it be she was having doubts? Doubts which made his silly heart soar. 'Should you be planning to spend eternity with a man you aren't sure about?'

'I don't think Westbridge will make a bad husband—not like Penhurst.'

'Hardly a glowing endorsement.'

'I know.' She dropped the telescope and stared at him. 'I have been trying to make a list of pros and cons in my head. He is a *duke*. He is rich and he is well respected within society.'

The title. As if that somehow made better men. 'And the cons?' Please God let there be significantly more.

'I'm still working on those.' She didn't want to share them and Seb saw that as a very good sign indeed. So he pushed some more.

'Tell me—does he know anything about the real you? The woman whose hair is naturally straight, who has a sweet tooth and a thirst for adventure?' The one whose kisses sent Seb mad with desire. 'I doubt he shuts up long enough to hear a word you say.'

Her silence was deafening.

'Do you love him?'

More silence broken by the ominous rumble of thunder in the distance. A well-timed omen of doom if ever there was one, although whether that doom was aimed at the windbag or Seb he couldn't say. 'Not yet.' A fat drop of rain splattered on the oilskin, closely followed by another. 'Perhaps I will. In time.' When the next droplet hit her face she pulled the oilskin up to cover her head.

'And if you don't?'

She didn't answer, but the sky did. The thunder was closer this time and cued the heavens to open, decisively killing their enlightening conversation stone dead. After one determined raindrop caught him on the back of the head and trickled coldly down his spine, Seb pulled the collar of his coat up and did his best to burrow within it.

'You should get in before you get soaked.' Gem shuffled over, innocently unaware the prospect made him instantly hard.

'I'll get one of my men to escort you back. There's no point in both of us suffering.'

'You're not getting rid of me that easily. Besides, a little rain never hurt anyone and neither of us will get soaked under here, will we?' She patted the space next to her, looking decidedly pleased with herself, clearly intent on torturing him for the duration. 'Isn't the whole point of oilskin that it is waterproof?'

As there was no arguing with logic and further resistance would require explanations he wasn't brave enough to give, like a man headed to the gallows, Seb edged his body beneath the oilskin and prayed for strength. At least the sudden downpour had killed the topic of Westbridge. Seb pulled the fabric up enough to shelter their heads before he relieved her of the telescope. Better to focus on the job in hand rather than the beautiful woman whose warm body was now inches from his in their own intimate, oilskin world. Wearing breeches. Tight, revealing breeches.

Two painful minutes ticked by, then she rolled on her side to stare at him again. Without the hat and with all the moisture in the air, her curls had begun to drop. She was vexingly beautiful and, for once, blissfully unaware of it. 'The troubling thing is, if I'm being completely honest with myself, I don't really find Westbridge particularly attractive. Do you think that will come with time as well?' Seb grunted in response. Whilst a huge part of him was delighted at this revelation, he didn't quite know how to answer. Like a coward he changed the subject.

'The sea is whipping up.'

'Do you think attraction is important in a marriage?'

The woman was going to kill him. 'I believe it certainly helps.'

'Why?' At his outraged glare she looked away. 'Ah, yes. I suppose it does help with the…um… physical side of things, doesn't it?'

'If you don't mind, I really don't want to discuss *that* side of your relationship with Westbridge. Not *now.*' And not ever if he had any say in it. Imagining Gem engaging in intimacies with anyone other than him would make his blood boil—which was ironic, as imagining her in his bed heated it in an entirely different manner.

'Yes. Of course. Sorry. A totally inappropriate topic of discussion. We should focus on the mission.' She stared back out to sea and he slowly inhaled in an attempt to banish all thoughts of intimacy from his mind. 'Not that we have *that side* yet.' The calming breath came out on a whoosh. 'That wouldn't be at all proper before marriage, would it? And Westbridge is predictably proper. Which is a good thing, I think.' She chewed on her bottom lip as she rolled back on her front and gazed off into the darkness, looking thoughtful. Seb doubted her thoughts and his were aligned.

She was pondering propriety while he was considering all manner of improper things he would happily do to her beneath this oilskin, married or not. But then he was no gentleman by society standards and, in his defence, the woman of his dreams was lying inches away and tempting him. Intent on discussing marital relations while wearing breeches that moulded perfectly to her delectable backside. An image his brain apparently refused to forget.

Bringing her had been foolish. Bad for his sanity.

Where were the blasted smugglers when you needed them? A boat, some miscreants and the illicit offloading of illegal cargo would take his mind off her and the uncomfortable bulge in his trousers. Why, through several layers of clothes, was his body so conscious of the soft, warm heat of hers? His skin positively prickled with awareness. He sensed her watching him and risked taking his eyes off the horizon to glance at her. It was another mistake.

'Do you know Westbridge is so proper, he hasn't even tried to kiss me? Not once in almost two years.' His own incredulity was met simultaneously with a shaft of lightning, which thankfully drew her gaze away from his stunned yet relieved face. His slack mouth was closed again by the time she turned back. 'Is that odd?'

Yes, of course it is odd! If you were mine I would kiss you senseless at every available opportunity.

'No.'

Westbridge is even more of a blasted fool than I first thought!

His eyes dropped to her lips hungrily before he tore them away and gripped his telescope for all he was worth.

'Did you get a chance to go over the dates I gave you with Penny?' Talking business might just take his mind off his desperation to bury himself inside her. If nothing else, those dates would link Penhurst to the Boss.

'Not yet.' Her jaw clenched as she stared out to sea. As an afterthought she took the telescope from him and peered down it.

'It's important, Gem. Can you make sure you ask her tomorrow?'

'I'll try.' She adjusted the focus, but Seb had the distinct impression she was fobbing him off.

'I need a definite yes. I'm relying on you.'

She stared resolutely at the horizon, chewing her lip thoughtfully. After an age she dropped the telescope, but still refused to meet his eyes. 'It's probably best you don't rely on me to read anything.'

Chapter Nineteen

'The list you gave me…well…' She raked a hand over her face, then seemed to deflate into the collar of her dark coat. 'The truth is I haven't read it because…'

'Because?' She looked so bereft it was worrying him, although for the life of him he couldn't understand why talking about a simple list should fill her with dread.

'Can you keep a secret?'

'A stupid question. I'm a spy, remember.' As she seemed to need reassurance he reached out and used one finger to turn her head to face him. Lord, she was beautiful. 'You can trust me with anything, Gem.'

She searched his face, then looked away, her words tumbling out. 'The truth is I can't read properly.'

Seb blinked twice, then ruthlessly forced his eyelids to remain static. He hadn't expected that, but knew instinctively that if he said or did the wrong thing in response it would break her heart. He had never seen her so vulnerable. 'Ahhh.'

'I know that probably makes me stupid. I mean I *know* I am stupid. I can read a little bit. Painfully slowly as long as I put a ruler or my finger beneath the words, but the letters always seem to spin and swirl in front of my eyes and then I panic and they make no sense.' There were tears glistening on her lashes now. Tears of shame which tugged at his heartstrings. 'I'm not very bright.'

Utter nonsense. She was brighter than the sun and the moon combined. 'I don't think you're stupid. Far from it, in fact. Actually, if you must know...' He took a deep breath. Now might well be the opportune moment to bare his soul and admit his feelings. 'I actually...' *Tell her, you useless fool!* '...think you are fabulous.'

'Now you are just being kind.' The telescope went back to her eye in a brisk, no-nonsense, I-would-prefer-not-to-discuss-this-further way, but not before the single, fat tear she had intended to hide shimmered as it rolled down her cheek. 'But I would appreciate your absolute discretion.' She swiped the tear away with the back of her hand and the well-practised haughty tone she had first used to put him in his place replaced the uncertainty. 'Nobody else knows. Not even my family. I've managed to convince them all I'm simply flighty since I was ten. *Incomparables* aren't supposed to be illiterate.' For her own protection she shuffled away and focused on the task in hand. That stoic bravery, buried in dismissive humour, was killing him. The knowledge she had entrusted the truth with only him humbling. And touching.

She had chosen him.

Above all others. Seb decided to take that as a very good sign.

'You can't read. So what? You are good at so many other things such a tiny flaw hardly matters in the grand scheme of things.'

She snorted her dismissal, shaking her head emphatically as if she firmly believed she was worthless, but was determined to rise above it. 'Unfortunately I merely put on a good show. It's all a façade. I can't paint or embroider. I have no musical talent aside from the ability to butcher any piece I attempt to play. Obviously, I'm no scholar, which makes learning things impossible. I'm good at nothing aside from being pretty. That is the only talent God gave me and thank goodness for it, else I really would be done for.' The saucy smile was all bravado and all credit to her acting skills, it almost reached her eyes.

Suddenly the vanity and the need to be admired made perfect sense. In her world, where the measure of a woman was determined by her *accomplishments*, Gem felt she had little to offer.

She didn't see what his heart saw clear as day. His arms ached to hold her so he could kiss the doubt away.

'You are brave and tenacious. Maddening. Obviously, but only because you have a canny talent for being right more often than you are wrong. You have a way with people which I envy. A natural charm that makes them want to be with you. I've never known a person be able to think on their feet as quickly as you do, or to come up with excellent solutions so fast. The fake tryst when we were about to be discovered, for example, was the perfect ploy. You saved the mission. A mission that would have been shot in the paddock had you not stepped in and saved me from the outset. You keep saving me, whether that be navigating me through society or saving me from murdering my brother. You might not be an accomplished young lady, Gem, but you are a damn good spy. One of the best.' She seemed to light from within at the compliment, dazzling him and knotting his damn tongue. 'And…' *I think I might be falling in love with you.* 'His Majesty's government owes you a huge debt of gratitude.'

The smile that bloomed on her lovely face warmed him, then her fingers touched the back of his hand and his common red blood burned hot with instant desire. 'I suppose it does. Thank you, Seb. You always manage to make me feel better. You are a good friend.'

'If they are going to offload tonight they had better be quick.' Seb turned away to stare back through the telescope, his expression unreadable. The abrupt change of subject a definite reminder that he was keen to focus on his mission, not her problems and certainly not her conundrum over Westbridge.

And him. It was plainly obvious her growing confusion since the Duke's unromantic proposal was mired in her feelings for Seb. Feelings so intense, Clarissa had to confront them.

She had certainly never confided her innermost secrets to another living soul before. Never dared! But for some reason she had just confessed everything. Had needed to confess everything, but only to him. A test perhaps to see if he could truly be trusted with all of her. Now she knew she could trust him, implicitly, there was more that urgently needed considering. All-encompassing and overwhelming new feelings. Was this born out of physical desire? Or was that desire, fuelled further by his sweet and loyal defence of her abilities, scrambling her wits and clouding her judgement?

'The wind is picking up.'

Was it? Clarissa hadn't noticed. She was too busy trying to make the most important decision of her life and the current situation wasn't helping her do that. With hindsight, coming here had been a mistake. He was plainly too much of a distraction. How was she supposed to consider the Duke's proposal with him lying beside her? Now that she had unburdened herself of her darkest secret and had been delightfully relieved at his calm reaction, she was becoming supremely aware of his big body next to hers with each passing minute. The clean scent of his cologne. His strong, capable shoulders. His clever lips. Kind, generous heart.

There was so much to like about her spy. Too much if she was being brutally honest. It both excited and befuddled her in equal measure.

They watched the rapidly brewing storm for several minutes in an odd, tense silence which seemed to weigh down the oilcloth which cocooned them. If Clarissa had to take a stab at gauging *his* mood, she would have to say he was angry, but whether that was at her babbling, Westbridge, the rain or the smugglers she couldn't be sure. She wanted it to be about Westbridge because she was angry at him herself. Only a small proportion of that was down to his assumptive proposal. The rest was for all the things which had been quietly bothering her, but which Seb had succinctly put into words. Vocalising her doubts cast them in sharp relief.

Westbridge didn't know her at all because he had never taken the trouble to learn. He did lack compassion and an overall awareness of anything outside of the bubble he lived within. He had left her dangling on the hook for months and was not the least bit remorseful for openly courting another woman while he made up his mind. She could never envisage confiding her darkest secrets to him because…well a duke who prized perfection above all else would be horrified to have been tricked into marrying a mirage. He was dull and cold and pompous, and she didn't find him the least bit attractive. The idea of intimacies with him was distasteful and she was suddenly glad he had never bothered trying to kiss her.

Unlike the man lying next to her.

The one her errant body ached to kiss again. Why, if her heart's desire was to marry a duke, was she so infatuated with Seb? And was it fair to dismiss what she was feeling as mere infatuation when both her head and her heart were screaming differently? The overwhelming need to be with him tonight, the worrying when he wasn't around, the confessions, the scandalous thoughts involving his mouth and hers, the comfortable sense of rightness in his company, the complete immersion in him to the exclusion of everyone else when they were together… What did all that mean?

If all that was between them was a growing

friendship, why was her body now reacting in a manner which suggested blatant carnal desire? The rapid heartbeat, skin newly sensitive and desperate to be touched, an intoxicating awareness of her own womb—all evidence of a woman who wanted a man. Should she be wanting another man when considering marriage to someone else? And more importantly, exactly what did she feel for Seb?

Gratitude?

Kinship?

Lust?

There was no denying the lust. While Westbridge might well be a stickler for propriety, Clarissa was prepared to concede that with Seb right at this moment, or during their one incendiary kiss, she had no such qualms. Lying next to each other almost touching, nothing but stark honesty and a few layers of clothes between them, every nerve ending was positively humming with lusty curiosity for this man who knew the real her and accepted her regardless. To truly be herself for the first time in years…

That was a heady aphrodisiac.

Should she tell him she had a *tendre*?

Yes!

No.

Maybe… Just not now. He was working. Doing his duty—but once they were done Clarissa made up her mind to confess the final secret as yet unsaid. She wanted him. And she didn't want Westbridge. There was no way she could settle for the sort of marriage the Duke offered, not when she would always yearn for her spy and those laughter lines.

'I can see movement.' Seb's voice cut through her thoughts. He pointed to the furthest visible edge of the cliffs. 'Look. Is that a ship?'

Clarissa stared intently, trying to separate the waves from the shadows in the blur of the rain. With no moonlight and the dense blanket of low clouds, visibility was poor to non-existent. It was the brief bright flicker which confirmed it, casting the bottom of the sails and the rigging in an eerie, lacy light for just a second before the sky was plunged into blackness once again. After that, it all happened quickly.

The answering flash on the cliffs was less than half a mile from where she and Seb were hidden, followed by the ghostly spectre of a ship gradually looming closer to the shore until it weighed anchor and bobbed several yards from the cliff on the storm-whipped waters below. From their vantage point it was impossible to see the thin strip of beach which separated the cliffs from the sea without emerging from their cocoon and risking being seen. There was no movement above, suggesting that whoever was waiting to meet the vessel had not come by route of the Downs. But their view of the ship was spectacular. Like ants, the crew swarmed across its deck. It was difficult to make out exactly what they were doing, suffice to say whatever it was it was being done in a great hurry. Within minutes, three large rowing boats drew up alongside the ship and were quickly involved in receiving whatever was being winched down to them.

Almost as quickly as it had arrived, the ship began to sail away while the men in the smaller boats rowed to shore and out of sight. 'Stay here. I'm going to see if I can get a better view.' Crouching low, Seb took himself to the edge of the cliff face and peered dangerously over the side to the steep drop beyond. The dratted man knew no fear, yet his carelessness terrified her.

'Come back here!'

The wind ruffled his dark hair and blew her whisper back into her face.

'Seb!'

Either he couldn't hear or he was purposefully ignoring her, crouched as he was on the precipice while the weather billowed around him. There was nothing for it, she was going to have to drag him back. The wind, the cliff edge, the perilous rocks and churning water below were all too dangerous and making her nauseous. Things he appeared blissfully ignorant of. At the same moment she scrambled out of the oil skin, Clarissa felt all the tiny hairs prickle on the back of her neck a split second before the enormous fork of lightning split the sky overhead. The image burned itself on to her eyes, forcing her to blink to clear it, while the wind plastered her hair against her wet face. She swiped it away and then suffered the agonising pain of her heart ripping in two.

Because the edge of the cliff was eerily empty and the love of her life was gone.

Chapter Twenty

'There's a hole in the rock near the top. A cave of some sort. Large enough to allow a man to pass through, but concealed enough not to be obvious.' Seb hoisted himself back over the ledge and grinned. None of his men had noticed the opening, hardly surprising when it was so well hidden. 'They hoist the barrels from the rowing boats into the cave. Once it's light, my men will have to do some proper recognisance. All we need to do is link it to Penhurst.' His pleased expression changed to outright confusion when he felt her finger poke him hard in the chest.

'I was worried sick about you!'

'Whatever for?' She resembled a bedraggled rat, her long hair hanging in dripping ropes around her face. Her slim shoulders rising and falling rapidly.

'You disappeared over the side of the cliff.

Over. The. *Side!*' The prod turned into a full push. 'I thought you had fallen! Or been captured!'

For a little thing, she packed a punch, although why she was fuming Seb couldn't fathom. He'd only been gone five minutes. Fallen? Captured? 'I was sat on that ledge watching. The view is much better down there.' He gestured towards the rocky outcrop a few feet below.

'You have a reckless regard for your own safety!' The second push was done with both of her hands and he had to take a step back to avoid falling on his behind. 'You could have died!' Another push. 'Was the bullet that almost killed you not enough?'

It was only then that he heard the tremor in her voice. 'Are you crying?'

'Of course I'm crying, you stupid man! I thought you were dead!' The final push coupled with his shock at seeing her so distraught did send him backwards and he landed with a painful thud on the ground. 'I hope that hurt!'

Before he could stand she was off, fists clenched at her sides as her legs pumped the ground, her delightful bottom wiggling with indignation as she stomped back the way they had come. Seb stumbled to his feet and ran to catch up with her. 'Gem—I'm sorry. I didn't mean to make you worry. I thought you were watching.'

She didn't slow her pace. 'I wasn't being reckless. I was perfectly safe at all times.'

That made her stop dead. Even in the pitch black and the storm he could clearly make out her fury. 'Were the rocks wet and slippery? Was the wind howling? Were the waves smashing onto the beach below?'

'Well…' The stinging slap across the face came out of nowhere.

'I thought I'd lost you!' The hand she had just smacked him with clutched at her chest and tore at her wet shirt. 'It broke my heart!'

Like a dam bursting, all her molten anger turned into racking, violent sobs. It wasn't pretty. Stunned, a little bit shaken by the dramatic turn things had taken, his mind whirring with the staggering possibility that he had the power to break her heart, Seb wrapped his arms around her and tugged her close. He was at a loss as to what else to do. To his greater surprise she coiled hers tightly around his waist and buried her head against his chest, noisily crying into his coat.

I thought I'd lost you.

It broke my heart.

Did those words mean what he hoped they meant?

He found himself kissing the top of her head and rocking her in his arms, oblivious of the rain that lashed his face. 'I'm sorry. Don't cry. Please don't cry.' The sound of it was tearing him to pieces and making him hope. 'Slap me again. Push me. Kick me, just please don't cry.' Beneath his chin she had started to make a strangled sound which began as a hiccup and ended on a snort, her slim shoulders convulsing with each one.

'I—I—I th-thought you were d-dead.'

'I know. I'm sorry.' Needing to see her face and reassure her of the earnestness of his apology, Seb smoothed the sodden strands of hair out of the way and tilted her chin up gently with his finger. 'Believe me, if I had known that you were worried…'

'It doesn't matter. You're safe. All that matters is you're safe.' Her fingers tangled in the wet linen against his chest and she offered him a cross between a smile and a grimace. It was the most beautiful expression he had ever seen. Of their own accord, his thumbs brushed away the fresh tears on her cheeks and then the raindrops glistening on her cheeks and lips. When her head turned and she kissed his open palm, he simply stared down at her in wonder. This was all so unexpected. Longed for, but never in his wildest dreams did he dare give credence to the idea of her reciprocating the emotions which Seb had suffered from the outset. The desire and need. The wanting.

It was Clarissa who tugged his mouth down to meet hers. It was her lips that hungrily slanted over his, but it was Seb who hauled her against him like a starving man and feasted. Like the first fateful kiss, this one banished all reason and burned, only this time he recognised she was as active a participant as he was. As needy and as consumed with desire as he was. He laughed as he kissed her, overcome with the sheer joy of the impossible becoming glorious reality.

Gem wrestled with the wet linen of his shirt and tugged it out of his breeches, then tunnelled her hands beneath to explore his skin. Boldly, her splayed fingers traced the muscles on his chest and abdomen, her hips pushed against his hardness with wanton abandon as the downpour soaked them both. She wasn't the only one who needed to feel skin. On a guttural moan Seb tugged at the hem of her shirt, and when it caught on something, she helped him to pull it up and groaned as he filled his hands with her naked breasts. The nipples hard and wet with rain, so sensitive she shuddered at the merest graze from the pads of his thumbs. Gem, too, was eager to explore. Her palms smoothed down his abdomen, feathering the hard length of him over the top of his breeches shyly.

It was ecstasy.

It was agony.

It was utter perfection.

A dazzling burst of lightning brought him back

to earth with a bang. They might think they were alone, but they weren't. His men were out here on the Downs, hidden from view and watching. The hazy cloak of the storm wouldn't camouflage everything.

On a ragged breath, he pulled her clothing back down and recognised the exact moment she realised they were not alone, too, because she took a hasty step back and pulled her coat around her, giggling. 'We should get back.'

'Yes.' But neither of them moved, instead they stood staring at each other in wonder, trying to make sense of what had spontaneously happened between them. To his delight, Gem was smiling. What started as a tentative curve of her mouth bloomed swiftly into a broad grin that mirrored his.

Because it felt right, Seb took her hand in his. Linked their wet fingers before kissing hers. 'We need to talk, I think.'

'Yes. Yes, we do. But somewhere warm and dry perhaps.' She was still smiling. Not angry or disgusted, but an intimate and contented smile before she tugged him to follow.

The mile between them and the house didn't feel like a mile, nor did the pummelling rain or the random bursts of thunder and lightning diminish the peculiar atmosphere now surrounding them. They held hands all the way, but never said a word, letting go only out of necessity when they reached the rope. He had to help her to climb it, which was a delightful excuse to touch her body again. Only her waist and hips this time, but enough to relight the fires of desire as she disappeared over the window sill back into her bedchamber. Then he took a moment to pause and consider what he was going to say.

There was no denying his feelings now. Not to himself. She was his everything and more. So much more than he had ever dared dream of. Beautiful, funny, a joy to be around. No wonder she had been declared an *Incomparable* so long ago. To Seb she was beyond compare. Did he risk telling her?

Was such a declaration too soon? It wasn't for him, but this wasn't all about him and for all he knew she still had her sights set on the fool Westbridge. Away from the fraught emotion of the clifftop, she might already have second thoughts. Perhaps a more measured and cautious approach was best, all things considered. Seb would listen first to what she had to say, then respond accordingly. *How are you feeling about what we just did?* Of course that all hinged on whether she immediately regretted it. Westbridge might well be a fool, but he was a legitimate one. He had a title, a huge estate, wealth. Things Seb couldn't compete with. Could Gem forgive him for the circumstances of his birth? She hadn't seemed to mind it before now—but then romance had not been on the cards then. Was it now? Did he dare to dream? *If you are agreeable, I would like to... What? Marry you? Make love to you? Court you? Yes to all three.*

Baby steps were probably best while he gauged the lie of the land. No heartfelt declarations should be made until there had been thorough recognisance. Subtle enquiries, careful observation and gentle hints were the way forward. He would be a gentleman about the kiss and remind her it had happened in the heat of the moment, then see what she had to say about it. Content he had a plan of action, Seb braced his arms on the stone and heaved himself inside.

'I was beginning to think you weren't coming.' She was sat on the bed wringing out her hair, the stolen coat a soggy heap at her feet. Had he not already known she was gloriously naked beneath the shirt, the translucent wet linen would have told him in no uncertain terms. The dark circles of her nipples were obvious in the candlelight, the fabric clinging to her breasts and leaving nothing to his imagination. His intended words dried to dust in his throat and with it came the return of his crippling awkwardness. It securely nailed his boots to the floor and bound his jaws with wire.

'I do love it when you blush. It's a very endearing quality.' He could hear the laughter in her voice and forced himself to meet her gaze. If he couldn't overcome the shyness, then he would never choke out the words he intended to say.

'I…er…' He gave up trying to speak and went back to staring at the floor, which stalwartly refused to open up for him.

'Do I need to fetch you some brandy? A little Dutch courage…' What did that mean? What *did* she want him to say? 'Oh, for goodness sake, Seb!' She was giggling now and patting the mattress next to her. Then her blue eyes darkened and her expression became all serious. 'Come here. Let's get you out of those wet clothes.'

'Your clothes are wet, too.' Where had that voice come from? It almost sounded flirtatious.

'They are. I shall probably need your help to remove them.' Gem was looking at him through her lashes, spiked with rain, her own voice laced with the sultry coquettish edge which she wielded with such precision—except this was no harmless flirtation or a contrived one intended to put him in his place. Seb might be famously useless around women, but he recognised an invitation when he heard one. Even if he hadn't, the moment she leaned back on her hands and the translucent shirt stretched across her bare breasts there was no denying the movement had been deliberate.

She knew exactly what he saw. Knew and revelled in it.

'It would be my pleasure.' All at once, his awkwardness evaporated, replaced by sheer carnal desire which needed to be slaked. With more confidence than he had ever displayed towards the opposite sex, Seb walked slowly forward, his eyes devouring the sight of her shamelessly displayed before him. He shrugged out of his wet coat and let it drop loudly on the floor, then reached out a hand. When she placed hers in it he tugged her to stand and pulled her so close she had to tilt her head to look him in the eye. The few inches of air between their bodies seemed to crackle with the anticipation, but despite his rampant arousal, Seb had no desire to rush.

This miracle needed to be savoured.

He began by removing the wet ribbon from her hair, then unwinding what was left of the thick plait. The weight of the rainwater had completely undone the work of her curling iron and it hung in a ruler-straight curtain almost to her waist. Seb rejoiced in the lack of ringlets, allowing the silky, damp strands to run through his fingers, knowing no other man had ever been granted the image of her as nature intended. To torment them both, he nuzzled her neck and nibbled on her ear, enjoying her soft exhale of breath as she swayed towards him.

With aching tenderness, he began to peel the wet linen from her body. As if in a sensual trance, Gem raised her arms the second her beautiful breasts were exposed and shivered as the air whispered over her pebbled nipples. Seb's sharp intake of breath at their perfection made her smile before her face disappeared briefly as he lifted the shirt away. Wearing just that knowing, feminine look and breeches was the single most erotic thing he had ever seen. Even his wildest fantasies had not prepared him for the reality.

Pert, rounded flesh capped with dark-pink, saucily erect nipples he ached to touch. And taste.

As if reading his mind, she wound her arms around his neck like a temptress, flattening her needy breasts against his chest and depriving him of the view. 'Kiss me.'

Who was he to argue? His mouth grazed hers gently and she sighed into it, clearly in no hurry either. This kiss was different. It still burned, but with the slow heat of anticipation rather than the fiery need for satisfaction. They had the rest of the night. No need to rush. The tip of her tongue lapped at his. He could feel the aroused peaks of her breasts through the damp linen of his own shirt. The bold press of her hips against his hardness. When her hands began to explore his skin beneath the fabric, he let her without interruption. The shirt slid upwards and her nipples brushed his abdomen. Seb tossed the shirt to the soggy heap of clothes on the floor and filled his hands with her deliciously curved bottom, pulling her hips flush against his. She undulated against him, those perfect breasts rising and falling as she explored his chest. Bizarrely, the starburst scar from the bullet was super-sensitive. His throaty groan as she traced the shape of it empowered her and she replaced her questing palms with her lips.

Pure heaven.

Without him realising it, his fingers had begun working on the buttons of her breeches at the same time as she began to work on his. Suddenly the need to feel naked flesh from head to toe made them both hurry. Both clumsy. They laughed as they wrestled with the clinging fabric, momentarily abandoning the luxury of undressing one another as they hastily stripped the last remaining wet layer off, then the laughter died as they took a few seconds to simply stare at each other. Stripped bare in every way.

Seb was big. Very big. His height. The broad shoulders and strong arms. Muscular legs stood slightly apart and that part of him jutting proudly. Intimidating yet exciting. Six feet plus of very aroused male. She had put him in that state. He had bewitched her in much the same manner. Her desire for him, for what would come next, overruled her apprehension that they wouldn't fit together. They had to fit together or her body would spontaneously combust from the wanting.

But laying with him was a huge step. Her tummy fluttered at the enormity of what it all meant. She was throwing away the security of being a duchess for a man who made her heart sing. Hoping laughter lines and love would be protection enough.

He must have seen her trepidation.

'I won't hurt you.'

'I know.' As if he could? In a rush, all those doubts dissolved. Seb was the better man. The only man she needed. With him she would be safe and protected and gloriously happy rather than ashamed of all she was not. Seb saw what she was, flaws and all, yet wanted her regardless. That glorious acceptance set her free.

Her hands came up to frame his face. There was no more doubt. Seb was a gentle giant. Her gentle giant. No other man would do. Clarissa stood on tiptoe to kiss him and then threw her head back and laughed as he lifted her into those powerful arms and gently placed her on the bed. Then the awkwardness she adored about him surfaced once again as he hesitated.

'We don't have to do this, you know. I'm happy to wait...'

'Well, I'm not.' As if she could. 'We both know

I'm intrinsically selfish. I want you now. This minute, in fact.'

To prove her point Clarissa shuffled over to make room for him on the mattress, then delighted at the way his eyes darkened with desire when she shamelessly stretched out, lying propped on one elbow in naked invitation. 'You have the oddest effect on me, Seb Leatham. Look at me.' He did, with such intensity it made her womb ache and her breasts throb. 'I've never been with a man before. Never ever been naked in front of another person before—yet I am apparently quite content to be so with you.' Because he made her feel more beautiful than she had ever felt in her life. All the thousands of compliments, all the flowery words, bouquets from admirers, all the nonsense that came with being an *Incomparable*, all of that paled against the way Seb looked at her. He was no wordsmith, but he was perfect that way. He couldn't say them and she couldn't read them. What a splendid pair they made!

Clarissa didn't need his flattery to know he appreciated every single inch of her. Adored and desired every single inch. It was all there in his intense, unwavering stare as plain as day, in the deep and rhythmic rise and fall of his impressive ribcage and the steely, velvet hardness of his erection. Genuine evidence that she was the only woman in the world for him.

His Gem.

Not a diamond of the first water, but a real woman with her own thoughts and flaws and attributes. Seb knew she could be shallow and selfish. Vain. Vulnerable. Resourceful. Had watched her scheme to catch a duke, bind her straight hair in rags and act out the part of the *Incomparable*. Knew only too well she wasn't perfect and yet somehow his casual acceptance of her flaws made her forgive herself for them. With Seb she was a better person. He appreciated her and understood her in a way no other soul ever had. No artifice. No affectations. Just as nature had intended. 'Come to bed, Seb.'

Without taking his eyes off her, Seb lay down, mirroring her position. She could feel the warmth of his body although neither of them was touching. He reached out his hand and ran his fingers once again down the length of her hair where it trailed onto the pillow. 'I love your hair like this.' The pad of his index finger trailed down her neck and across her collarbone as his gaze dipped to her breasts, lingered, before raking slowly down her body to the triangle of curls between her legs, then back up to her face. Every inch of her tingled with anticipation. Every inch of her screamed for his touch. Seb withdrew his hand and grinned. 'You should also know I loathe your ringlets.'

'Has anyone ever told you that you talk too

much?' Because there were a hundred and one things she would prefer he did with his mouth at this precise moment and none of them involved discussing hair styles. The arrogant smile suited him. In that moment she realised he enjoyed teasing her and was well aware she was desperate for his touch and was denying it on purpose, the wretch. But Seb's restraint was paper thin. A rapid pulse beat in his neck and there was a tenseness around his jaw which he struggled to hide. Wasn't it wonderful that she knew him so intimately already? Confirmation that they were meant to be.

To torment him, Clarissa smoothed her palm down his abdomen and felt the taut line of muscles bunch beneath her fingers, then gave in to the temptation of touching him lower. His eyes closed and he sucked in a breath as she openly explored the length and shape with her fingertips with such deliberate slowness that his control soon snapped. On a growl, he rolled her to lie beneath him and plundered her mouth, his own hands doing some exploring of their own, smoothing over her body possessively.

When his lips closed around her nipple it was she who growled in appreciation, her body writhing on the mattress as he took his time to worship both breasts while her nails raked his back and scalp to anchor him in place. Her legs fell open and her hips bucked when he touched her sex, welcoming the strange intrusion and the new sensations it elicited, yet needed more. So much more.

Instinct made her position her body beneath his, made her hook her legs around his. Her body cradled his naturally, her hips rising to signal she was ready. Wordlessly, Seb gazed down into her eyes and began to gently edge inside, his arms braced and big body taut with the effort it took to give her the time she needed to become accustomed to his intrusion. Then he stilled, his expression pained. 'This bit might hurt at first. I'm sorry.'

'I'm not.' Clarissa grabbed his hips and lunged hers towards him, biting her lip against the slight discomfort and then marvelling at the intimacy of being wholly possessed by him. Only when he was certain the pain had passed did he begin to move and a whole new world of pleasure opened up. One that her body was apparently beyond ready for because it was wildly out of her control. Instinctually, her pelvis tilted to meet each thrust, her body tightening around his as all rational thoughts evaporated.

Open-mouthed kisses.

Needy sighs.

Nerve endings dancing with the strength of their passion. Nothing in the universe existed except him. She chanted his name over and over again like a mantra. Tears pricked at her eyes at the intensity of the emotion which seemed to fill her heart and clog her throat, merging with the physical and the carnal until Clarissa thought she would die from the joy of it all. The wonder.

Then he spoke. Just three simple words.

'I love you.'

Words she had never dared hope for, but which gave her battered soul absolution. And the brittle universe in which only they existed shattered into a million brilliant and blinding stars.

Chapter Twenty-One

Clarissa floated into the breakfast room, rejuvenated despite the few minutes of sleep she had managed to snatch between bouts of splendid lovemaking. Seb was already seated, looking more handsome than he ever had. She had watched him swallow at the sight of her, pleased that the simple, loose knot Agnes had arranged her hair in perfectly displayed its lack of curls. It was a statement. A declaration of love. One it was obvious he appreciated.

Breakfast was the least formal meal in the Penhurst house and guests seated themselves. This morning's bunch was sparse. Penny sat at the head of the table, Westbridge and the young usurper on one side and Seb sat alone on the other. Supremely conscious of his eyes on her, Clarissa loaded her plate with all the foods she usually deftly avoided. Because he adored her curves, and to her maid's utter consternation, she had insisted her stays should be looser and more comfortable this morning. It was a good job. Clarissa was famished. In fact, she could not remember a time when she had been this hungry. Confession truly was good for the soul. So was pleasure. Seb had invented a scandalous way of helping her consign his questions for Penny to memory. She had remembered them all much earlier than she let on, prolonging the sweet torture until all rational thought was impossible. She was going to thoroughly enjoy being his wife.

Not that he'd asked.

They had been too busy exploring each other to discuss the inevitable formalities.

Balancing a slice of toast onto the mountain of eggs and bacon on her plate, she took herself to the seat next to Seb.

'Good morning, my lord. How are you?'

'Never better, my lady. Yourself?'

'In fine fettle. The finest, in fact.' Thanks to his talented mouth and the glorious other parts of his anatomy. His knee came to rest next to hers proprietorially and desire bloomed afresh. Would they be able to sneak away some time this morning? Clarissa certainly hoped so. Making love to Seb was her new favourite form of exercise.

'Good morning, Lady Clarissa.'

The clipped tones of the Duke of Westbridge reminded her of his existence and reluctantly she tore her eyes away from her handsome lover to politely smile down the table. What on earth had she ever seen in the man? In a ridiculous profusion of lace, the Duke appeared annoyed. She couldn't muster the enthusiasm to care what about. 'Good morning, your Grace. And Lady Olivia. You look lovely today.' Clearly her good mood knew no bounds if she was tossing out compliments so blithely. But then Olivia was no longer competition now that Clarissa had won the real prize.

'You look…*different*. What *have* you done to your hair?' The younger woman's smile didn't touch her eyes.

'Nothing whatsoever. I left it as nature intended. It's wonderfully liberating. You should try it.'

'Alas, my hair is naturally curly.'

She felt Seb's warm palm smooth up her thigh under the table and swallowed the bubble of laughter that threatened. 'Lucky you. I have to sleep in uncomfortable rags to get mine to curl. I've decided to dispense with them henceforth.' Alongside her tighter corsets and her virginity. And the ridiculously constricting label of *Incomparable*. That, too, was part of her past and she was done pretending. Clarissa was going to be herself from now on. 'Could you pass the jam, Lady Olivia? I have a sudden craving for sweet things.'

The table fell silent as she smothered her toast

in a thick, crimson layer of raspberry preserve as if the concept of a young lady indulging in sugar in public were entirely alien. She supposed it was. They all curbed their natural desires and personalities to secure the right husband, a wholly pathetic notion now that she thought about it properly. Thanks to Seb, the blinkers Clarissa had worn for a decade had been totally discarded. There was a whole world outside of the claustrophobic confines of polite society where a woman's life was dictated by unreasonable expectations.

Frankly, it no longer mattered that she couldn't speak French or play an instrument, paint or embroider. She was loved rather than admired. Respected for her quick thinking and canny insight. Her new world involved espionage and excitement, passion and laughter. A meaningful sense of purpose. Love. None of those meant she needed to abandon her desire to have a family—only now she would be having a family with a man she adored rather than one who loved the façade she had painstakingly constructed and hidden behind all her adult life. The urge to paint a garish and childish rainbow was overwhelming.

'Penny, can I borrow your watercolours this morning?' With Seb off to meet his men this morning, she might as well indulge her whim.

'I didn't know you could draw?' Her friend sounded amused at the uncharacteristic request.

'I can't, but that doesn't mean I shouldn't.' She might even take a Mrs Radcliffe novel out on the lawn and struggle through it at a snail's pace. Feeling loved made Clarissa feel invincible.

'Then perhaps we should take a ride across the estate?' Never one to miss an opportunity, Lady Olivia pawed at Westbridge's scrawny arm.

'Would you care to ride with us, Lady Clarissa?' The ugly vein next to Westbridge's eye was pulsing. It almost put her off her jam.

'No, thank you. But the pair of you should go.' And ride off into the sunset together towards their inevitably miserable society marriage. With her blessing. 'I'm sure dear Olivia would prefer having you all to herself, your Grace.'

'I shall go and change immediately!' The barnacle practically bolted in case anyone changed their mind, her bird-sized breakfast already forgotten.

Penny was watching her intently, a question in her eyes. 'If you don't mind the company Clarissa, I should like to paint, too.'

'I should love some.' Although the prospect did dampen her buoyant mood, Seb needed answers and Clarissa needed to find a way of forewarning her friend of the chaos to come without compromising the mission. Seb squeezed her thigh in sympathy, then stood.

'I shall see you later, ladies.' His head tilted ever so slightly. 'Your Grace.'

She watched him leave with a definite spring in his step and grinned into her napkin. 'I should change also. Excuse me.' Westbridge clicked his heels like a Russian Prince and strode out as well, clearly fuming. That, too, made her smile.

'What's going on?' Penny darted from the carver chair at the end of the table to the one Seb had just vacated.

'I'm not sure what you mean?' The smug, satisfied smile refused to fade and she found herself grinning openly at her friend.

'Oh, really? The intensely longing gazes? The flirting? The surreptitious touching under the tablecloth! Are you enamoured of Lord Millcroft or is it just another ploy to force Westbridge's hand?'

'Westbridge proposed last night.' A bubble of laughter escaped. 'I said I needed to consider it— but I'm going to turn him down, Penny. Isn't that marvellous?'

'Because of Seb?'

'Yes, because of Seb! I'm in love, Penny. Deliriously, hopelessly head over heels in love with the man.' Something she should probably tell him at her earliest convenience, too. Last night he had barely given her time to breathe, let alone speak.

'You scarcely know him.'

'I know enough.'

Penny's voice dropped to a whisper. 'He has made fast friends with my husband.' Under normal circumstances a valid note of caution. 'I would hate for you to make the same mistakes I did.'

'Oh, Penny…' The guilt was unbearable. 'Leave Penhurst. Today. I'll help you. I'll buy you a cottage somewhere well away from him, you could change your name…'

'We have a son, Clarissa. I could never leave my baby behind.'

'I wasn't suggesting you did. I'm sure you'd both have a much happier life out of Penhurst's clutches.'

Penny glanced down at where Clarissa's hands had gripped both of hers tightly and stared. 'If only…'

'Let me help you. I guarantee I can have you out of this house before dinner.' If Seb could help a harlot escape he would help her friend, she knew that with the same certainty that she knew he loved her. 'Pack a small bag and…' She felt Penny's hands slide out of hers.

'If I did that, then he would hunt me down. Not for me, but for his heir. He has powerful connections and the law would be on his side. I would spend my whole life in fear, looking over my shoulder. When he caught me, and he would catch me, I'd lose my son for ever.' Resignation. Acceptance. Another forced sunny smile. 'Besides, it's not so bad. Penhurst spends so little time here that I frequently get to forget he exists.'

As one door closed, another always opened. 'How often is he here?'

'Millcroft. A word.' Seb felt his hackles rise at Westbridge's summons, but forced a bland expression as he turned around.

'Your Grace?' He made damn sure he didn't incline his head one jot this time and pulled himself to stand at his full height for good measure.

'In private. A gentleman doesn't discuss matters of import in the hallway.' The Duke barged past into the morning room, expecting Seb to follow.

'Is this going to take long, only the stables are expecting me and I had planned a morning ride myself.' Folding his arms, he sat on the arm of a convenient sofa and looked bored.

'I wish to talk about your inappropriate relationship with Lady Clarissa.'

'That is none of your business.'

'I'm afraid it is. We are betrothed.'

Impossible. 'Does she know?' The flippant tone made the Duke turn bright red with indignation.

'Of course she knows. I proposed yesterday.

The banns are being read at St George's next Sunday. We agreed to keep the engagement a secret until she could speak to her family in person.'

The bile rose in Seb's throat. Gem had made no mention of it yesterday or last night as she lay in his arms. The windbag was lying. He had to be lying. 'If I were you, I would talk to her again.'

'I have. Just now, as a matter of fact, and she reiterated her joy at becoming my duchess. The Countess of Penhurst will bear witness as she was there and sworn to secrecy.'

The room tilted and for a moment Seb feared he might see his breakfast again. Only stubborn pride covered the pain. 'Congratulations.'

'Thank you. I shall pass on your felicitations to *my* fiancée.'

'I would rather pass them on myself.' He wouldn't believe it. She had given him her innocence. Flirted with him this morning. Entrusted him with a secret she hadn't dared confide to another soul. He loved her. He'd told her. She hadn't reciprocated the declaration…

'I'm sure you would. Which brings me to my main point—Clarissa has asked me to inform you that your attentions are no longer required. They served an *obvious* purpose—' the Duke smiled in that condescending manner the aristocracy did so well '—because your little ruse worked, but frankly she was never going to consider a mere lord now, was she?'

He's a duke.

How many times had Gem uttered those words? Too many—as if dukes were the be all and end all...but would she be that callous? The nagging voice of experience in his head spoke with bitter memories. People of his lowly status *were* insignificant and disposable. Shamelessly cast aside when they had served their purpose. 'What ruse?'

'Her little plan to make me jealous. She confessed it all a few minutes ago after your outrageous display at the dining table.' If Westbridge knew that then she had told him. The betrayal was like a knife in the back. 'Obviously, propriety dictates that such behaviour has to cease immediately. Duchesses need to be beyond reproach. Clarissa understands that and therefore has decided to sever all ties with you.'

He was disposable.

Of course he was.

Like his mother before him Seb had been a means to an end. Entertainment. Callously tossed aside now that he had *served his purpose.*

Even though he was dying inside, he returned the smug smile. 'Tell my lady that I was glad I could be of service.' Blessedly, his legs still worked, allowing him to stand and saunter to the door. They carried him at a respectable pace to the stables, got him astride his horse and made that horse trot sedately out of sight of the house.

Only then did he allow the molten rage at his own stupidity to vent as he kicked his mount into a gallop and howled at the sky, his heart sliced in two.

Chapter Twenty-Two

Seb failed to materialise for luncheon as he had promised. Clarissa tried not to be concerned. After the smuggling ship had offloaded last night she supposed the mission was at its most critical stage. Plans would need to be put in place. Reinforcements and the proper authorities would have to be summoned. Instead she helped herself to extra potatoes and did her best to appear interested in Westbridge's conversation. Annoyingly, he was seated beside her. More annoyingly the other Duke, the one she ferociously hated, was sat the other side. Feigning civility to the man who had beaten Seb and ruined his childhood was proving to be more difficult with each passing minute. Each time he spoke, the urge to stab him in the forehead with her fork was overwhelming. In fact, the urge to stab a few of the so-called gentlemen seated at this table with a fork was overwhelming.

Penny was subdued. They'd had a long and frank discussion about the state of her marriage and the perils of marrying the wrong man, and whilst her friend was still convinced Seb was the wrong man, discussing her own troubles, so long bottled up, had stirred up emotions that up to now had been private. As Clarissa had long suspected, Penhurst's cruelty was physical as well as mental and he was not averse to beating her if she spoke out of turn or displeased him. Which she apparently did without trying.

The viscount's infidelities were more than an open secret. They were another stick to beat his wife with. The monster revelled in telling his wife all the sordid details of his affairs, comparing her body to the harlots he preferred as he forced himself on her. Those debasing violations, Penny had assured her, weeping, happened less and less, and she would still not hear of leaving him because of her son. That baby and the long stretches of her husband's absence were Penny's salvation. His visits home a nightmare. All bar one of the dates Seb had given her married with the days Penhurst had graced his wife with his presence and subjected her to his abuse.

Clarissa hoped he hanged and was more resolved than ever to help free her friend from the life she had never deserved. It was an extreme solution, but a fitting one for Penhurst. He caught her looking at him and raised his glass, already drinking wine in the middle of the day.

'Do you have any idea when Millcroft will be back?' It was the third time he had enquired in the space of an hour. Penhurst's interest bothered her.

'Soon, I am sure.'

'I hope so, for I have something to… Ah! Talk of the Devil and the Devil shall appear.'

Seb strode in and little bubbles of excitement popped in her belly as she waited for him to glance at her in the same heated way he had over breakfast. He didn't look at her. 'I'm sorry I'm late— but it is a lovely day and I lost track of time.' He snapped open the napkin as he sat in a chair next to Penhurst at the opposite end of the long table.

'Better late than never, old chap.' The viscount leaned his head and whispered in Seb's ear. Clarissa strained to hear, but had to settle for seeing Seb nod and then whisper back. Their covert conversation paused as the servants dished up his food and then it continued in earnest. Once it was done, he concentrated on eating, a tightness about his jaw and brows she had never seen before.

'Did you have a pleasant ride, my lord?' It wasn't strictly polite to talk down the table, but then as it wasn't polite to whisper either, Clarissa didn't care. For the first time his eyes lifted to meet hers and burned. But not with passion or longing or shared secrets. The venom in them shocked her.

'Very.' And as if she were suddenly as insignificant to him as Penny was to Penhurst, he turned his head and plunged head-first into a mumbled discussion with Lord Gaines. Whatever he was talking about, it had all of Penhurst's odious cronies chortling to the exclusion of the rest of the diners, Clarissa most definitely included.

It had been a pointed cut, and a public one, although she didn't know why. Rattled, she went back to her plate and tried to ignore her own hurt at the slight and Penny's weighted stare. There was probably a very good reason why he was ignoring her. Hadn't he once cautioned that if he ever appeared rude or obnoxious she should pay it no mind because he was playing Millcroft?

As soon as the meal ended, he was off as if his breeches were on fire, and his foot was already on the stairs to the east wing before she caught up with him. 'Seb!' He stilled, but didn't turn around at first. When he did, his hostile expression had been replaced by one of bland indifference.

'My lady.' No mischievous stare. No warmth. No nothing.

'Is something wrong?'

'Should there be?'

'I don't know.' He was being Millcroft yet

there was nobody close by to witness it. Just to be sure she scanned the hallway. Aside from the ever-present footman at the front door they were alone—but the footmen had ears and he was right to be cautious.

'You are acting very peculiarly... The morning room should be empty.' She tugged at his arm and felt it stiffen to granite beneath her fingers. The icy coldness made her panic. 'Please, Seb.'

'We have nothing to talk about, *my lady*.'

'Of course we do...' How dared he? They had *everything* to talk about. Their future. Their hopes and dreams. Their wedding. 'Why are you angry?'

'Stop playing games. *I know*.'

'Know what?' Now he was talking in riddles and her own temper flared. 'Stop this nonsense. What happened this morning? What is the plan?' She was aware she was babbling, but his behaviour was so uncharacteristic it was frightening.

With deliberate slowness he uncurled her hand from his elbow and stepped away. 'Stay in your room tonight. By tomorrow it will all be over.'

'Stay in my room!' Had he lost his wits? 'No!' She reached for him and he stepped away. 'I want to be with you. Don't you dare try to shut me out! I'm helping you. You *need* me to help you!'

'I don't *need* you at all!' He spat it with such venom she recoiled. Seb's cool, detached composure had cracked and his face contorted into a snarl, one he tempered as the two Dukes entered the vast hallway and began to walk in their direction. He barely inclined his head to them, adjusted his cuffs and turned his smile to her. His usually dark, stormy eyes were dead behind the irises. 'We are done, Gem. We have *both* more than served our purpose.' Then he calmly, cruelly, walked away.

Clarissa wanted to go after him and demand an explanation but a public slanging match—because that was what Seb's dreadful behaviour warranted—was out of the question in front of witnesses. One of them would let slip something in anger and potentially jeopardise the mission. She swallowed her temper and stalked to the opposite staircase.

'Clarissa?'

'What?' She didn't bother smiling at Westbridge.

'If you have a moment I would like a word.'

'About?' Not that she cared, her mind was too busy trying to work out why Seb was fuming. What exactly had happened between breakfast and lunch to turn him from an adoring lover to a snarling stranger? It was so out of character. Something must be very wrong.

'The question I asked yesterday.'

Oh, good gracious—she had completely forgotten about that. Westbridge's lacklustre proposal

was so low on her list of priorities it had not occurred to her to respond. Not when there had been
Penny's woes, smugglers, and scorching kisses in
the rain and earth-shattering passion in her bedchamber. 'Thank you for your proposal.' Because
Lord only knew she had waited long enough for
it. 'But the answer is no.'

'No?' The Duke gaped, incredulous. 'Are you
toying with me?'

'Not at all. I gave the matter careful consideration…'

'Hardly careful consideration if your answer
is no!'

Pompous windbag! 'I do not love you, your
Grace. If I am honest, I am not altogether sure I
even like you.'

The ugly blood vessel next to his eye rose and
began to twitch with indignation. For the longest
time he said nothing, then his face changed. 'I see
what this is about.' His finger wagged amongst
the profusion of lace. 'I made you wait—ergo, you
are getting your own back.'

'Not at all…'

'I shall redouble my efforts to court you.'

'That would make no difference!' The stupid
man wasn't listening to her at all. As usual. 'I
don't want you to court me. The truth is…'

'The truth is as plain as the nose on your face

and I will enjoy the chase. What would you like? Flowers? Jewels?'

'Nothing. I want nothing from you.'

'Love poetry, perhaps? Something that does justice to your beauty.'

Good grief, she could think of nothing worse. 'You are quite mistaken, your Grace. I want nothing from you. Not even your company henceforth…'

He grinned. It didn't suit him. 'Leave it with me. I shall surprise you.'

'Oh, for pity's sake!'

'And I shall begin at once.'

'You would be wasting your breath.' But Clarissa was talking to his back. Imbued with a sense of purpose, the Duke was off on a mission of his own. So be it. She had better things to do than chase after the fool and correct him. He would get the message soon enough when she became Mrs Leatham. And she *would* become Mrs Leatham because Seb loved her. The real him had said so and he had meant it regardless of the nonsense he had spewed just now. A man who made love to her so ardently and with such tenderness couldn't fake those feelings. Seb adored her. The real her. And she adored him, too. Something that was far too precious to lose. She would let him cool down, then have it out with him, and if that failed she would knock him over his thick head with her redundant curling iron and drag him to the altar.

Men!

'The Excise Men will arrive here at eight just after everyone is seated at dinner.'

The sight of Gray in his bedchamber, diligently cleaning his pistols, was not what Seb wanted. Not yet. He needed at least twenty minutes to smash every stick of furniture in the room before he was truly capable of reason. Perhaps an hour. Three. Twelve. He suppressed the rage and the pain and grunted in response.

'What's wrong?' His second paused, dropped the rag and frowned. 'Do we have a problem?'

'No.'

'Really? Only you look ready to commit murder.'

He was. Westbridge, his long-lost brother. Gem. He wanted to wring her damned neck. He knew better than to expect, to covet what he couldn't have, yet the ache in his chest was crippling him. 'I'm merely eager to get this mission over with.' Which was why Seb was rushing the conclusion when all they really had was more circumstantial evidence. Nothing a thorough search of the Penhurst cellar wouldn't remedy if his gut instinct was correct. Nothing had left by road, so the illegal brandy still had to be there. The viscount was

probably waiting for all the guests to leave before
he shifted it. Most were leaving tomorrow. He had
already informed the butler and his brow-beaten
hostess he would be one of them. If the contraband wasn't in the cellar, then he'd deal with the
dire consequences later. It wasn't as if he could
feel any worse. 'I've had about as much of society
as I can stomach.'

'Not all society though.' His friend winked.
'Dawkins mentioned he saw you kissing a certain
lady on the Downs last night.' The reminder was
like a blow that winded him. His grief must have
been obvious because Gray's roguish grin was replaced swiftly with sympathy. 'Oh…right…well,
I've cleaned all the guns. I'll hang around here,
watch the cellar, etcetera, until they arrive. The
rest of the men will make their way towards the
house later. There's a coastguard vessel anchored
in the harbour as plain as day in case they get any
ideas of moving the stuff before tonight and, of
course, the other ships will flood the bay just before the off. Lord Fennimore has been summoned
and should be well on his way by now. Anything
I've missed?'

Only the complete annihilation of hope. 'No.
We're all set.'

'What are you plans for the afternoon?'

To die inside. 'Act normally. Penhurst has ar-

ranged a shooting competition for the gentlemen.'
Which blessedly spared him the sight of her.

'A timely bit of target practice will warm you
up for tonight.' Gray watched him tear the cravat
from his neck and throw it to the ground, then
slam the wardrobe door shut after he had grabbed
the 'shooting' clothes the tailor had made for him.
So many stupid outfits. So many stupid rules. Oh,
how he hated the aristocracy! 'Do we trust you to
hold a gun? In your current mood...'

'Back off, Gray!'

His friend's dark eyebrows raised, but he wisely
clamped his smart mouth shut. As Seb quickly
dressed, he went back to cleaning the pistol. Just
as well. The need to resort to violence to relieve
the agonising tension in his body was palpable.
But this wasn't Gray's fault. It was his. He'd allowed himself to be seduced by the exact sort
of woman he loathed the most. The judgemental,
spoiled, pampered princesses of society. Gem
wasn't from his world. Didn't adhere to the same
rules of conduct he did. Her blood was as blue
as her eyes and his, as far as her world was concerned, didn't pass muster.

And she had lied to him.

Perhaps not with actual words, but certainly
with her deeds. Last night, during all the time
they were alone together, while they had discussed
her doubts about her Duke and lost themselves in

each other, she had omitted telling him one significant yet fundamentally critical detail. Westbridge had proposed.

And she hadn't said no.

Which explained their lengthy discussion about the pros and cons of marrying the man, yet clearly being pompous, self-centred and devoid of all emotion paled into insignificance because of the lofty fact he was a duke.

It didn't make Seb feel any better when he slammed out of the bedchamber and stamped down the stairs, but when he saw Westbridge and his awful brother guffawing next to Penhurst and his cronies on the lawn a part of him died inside. It took all seven years of his training to strap on the mask of Lord Millcroft. There was nothing left but to act like Millcroft, as well.

'One hundred pounds says I can outshoot any man here!'

Chapter Twenty-Three

The commotion on the back lawn made small talk with the other ladies over afternoon tea on the terrace problematic. The tea long drunk and the balmy afternoon now definitely early evening and they were still at it while the ladies waited for them. Random gunfire followed by raucous shouting and laughter peppered the air while Seb's name was mentioned many times. He was in the thick of it which was galling in the extreme. Knowing he was having fun while Clarissa was still fuming didn't improve her mood.

'Well, ladies, as it doesn't look like the gentlemen will be joining us after all, I suggest we all retire to change for dinner.' Penny stood, signalling the end of their interminable gathering and one by one the ladies drifted off. Clarissa lingered, waiting till she was all alone before vacating the chair which had become part of her backside and marching with purpose towards the furthest end of the garden. Surely the silly shooting match couldn't go on much longer?

But when she rounded the shrubbery it was apparent it could, although seemingly nearing some kind of crescendo as only Seb and the Duke of Thetford were still armed. The others were all huddled together, watching intently as a pair of footmen heaved a target further away. Spotting her, Westbridge broke away from the pack and strode towards her.

'You picked an excellent time to spectate. Thetford is about to issue that upstart his well-deserved comeuppance.'

'Really?' Of all the opponents Seb could be pitted against in the grand finale, it had to be his brother. That couldn't be good, especially if Seb lost. 'Who's winning?'

'It's a tie so far, but Thetford is a crack shot.'

If he was one of the last two men standing so was Seb, although that fact didn't surprise her. In his profession, his life and that of others probably depended on him being handy with a gun. His skill would have been honed out of necessity rather than picking off partridges and pigeons for fun. As if he sensed her, Seb's eyes turned to where they were standing. His expression might be blank, but his eyes were shooting daggers. His free hand formed a fist where it hung at his side. To vex him she smiled at the Duke and saw those frozen eyes narrow to slits. 'Penny sent me to re-mind you all that dinner is in less than two hours.'

'I'm looking forward to dinner.' Westbridge said this with the contrived smugness of a man who knew something she didn't—or thought he did. It served as a timely reminder to check the seating arrangements with Penny in case she got saddled with him again. Now that there wasn't a hope in hell she was going to marry the man, Clarissa would be damned if she would endure an-other one of his self-centred and self-aggrandising conversations. Nor would she suffer through an-other futile attempt at turning him down. If West-bridge didn't listen that was his problem, not hers. Clarissa had enough of her own. And one in par-ticular that was still glaring at her with a pistol in his hand.

'Are you ready, gentlemen?' The timely call from Lord Gaines saved her from Seb's accus-ing stare—because it *was* accusatory, she now realised—despite now being focused on the tar-get. What had got his hackles up?

His half-brother stepped forward, rotated his fat neck and aimed. The bullet hit the target, but it was hard to make out where because of the dis-tance. The two footmen merged from the side, picked it up and jogged with it towards Lord Gaines, who seemed to be the referee.

'A splendid shot! Bravo!' Westbridge began to

clap his hands next to her, then as an aside said, 'He's clipped the outer edge of the bull's eye', in case she was too stupid to have seen the gaping hole for herself.

Gaines pulled out a ruler and measured. 'Two inches shy. Well done, your Grace.'

Thetford inclined his head regally as the other gentlemen cheered and then offered Seb a patronising smile, completely unaware that in doing so he had probably signed his death warrant. Seb wouldn't allow himself to be beaten by a duke, especially when that Duke was the one he hated the most. The steely determination was written all over his face as the poor footmen did another dash to the furthest end of the garden and repositioned the target in the same spot. He stepped forward. The men immediately hushed when he aimed.

'Millcroft lacks the finesse of his opponent.' Westbridge practically bellowed his criticism into the silence, oblivious of his rudeness, but clearly intent on putting Seb off his shot. His dark head whipped around to glare, his eyes narrowed and then it whipped back. In that same moment he squeezed the trigger, barely taking aim. The musket ball whizzed through the air and exploded through the target. Then he dropped the pistol on the ground and stood arrogantly with his arms folded as the servants scurried to fetch it back.

'Your plan backfired.'

'Excuse me?'

'You tried to give the Duke of Thetford the advantage. That was very unsporting, your Grace.'

'I'm not sure what you mean?' Westbridge had the nerve to look affronted at the suggestion.

'Then let me say it plainly. If Lord Millcroft's shot is off, then it will be as a direct result of your flagrant cheating on Thetford's behalf.' But she could already see that the Duke had failed. Seb's bullet had gone clean through the centre of the bull's eye. Lord Gaines pulled out his ruler for effect, then tossed it away.

'I declare Lord Millcroft the winner!'

Seb was immediately surrounded by every gentleman accepting their hearty congratulations bar the two vile Dukes. In a shocking display of equally unsportsmanlike belligerence, Thetford turned on his heel and stormed off into the trees.

'How dare you call me a cheat!'

'I merely say it as I see it, your Grace. You timed your outburst to put Lord Millcroft off. It was a low blow and you should be ashamed of yourself.' Out of the corner of her eye, Clarissa saw Seb striding across the lawn at a tangent towards the house. Any faster and he would break into a run. The dratted man intended to avoid her again and had plotted his course accordingly. 'If you will excuse me.' She picked up her skirts and followed him at pace, but her legs were no match for his significantly longer ones.

'Lord Millcroft! Wait!'

He heard her, she saw, because he stiffened before he sped up, then darted out of sight behind the shrubbery. By the time Clarissa got there, there was no sign of him. She stopped dead and checked left and right, cursing him silently for his well-honed skills at blending into the shadows. Trust her to fall in love with a spy! And one who headed a group of men called the Invisibles! He was probably lurking in the bushes right now, watching her and biding his time until she gave up. 'When I get my hands on you, I am going to strangle you!'

Silence.

'I know you can hear me, Seb Leatham!'

Behind her a twig snapped and a boot emerged from the bushes. 'Leatham?' Her initial relief quickly turned to fear at the sight of the Duke of Thetford's outraged face. *'Sebastian Leatham?'*

Seb knew he was being cowardly as he darted into the door next to the kitchen. Yet he still took the dark servants' corridor and stairs back to his bedchamber. Watching her cosying up to that fool Westbridge in plain view was horrendous. The fact that she would do so right under his nose after last night was just plain cruel. His bedchamber was thankfully empty when he arrived in it, although Gray had laid out his evening clothes before disappearing.

He dressed quickly and, for the first time since he had met her, without any thought. Or so he told himself as he stubbornly refused to check his reflection in the mirror. What difference would it make if his hair was mussed or his chin needed shaving? A quick swipe of a razor over his stubbly jaw wasn't going to alter things. If he looked a wreck, it matched how he felt. Wretched and broken. The bullet which had almost killed him had hurt less.

But he had nearly gone back for more.

When she had followed him across the lawn and called to him, Seb had wanted to stop and forgive her, accepting whatever half-cocked and shoddy explanation she gave him simply because he couldn't bear the thought of tonight being the end. What if she had wanted him again tonight or in the future when the bloom had faded from her advantageous, passionless marriage to her Duke? The married women of the aristocracy took lovers all the time. Both partners did. It was the way of things once the obligatory heir and a spare had come squalling into the world. But then what? Having part of her rather the whole would be torture. Never-ending and soul-destroying torture. Yet he was tempted. That was why he had quickened his pace and effectively hidden himself away for the better part of an hour. Self-preservation.

Perhaps this was how his mother had been with his father? Devastated at not being important enough to truly matter but so hopelessly in love that she accepted whatever crumbs he tossed her way? Seb had seen how tragically that had ended and had no desire to allow history to repeat itself. Ultimately it was better this way. Sever all ties cleanly and then let this new and agonising open wound heal over. He snatched up his pocket watch and glanced at it impatiently.

Dinner started in five minutes; many of the guests would already be seated. In twenty, the King's Elite would come and within an hour his mission would be over. All he had to do was avoid her till then.

He took the servants' stairs back down just in case and emerged near to the door of the dining room, only to stop dead in his tracks. Gem was there waiting for him, watching the grand staircase while wringing her hands as if in the same turmoil as him. Wearing the same dress she had worn on the shooting field, her usually perfect coiffure wilting. The loose tendrils framing her face poker-straight. Seb considered retreating back the way he had come, but she sensed him and turned around. Her lovely eyes wider than he had ever seen them.

'Oh, Seb! Thank the Lord...'

He couldn't do this. Wouldn't do this. He held up his hand and surged towards the sanctuary of the dining room. 'Not now.' And not ever.

'But, Seb!' She grabbed his arm and tugged. 'Something unexpected has happened that I really *need* to tell you about.'

Ruthlessly, he used his superior strength to escape and straightened his coat. Then ploughed through the door, fighting to compose himself in front of the sea of aristocratic faces sat at the table. 'Good evening.'

'There you are, Millcroft!' Penhurst stood and stepped away from his chair. 'You've been a difficult fellow to peg down today. My wife tells me you are leaving on the morrow. Early.'

'Indeed. I have neglected my affairs long enough.'

'Talking of which, I have something I have been meaning to discuss with you. Do you have a few minutes?'

'But, my dear, the soup is about to be served,' Penny stated.

'Then tell the kitchens to wait!' Penhurst snapped at his wife as if she were a servant and just like one she shot to her feet and went off to do his bidding. He leaned closer and whispered in Seb's ear, 'I think you will be very interested in what I have to say. Especially after you see the contents of my cellar.'

Chapter Twenty-Four

Seb re-emerged into the hallway with Penhurst just as Clarissa had steeled herself to go in and try to find a way to drag him out. He stopped dead and stared at her for a second, then the pair of them walked away as if she didn't exist. They rounded the corner and she heard his deep voice.

'If you will excuse me for a moment, I believe I dropped something...' Miraculously he darted back towards her, but his expression was determined rather than angry. 'Ah—there is my stick-pin!' As the diamond was safely nestled in his cravat, she knew instinctively something was afoot. Seb kneeled before her and pretended to pick it up, then still on the floor made a show of replacing it. 'Go to the drive. Find Gray.' His voice was so soft she had to crane her ears to hear him. 'Tell him to delay for twenty minutes.' He stood and bowed. 'Warn him I will be in the cellar.' His eyes flicked subtly to the side where Penhurst stood waiting.

She swept into a curtsy of acknowledgement. 'My lord.' The Duke of Thetford could wait. She hovered until both men were safely out of sight, then headed to the front door. Two footmen stood guarding it, so she changed direction and, thinking on her feet, veered back towards the dining room and the servants' door Seb had emerged from. There had to be a better way out of this house than in plain sight and the Penhurst servants were excellent at blending into the background. She followed the sound of the kitchen and found a door out to the garden, then, keeping low and close to the house, she skirted its perimeter until she saw the drive ahead.

'Can I help you, my lady?' Another footman stepped away from his sentry post. She sailed towards him, looking pained.

'I have a headache. I thought a little air might clear my head before dinner.'

'Then surely the gardens provide a better view?'

The faked sneeze was wet and explosive. 'The evening pollen…' She aimed the second sneeze to hit his face. 'I'm so sorry… I'll ju-ju-ju-just…' he instinctively backed away while she rummaged in her pocket for her handkerchief '…walk on the gr-gr-gravel if you don't mind.' She buried her nose in the linen and blew and he waved her on. Still sniffling, Clarissa didn't wait for him to change his mind.

'Gray? Gray?' She kept her head straight ahead, her eyes searching the bushes. 'Anyone?' She was a good three hundred yards from the house when one of the Invisibles appeared, still shrouded by the foliage he was hiding in.

'He's still watching you.'

She stopped and sneezed again, noticing that indeed the footman was scrutinising her every move. Wiping her nose, she whispered the message, then dithered as the Invisible blended back into the shadows. Then she casually sauntered along the drive a bit more before turning around and making herself stroll slowly back, offering the footmen a sunny, bunged smile as she wandered past him.

'Shouldn't you go in the front door, my lady?'

She paused mid-step and grinned, nodding. 'Probably wise. I don't want to set off another sneezing fit.'

The footman accompanied her to the heavy oak door and used his fist to bash on it, effectively transferring her into the care of one of the other guards, then bade her a good evening. Back in the house, the most prudent course of action seemed to be to go back into the dining room and wait, but Seb was in the cellar with Penhurst. All alone.

Who knew what dangers lurked there? She had her fingers around the door handle when she decided prudence could go to hell in a handcart and, when the footmen turned, swiftly escaped through the handy servants' door again.

The kitchen loomed brightly ahead, the door now flung open to let out some of the heat. Quite rightly, the kitchen staff were grumbling about the delay in service, the cook the most vocal. Her cream soup would curdle if she kept it on the heat much longer, yet doubtless they would all be blamed for their ineptitude by the master when he was served a disaster. Clarissa inched her face around the corner and waited until the coast was clear before daring to cross the narrow space to the staircase that led down to the cellars. Silently she tiptoed down, then pressed her back against the wall at the sound of voices, neither of which she recognised. More sentries, no doubt. A man who guarded all exits and his gardens wouldn't leave the place he hid his smuggled brandy unsecured.

It also presented Clarissa with a very real problem. Theatrical sneezing wouldn't get her past the guards. Nothing would. Venturing further down would put Seb in jeopardy. For now, Penhurst had no reason to suspect he was a spy, or at least she hoped he didn't. Therefore, until Gray arrived with the cavalry, all she could do was wait. Preferably close by. Back in the corridor, she tested the other doors. The linen closet would have to do for now.

Penhurst said nothing as he led Seb down the cavernous tunnel chiselled into the chalk. He had already been warned that his life henceforth depended on his silence and had agreed that, if the pickings were as rich as the viscount had alluded, then he was prepared to take the risk. They had long left the empty cellar behind—barren aside from the four burly and armed individuals who nested there—and if he were to hazard a guess at his actual location he assumed he was either under the gardens or under the Downs beyond. A solid white wall of chalk loomed ahead of them, a small padlocked door sat central in the rock. Only then did Penhurst stop.

'Before we go any further, let me explain what I need. If you are not the man to provide it, then our little tour ends here.'

Seb folded his arms and said nothing.

'How serious are you about investing in more hells?'

'Serious enough to have purchased a building in Covent Garden. I sign the papers tomorrow evening upon my return to town.'

'Just the one, then.'

'For now, although it won't be long before I

have a string of them. I have the capital. All I need to do is buy more buildings and persuade the current owners of the established houses to sell theirs to me.'

'You seem arrogantly sure that will happen.'

'I can be very persuasive. Either they sell the businesses to me or I sell them down the river. Or I destroy them with the competition. My fortunes can withstand a year or two of drought while I undercut their prices and lure their clientele away. Give me two years and I'll have a controlling hand on every lucrative hell in London. That's what I did in Sydney. Some I built from scratch and some I procured along the way. Once I set my mind to something, I do whatever it takes.'

'Just as you did with the delectable Lady Clarissa. One of my servants saw you leaving her room before the sun came up this morning. Seems you got to sample the goods before she skips down the aisle with Westbridge.' The knowing leer made Seb's blood boil both at the insult to Gem and the reminder of her treachery. But she wasn't his to avenge. Never truly had been.

'As I said, once I set my mind to something… The lady was ripe for the picking and now that she has been *thoroughly* picked he's welcome to her. She'll warm my bed again if I click my fingers, which I might do for my own amusement. Cuckolding a duke might be fun.' The smug, satisfied grin must have been convincing because Penhurst threw his head back and laughed.

'You're a ruthless bastard, Millcroft. That's what I like about you. I think we will make a good partnership.'

'You are assuming I will want to invest.'

'On the contrary, my dear fellow. I am assuming you will want to *buy*, because behind that door is your means to undercut your rivals with the finest French brandy for the cheapest price. Or the cheapest brandy for a pittance. Either way you can't lose. You can buy it all or sell it to the other hells for me on commission.'

'Wouldn't you get more on the open market?'

'I already sell vats of the stuff on the open market every day, but I'm pragmatic and always open to *another* market. The more lucrative the better. With your connections, and ruthless ambition, I could soon be the sole supplier of all the hells in London.'

Penhurst removed the padlock and pushed the door open, then hung back to allow Seb to enter, closing it swiftly behind him and securing the padlock. The cave was vast and stacked high with barrels. Hundreds of beautiful wooden caskets filled with conclusive, irrefutable evidence.

'Impressive.' Seb walked around the room as if taking stock, his eyes scanning the space for potential danger. No hidden guards. Another heavy, locked door, obviously leading to the cliffs, was directly opposite. Aside from that and the one they had just walked down there were no others. When his men arrived, Penhurst would be surrounded. Caught red-handed amongst his ill-gotten gains. All Seb had to do was keep him in the trap.

'Who does it come from?'

The viscount touched his nose in response. 'You are not the only one with contacts. Only a fool would cut his nose off to spite his face and I am no fool. My suppliers are mine to know, just as your contacts are yours. It's less messy that way.'

'It also keeps the overall power in your hands.'

'And minimises the risk. The Excise Men are damned idiots, but the less people know, the less chance there is of them learning about my little gold mine. And it is a gold mine. Be in no doubt.'

'I take it Lord Gaines is in on this.'

'You ask a great many questions when you should be chomping at the bit at the fortuitous opportunity I have just laid at your feet.'

'I'll be risking my neck. Only a fool would enter into a business arrangement with criminals without knowing all the pertinent facts and I am no fool either. I will need to know which men I am working closest with. If I don't trust them, then I won't put my money in. So I'll ask again—is Gaines involved?'

Penhurst shrugged, unoffended. If anything,

Seb's caution appeared to impress him. 'He is. Regis, too.'

'And Westbridge?'

Penhurst snorted and shook his head. 'Good grief, no! The man is an idiot. I keep him close because he's good for the reputation and useful to a man in my position. A convenient duke in the hand works wonders and opens so many illustrious doors. Only a fool lets a duke go.'

A bitter truth indeed.

Seb's well-trained ears heard a single footstep in the distance. Any second now and all hell would break loose. 'Any chance I could try before I buy?'

Chapter Twenty-Five

Clarissa wasn't entirely sure what she was expecting, but the sheer speed of the house being invaded and being completely overrun with what she presumed was uniformed men with guns was staggering. The noise of so many pairs of boots swarming through the rooms and corridor and up the stairs had to have tipped Penhurst off. Had Seb anticipated that? Had he planned for every eventuality or was he all alone, held hostage by the viscount and whatever guards were amassed down there?

Not being privy to the final preparations, she had no idea and the worry was killing her. When those heavy boots clattered towards her, she burst out of the closet, intent on telling them to hurry up, not expecting the barrels of six muskets to be immediately pointed at her face.

'She's with us!' Gray pushed to the front as the

Excise Men surged down the stairs towards the cellar. 'Are you all right?'

'Seb's down there all alone!'

'Not for much longer. We'll get him out safely.' To prove his point, Penhurst's guards emerged from the stairwell with their hands on their heads and muskets prodding them between the shoulder blades.

A shot went off, and she panicked, only to hear that the lock had been blown so that the King's men could file into the cellar. 'Stay here!' Gray left her to join the others and, as quickly as they had arrived, Clarissa found herself stood all alone again. Waiting.

She waited a full three seconds before she plunged down the stairs herself. With no clear plan of action other than being there in case Seb needed her, Clarissa followed the men through the cellar and then along the never-ending tunnel beyond. They all gathered at the impasse of the door. Gray stood with his back to the frame and bellowed. 'We have you surrounded, Penhurst! Open this door and come out slowly with your hands up.'

When there was no reply, he issued another warning, then motioned for one of his men to fire at the lock. He entered first, crouching low, then signalled with his hands. Two more men, neither in any uniform save that of a labourer, followed him inside. A few seconds later they declared the chamber safe.

Once again, Clarissa tacked herself on to the end of the line as they streamed into the hollowed-out cavern. Huge wooden barrels were stacked from floor to ceiling. Another door remained bolted and padlocked from the inside, but there was no sign of Penhurst or Seb.

An older gentleman Clarissa hadn't noticed before was in deep conversation with Gray and another man. 'There must be another cellar.'

'If there is, Lord Fennimore, then I haven't found it.' Gray looked baffled. 'Unless Penhurst took him somewhere else.'

'It's possible, I suppose. There are certainly no signs of a struggle.'

At the word *struggle* Clarissa instinctively scanned the ground for signs of blood. It was then that she saw something shimmer on the ground to the left. She stepped towards it and bent to pick it up. Seb's diamond stick-pin. It wasn't bent or misshapen. It hadn't been ripped off his cravat in a fight. Instead the little plug at the bottom had been carefully put back on the sharp end of the pin and it had been placed on the ground. Seb had left a clue.

While the men wasted valuable time pondering, Clarissa began to search the area where the pin had been placed, hoping it was significant.

Finding nothing, she got down on her hands and knees and began to feel the floor, the sides of the barrels. Her fingers found the latch before she saw it. 'Over here!' The barrel was sawn in two, one side was hinged. She pulled it open and revealed a small tunnel leading off it. Not wanting to trail at the rear, she lunged through it first, feeling her way with her arms extended, oblivious of the pitch-black darkness beyond. She stumbled as she hit a staircase and found herself bathed in dim lamplight.

'Wait.' Gray's voice was hushed, but his grip on her shoulder was insistent. 'If Penhurst escaped through this secret passageway, then we have the advantage. Let's not spoil that with hasty and ill-conceived rescue attempts. We have the element of surprise.'

They did and he was right. Behind him there was Lord Fennimore and the tall blond man. Both men had pistols in their hands. 'Leave this to us, young lady.'

'I'm coming with you.'

'You will only be in the way.'

'Did you see the stick-pin? Did you find the hidden doorway or this passageway?'

'She has a point.' The tall man smiled. 'And she probably knows this house and its occupants far better than all of us.'

Lord Fennimore sighed as if greatly put upon.

Then shrugged. 'A fair point, Flint. Make sure she stays safely behind us then.' The older man pushed past and forged forward, carrying the miserly lantern aloft. 'Let's see where this tunnel ends, shall we?'

The narrow passage twisted and turned. In places it was so low they had to drop on all fours to navigate it. After an eternity it branched out into two, but with no point of reference in this dark, subterranean world, it was impossible to know which to take. 'One has to be an escape route out to the Downs.' Knowing Penhurst as well as she did, Clarissa knew he would always consider his own skin above all else. 'The other probably leads back to the house or grounds somewhere.' Again, if he needed it, the viscount would have a contingency plan.

'That makes sense. But which would he take?' Lord Fennimore could apparently read her mind.

'Penhurst would run for the hills. Seb would want him back at the house—if he hasn't had to reveal his hand.' A man who was able to quietly remove his stick-pin and lay it on the ground was hardly a prisoner, or so Clarissa desperately hoped. Seb would play Millcroft to the end because he was stubborn and brave, with emphasis on the stubborn.

'Then let us assume Leatham has convinced

him and headed to the house.' Fennimore was clearly not one to waste time making decisions.

'If only we knew which way the house was. Perhaps we should split up?'

Lord Fennimore rummaged in his coat pocket and pulled out a compass. Flipped it open and then nodded left as if it was perfectly reasonable he had the instrument on his person. 'It's that way.'

In single file they climbed the steep incline until the older man halted them with a raised hand and swiftly blew out the lantern. Ahead a thin strip of light bled through what appeared to be floorboards. Being the tallest, Flint went to investigate, pressing his eye close to the wood and leaving Clarissa to wait with her heart in her mouth for what seemed like five minutes before returning.

'It's the study, I think. Just two men—Seb and Penhurst. It looks like they're making preparations to leave. Seb is holding open a satchel while Penhurst is stuffing money into it. Seb has positioned himself to shield the hatch, so he's expecting us, but we'll have seconds at most. Only Penhurst appears to be armed.'

He couldn't delay things much longer. It had taken all his powers of persuasion to convince Penhurst not to leave without funds to aid his escape and now that the satchel was stuffed with every note the viscount had stashed away for such an emergency, he would want to leave. For the hundredth time Seb cursed himself for his carelessness. Forgetting his pistol had been a ridiculous mistake. But his head had been filled with thoughts of Clarissa and his heightened emotions had made him sloppy. He'd had no choice but to play along and assist with Penhurst's escape, pretending his own safety would be compromised any other way.

Seb wrestled with the buckles, making a hash of closing the satchel. As he handed it to him, he would have to punch him square in the face and hope that he could grab the gun before Penhurst pulled the trigger. The man's index finger had been twitching on it since the moment they had heard the Excise Men rushing down the corridor.

Then the oddest thing happened. Seb knew they were there because he sensed her.

'Give it here, man!' Penhurst tugged at the satchel at the same moment the hatch flew open. Seb lunged for the gun, vaguely aware of Lord Fennimore's shout, but the viscount was too quick, whipping it back and sending Seb crashing to the floor. He felt the hard press of steel against his temple, holding him down.

'Back off or I kill him!' Gray, Flint and Fennimore stood with their own pistols aimed. Icy calm. Seb expected nothing less. No one would shoot unless necessary.

'Drop the gun.' With deliberate slowness Gray pulled the hammer back. 'This house and the grounds are filled with Excise Men. All have been instructed to shoot to kill if the situation warrants it.'

Penhurst's eyes were frantic, flitting from face to face as realisation dawned. He dragged Seb to his feet and used him as a shield, the barrel of the gun now digging into his neck. 'Get out of my way!'

His comrades began to move in a slow circle around them. 'Think about your situation, Penhurst.' Fennimore's tone was matter of fact. 'We have all the evidence we need to send you to the gallows. By now, my men will have rounded up everyone in this house. Secured the exits and already be scouring the grounds. The roads are blocked. We have ships anchored off the cliffs watching the beaches. More men are waiting below us. Wondering why we haven't returned. All it will take is one signal from me to unleash them.' He paused and stamped one foot loudly on the floor. Gray followed by bashing his fist against the door.

'He's in here!'

'Stop it!' The pistol jabbed into Seb's jaw. 'I'll kill him!'

'Go ahead.' Lord Fennimore sounded bored. 'My men know the risks of the job. They also know their deaths will be ruthlessly avenged. The moment you shoot you leave yourself exposed. He will die knowing we won.'

Behind him, Seb could feel Penhurst's heart hammering against his back, feel the way his breathing had become erratic. Cornered and panicked, he would shoot any second. Unlike the bullet that had ripped through his chest, the viscount's would kill him. Instantly his mind wandered to Gem and the grief at never seeing her again overwhelmed him. Seb should have fought harder to convince her he was the one, reiterated his love. At least allowed her to answer instead of storming off, bitterly regretting their last interactions had been mired in anger when there was so much still left unsaid.

Time seemed to stand still. Every sense was heightened. He heard Penhurst's finger begin to pull back the trigger. Saw Flint and Gray's eyes widen as they realised his number was up. Closed his own eyes to picture her one last time before his heart stopped beating and resigned himself to his fate.

Then there was a dull thud and the fingers dug like claws around Seb's neck suddenly loosened as the viscount crumpled to the floor.

When he opened his eyes Gem was stood like a warrior, teeth bared and wielding the bronze statue of Aphrodite like a tennis racquet, ready to bludgeon Penhurst if he moved a muscle.

Which he didn't because he was out cold.

'I knew she wouldn't stay put.' Lord Fennimore knelt down and felt Penhurst's neck for a pulse. 'He's alive, thank goodness. We can't interrogate a corpse.' From his pocket he produced some cord and looked up at them impatiently. 'Well? Is one of you going to help me tie him up or are you all just going to stand there?'

Seb didn't move a muscle and neither did she. Her hair a veritable bird's nest, a smudge of dirt on one cheek and what looked like a dusty cobweb hanging from her ear. He had never seen anything lovelier. His feet moved towards her and he found himself prying her weapon out of her clenched fingers by peeling them back one by one. She didn't want to relinquish it. 'It's over, Gem.'

Her forget-me-not eyes flicked to the viscount on the floor and then back to Seb, then she rushed at him and wrapped her arms tightly around his neck. 'I thought I'd lost you again.' She kissed him, smoothing her palms over his face and shoulders. Then she shook them. 'Every time I look away you put yourself at risk!' Another kiss. Longer. Perfect. Seb happily kissed her back.

'Do you two mind?' Lord Fennimore snapped, his exasperated face inches from theirs. 'Such nonsense should be saved for your honeymoon. We still have a job to do.'

The mention of a honeymoon cruelly reminded him of her impending marriage. 'You should get back to your *fiancé*. He's probably worried.' He sounded like a petulant child and didn't care. He'd almost died. He'd earned the right to be petulant. 'You could have told me yourself rather than making me hear it from him. I'm sure you and Westbridge will be blissfully…indifferent to one another.'

Her head tilted, then her mouth opened, then she pushed him hard in the chest. So hard he staggered backwards. 'For a man who claims to hold no *duke* in high regard, can you explain why you listened to that "windbag", as you are so fond of calling him, yet failed to ask me if it was true?'

She had a point, a glorious, wonderful point that made his heart soar with hope. One he would have told her, except she didn't give him a moment to get a word in. But then he had never been good with words so he let her give him both barrels and thoroughly enjoyed it.

'You are a stubborn idiot, Seb Leatham! Storming off and avoiding me after we spent the night together! Refusing to speak to me!' Another push. 'After everything we have been through, did you seriously think I would want him over you?' Her hands fisted on his lapels. 'And after I just saved your miserable life! Why, I have a good mind to strangle you rather than marry you! Not that you asked, of course. Which is another black mark against your—' Seb silenced her with a kiss. Like all their kisses this one heated immediately. Only the sounds of a veritable army storming the room broke them apart.

The commander of the Excise Men stepped forward to speak to Lord Fennimore. 'All bar one of the guests is accounted for, my lord. They are in the ballroom awaiting questioning.'

'Who's missing?'

'The Duke of Thetford. He hasn't been seen since late afternoon.'

'Oh, good gracious!' Gem's eyes were wide as she darted out of his arms. 'I completely forgot! He's in my bedchamber!' With that she dashed off, leaving Seb no choice but to follow. She took the stairs in a hurry, her skirts held so high he was rewarded with the delicious sight of her silk-clad legs before she skidded to a halt at her door, her expression pained.

'I might have accidently let slip to him your real identity.'

'It doesn't matter now.'

'Oh, I know that—but this afternoon, with things at such a critical stage, I thought it best to…um…contain the situation.' She flung open the door and revealed a completely empty room.

Just as Lord Fennimore, Flint and Gray arrived in the doorframe, all obviously more curious to see what she had done than remain downstairs, Gem went to the wardrobe and grimaced as she opened it. 'I might have lured him here with a promise of a full explanation, then clocked him over the head with my curling iron.'

There, crammed awkwardly in the bottom amongst an array of slippers, his fat hands and feet bound by what looked like stockings and ribbons, was his brother. Bright purple with indignation. His mouth stuffed with a lacy handkerchief.

'She's a canny one, your lady love.' Fennimore breathed on the lenses of his spectacles then polished them with the corner of his coat. 'Quick thinking. Resourceful. An asset, I think.' He wound the wire frames around his ears. 'The pair of you had best get yourselves downstairs with the other detainees while I sort out this mess. Gray—arrest them.'

'Arrest us!' Gem clung to his arm while Seb simply glared. His superior was up to something. 'He can't arrest us! Can he?'

'Of course he can't. There will be an ulterior motive. With Lord Fennimore, there is always an ulterior motive.' Seb folded his arms and pinned him with his stare. 'What is it?'

'Think about the possibilities...'

'Here it comes. Brace yourself. He excels at

bullying people into doing things they don't want to do.'

'At least hear me out. It's a splendid idea and nobody downstairs is any the wiser, so we must strike now and use the momentum. From the outset, Lord Millcroft has been a triumph in society. The arrogant, mysterious adventurer from the Antipodes. The beautiful *Incomparable* hanging adoringly on his arm. As a couple, the *ton* will love you. Especially after the scandal sheets are filled with the tale of how she tossed away a duke to marry for love! The pair of you will be invited everywhere—every hostess will be delighted to have you. So delighted, nobody will ever think you are working for the Crown. The possibilities are endless for Lord and Lady Millcroft.'

It was outrageous. Preposterous. Dangerous. Positively brilliant. Seb's temper flared, then was doused immediately. Because Gem's arms were outstretched and she was beaming. 'Don't tie my wrists too tight, Lord Gray. I don't want ugly bruises.'

'You don't have to do this.'

'Of course I do.'

Both Flint and Gray were nodding at the idea as if it was a *fait accompli*. 'Good men are dropping like flies! Another one of the King's Elite appears doomed to fall into the parson's trap!' Flint appeared appalled.

'It'll be you next.' Gray nudged him, winking.

'Over my dead body!'

Joking? At a time like this? Was Seb the only one thinking about the practicalities here? 'In case it has escaped your notice, my incensed half-brother is currently bound and gagged in the wardrobe! Once that gag comes out, believe me, he will shout the truth from the rooftops!'

'No, he won't.' Flint bent down and stared at Thetford like a specimen in a jar. 'He's been consorting with a traitor. There will have to be a thorough investigation. Every tiny detail of his life and finances will have to be publicly scrutinised. When the papers get hold of it there will be a huge scandal…not to mention the censure he will receive from the whole *ton* and even the King himself when it comes to be known how he shockingly abused and mistreated a national hero—his own brother, no less.' The Duke's terrified eyes were wide.

Lord Fennimore shook his head, looking very dour. 'Aside from that, in matters of *national importance*, spilling state secrets is, in itself, an act of treason. If he says a word, I'll have him tossed in Newgate. But he won't say a word, will you, Thetford?' The wily Lord joined Flint, bending over him. 'You will be an asset to the King's Elite and do your best to ensure that Lord Millcroft is welcomed everywhere he goes. You will take your secrets to the grave.'

As his half-brother was now nodding pathetically, Seb turned back to an indignant-looking Gem. 'This is a bad idea.' Although even he couldn't truthfully say that with much conviction. Together they were rather splendid. Better than splendid, they were perfect.

'I have a talent for spying, you said so yourself, and I have learned that I am so much more than a pretty face. Have you any idea how marvellous that is? And you need me around to keep an eye on you, else there is no telling what will happen. Besides, these last few weeks have been the most exciting of my life.' Her palms found their way to his chest. It seemed perfectly natural to loop his arms possessively around her waist. Despite their audience, his ears didn't redden and his tongue didn't feel tied. His usually shy eyes locked with hers and held. 'How many ladies in my position get to help the Crown doing something that they adore with the man they love?'

'You love me?'

'Don't sound so surprised by it. I turned down a proposal from a duke for you. A girl doesn't do that unless she's head over heels in love. Which I am. Completely. Hopelessly. Ecstatically. It's wonderful.'

'It is.'

She loved him. He could see it plain as day in her forget-me-not eyes. Miracles did happen. Gem stood on her tiptoes and pressed her mouth to his stunned one, giggling.

'I'm done with dukes and curling irons and pretending to be what I'm not. I want excitement and passion and purpose. I want honesty and trust. I want to work by your side every day and sleep next to you every night. And I want shortbread smeared in jam under oilskin in a thunderstorm. I want to love and be loved unconditionally. But more than anything, I want to grow old with you. Marry me, Seb Leatham. Let's make thousands of crinkly, wrinkly laughter lines together. We both know you want to.'

As usual she was right. He did.

* * * * *

MILLS & BOON

Coming next month

THE WARRIOR'S BRIDE PRIZE
Jenni Fletcher

'I won.'

'What?'

'The game. I won.'

'Oh.' Livia stared at Marius blankly. Did he expect her to congratulate him? 'And you woke me to tell me that?'

'No.' His expression shifted to one she hadn't seen there before, as if he were uncertain of himself. He seemed to be having trouble finding words. 'There's more...about Scaevola.'

'Has something happened to him?' She felt a fleeting, *very fleeting*, moment of concern. If he was hurt in some way then it would explain his absence. Although it might also postpone their wedding, she thought hopefully.

'Not physically, but, yes, in a manner of speaking. He ran out of money.'

'You mean he was gambling?'

He inclined his head and she rolled her eyes scornfully. Of course he'd been gambling and now he'd run out of funds again, just as he had in Lindum. She was amazed he'd had anything left to play with in the first place. Then she tensed as another thought struck her. Was *that* why Marius was there? Because Scaevola owed him money? Had he come to ask *her* to pay the debt? Her mouth turned dry at the thought. Surely that couldn't be the reason he'd come to wake her and yet...what else could be so important?

She pulled her shoulders back, bracing herself for the

worst. 'If he's indebted to you, then I'm afraid I can't help. I don't have any money of my own.'

He drew his brows together so sharply they met in a hard line in the middle. 'I'm not here for money, Livia. Is that what you think of me?' His gaze dropped to her mouth. 'After last night?'

She tensed again as the low, intimate tone of his voice sent a *frisson* of excitement racing through her body, though she forced herself to ignore it. They shouldn't talk about last night.

'No. You're right, I shouldn't have said that. I just thought...' She licked her lips, trying to put her confusion into words. 'I *don't* think of you like that, but why are you here, Marius? What's so important about a game? Did Scaevola lose so much?'

'Yes, but it's not about money...'

'Then what?'

He muttered an expletive before answering. 'He staked you.'

'What?' Her body seemed to go into shock, though it took her brain a few seconds to catch up with the words.

'He had no money left so he staked you.'

'In a game of tabula?'

'Yes.'

'You're saying that he offered me as a prize?'

'Yes.'

'And that you won?'

'Yes.'

'So you won...me?'

Continue reading
THE WARRIOR'S BRIDE PRIZE
Jenni Fletcher

Available next month
www.millsandboon.co.uk

COMING SOON!

We really hope you enjoyed reading this book. If you're looking for more romance, be sure to head to the shops when new books are available on

Thursday
4th October

To see which titles are coming soon, please visit
millsandboon.co.uk

LET'S TALK

Romance

For exclusive extracts, competitions
and special offers, find us online:

f facebook.com/millsandboon

📷 @millsandboonuk

🐦 @millsandboon

Or get in touch on 0844 844 1351*

For all the latest titles coming soon, visit
millsandboon.co.uk/nextmonth